BRAND-NEW EMILY

BRAND-NEW EMILY

a novel by

GINGER RUE

SCHOLASTIC INC.
New York Toronto London Auckland
Sydney Mexico City New Delhi Hong Kong

For my girls

The author wishes to thank Lois and Glenn Griffin, W. Glenn Griffin, David Weathers, Martin Chambers, Dorothy Ward, Thomas Rabbitt, Leigh Ann Hirschman, Mary Lou Carney, Edward Grinnan, Rick Hamlin, Betsy Kohn, Celeste McCauley, Allison Ruffing, Jennifer Griffin, Lynn Anderson, Maureen Kohl, Heatherly Whiteside (who is NOT a Daisy), Krutin Patel, Kailyn Brinyark, and Abigail Samoun and everyone at Tricycle Press.

ISBN 978-0-545-29155-2

12 11 10 9 8 7 6 5 4 3 2 1   10 11 12 13 14 15/0

Printed in the U.S.A.   23

First Scholastic printing, September 2010

Design by Toni Tajima
Typeset in Bigband, Minion Pro, Officina Sans and Serif, Preface, and Spoleto

I.
TACTICAL ERRORS OF THE UNDERDOG BRAND

One

EMILY SUCKS BIG TIME.

It was scrawled across my locker in black letters.

I crouched against the other lockers on the bottom row, furiously wiping the slick metal door with a wet paper towel. The harder I tried to rub the words away, the more everyone in the hall snickered.

Clearly, I was in need of marketplace repositioning, but at the time, I didn't even know what that meant.

I paused when three pairs of black high-heeled boots stopped in front of me. It was still February. I never would have dreamed that by the time boots were out of season, things around Wright Middle School would be a lot different.

"My, my," Heatherly Hamilton said. "That looks like permanent marker to me. Doesn't it look like permanent marker, Meredith?"

"Permanent. Absolutely," Meredith agreed.

I didn't look up. I didn't even move.

"Get up, snitch," said Alexa, grabbing my sweater and pulling me to my feet. "You're in our way."

Heatherly's eyes met mine. "You suck. That's permanent. Everyone knows it, and there's nothing you can do to change it."

One thing you never, ever wanted to do at Wright Middle was make an enemy of the Daisies.

You wouldn't think a simple thing like a can of Coke could make everyone at school hate you. All this had started a week earlier . . . when Alexa had perched her Diet Coke on the edge of Heatherly and Meredith's locker and the full can had cascaded all over me and my social studies project. Alexa managed a halfhearted "sorry" between uncontrolled fits of laughter, and the three of them went on their way, not even offering to help me clean up. I got to first period just in time to say "Emily's here" at the end of roll call. Mrs. Crutchfield called roll by having us call out our names. When I spoke, everyone stared at me.

"Emily, what happened to your project?" Mrs. Crutchfield asked. The cotton balls I'd glued on the poster board to represent Greece's major export had turned the brown of old women's pantyhose, and the information cards beneath each panel were smeared with incoherent blue ink. "It's ruined! And your hair is soaked! What's going on? This is your fifth tardy in two weeks." I didn't know what to say. Mrs. Crutchfeld looked at me a moment then said, "Why don't we go out in the hall for a minute." I followed her into the hall. "Is something wrong?"

"I can't get to my locker."

"Why not? Halls overcrowded?"

"Sort of," I said. And I should have stopped there. But I have a bad habit of talking too much when I get nervous. Silences make me uncomfortable, and I try to fill the empty space with words. I'm pretty good with words when I'm writing, but not so good when I'm talking. If you ask me, talking kind of sucks because you can't go back and revise. "Three girls are sharing the locker above mine, and by the time I squeeze under them, the first bell has already rung. Today, one of them had a Coke, and it spilled. Are you going to lower my project grade?"

"Of course not, Emily," Mrs. Crutchfield said. "This isn't your fault. I'm just trying to think if there's something I can do to help. Frankly, I'm surprised that this has escaped Mr. Warren's notice so long, the way he patrols the halls. I can't believe he'd miss three girls sharing one locker."

"I'm surprised I missed it, too," Warren said, appearing out of nowhere. Those elevator shoes with the rubberized soles were really quiet—he was like Ninja Psycho Vice Principal. "So who's sharing a locker without permission?"

"Oh, it's nothing," Mrs. C said. "Nothing I can't handle."

"I asked you a question, young lady," he said to me.

"Mr. Warren," Mrs. Crutchfield said. "I assure you that this isn't a matter you need concern yourself with. I know how busy you are, and I wouldn't dream of adding to your workload."

He ignored Mrs. Crutchfield, then said to me, "What's your name?"

"Emily Wood."

He wrote it down and walked away.

"What's he going to do?" I asked Mrs. C.

"I have no idea."

A few periods later, I was waiting for the Daisies to put away their things in their locker when Mr. Warren walked up to us.

"Ms. Wood, are these the girls sharing a locker without my permission?"

The three Daisies looked at me, shocked.

"My office," Warren told them. "Now."

"Thanks for telling on us, Emily," Heatherly said when they came into seventh-period choir. "Warren gave us two weeks' detention. Work detail." Heatherly was the most popular of the three, a blonde with plain features. None of them were particularly beautiful, in the sense that beautiful things are rare and delicate. I had secretly named them the Daisies, because they were attractive yet common and, unlike orchids or roses, had no layers or depth.

Work detail was the stuff of legend at Wright. Rumor had it that detainees had been forced to clean locker room toilets without rubber gloves, hose out the Dumpsters, dispose of the biology lab's fetal pig dissections, and any other horrific thing that occurred to Warren. Unapproved locker sharing may sound like no big deal, but to Warren, everything was a big deal. He even had a sign on his office door that said SWEAT THE SMALL STUFF.

"You guys, I promise I didn't tell," I said.

"Right. Like we're going to believe that," Alexa said. "We heard him ask you if we were the girls you'd told him about."

"I didn't tell him . . . ," I began. But how was I going to finish? By saying that I'd told a teacher instead? That would be just as bad. They didn't know Mrs. Crutchfield wasn't like other teachers.

"Do you even realize who you're messing with?" Meredith said.

Whom, I thought. With *whom* I'm messing. But I didn't say anything. There was no way I was going to get out of this. Nothing I could say would make them believe me.

"In less than three months, Heatherly Hamilton is going to be the May Queen!" said Meredith. "She's practically royalty at this school. The May Queen isn't supposed to clean the bathrooms and pick up garbage."

Heatherly said, "This little incident you've caused has upset me, and I resent that. Stress is bad for my complexion. My skin needs to be radiant when I'm photographed as May Queen. It always makes the front page of the paper. My dress is already hanging in my closet. It's going to go perfectly with that crown. All I have to do now is stay focused until Spring Fling. I don't like being distracted by this stunt of yours." She smiled. "But there's always one thing that relieves my stress. A little something called payback. I'm going to feel *so* much better when I've made you suffer."

"Consider yourself toast," said Alexa.

"Yeah, don't worry," said Meredith. "We'll get you for this."

They weren't kidding, either. Over the next several weeks, everything at school went from bad to worse to hellish.

When Dad got home that first night, I didn't tell him anything. It was Thursday, and he'd been late every night that week already. "I'm probably going to stay even later tomorrow," he said. "Do you want to sleep over at a friend's house?"

So many choices—which friend should I select from my extensive social network? Sometimes Nobody got jealous if I spent too much time with No One.

We'd moved from Pleasant Hill, three hours away, before school started last year so we'd be close to Uncle Sonny, Mom's brother. I'd tried to make the best of it—I'd even read an article in *Flirt* magazine about how to make friends at a new school. The article had a photograph of these five girls with their arms around one another's shoulders and their heads thrown back, their mouths wide open in gigantic smiles, as though someone had just said the funniest thing *ever* and being a teenager was, like, totally a superfun time! So either the editors had completely forgotten what middle school is really like, or their teenage years differed vastly from mine. It wasn't as if I was popular or anything in Pleasant Hill, but at least I had some friends. I'd even made a few superficial friendships the first semester at Wright, but once the Great Coke Debacle occurred, no one wanted to be associated with me, not even on MySpace.

"Maybe I'll hang at Sonny's," I told Dad. "Everyone already has plans, I think." He didn't need anything else to worry about. He'd almost made partner at his old firm, and moving away meant he'd had to start again somewhere new.

"When tax season is over, we'll spend more time together," he said. He always said that. Tax season was officially January 2 through April 15. Before Mom got so sick, she always took care of everything around the house because Dad worked such late hours. Every April 16, we'd go out to dinner, and we'd talk about the fun we were going to have until the next January. Dad meant it—he really did. Every year, we took some kind of family trip the weekend after the 16th; it was a tradition. He'd even pull himself away for a weeklong trip to the beach every summer, but other than that, he pretty much lived at the office, tax season or not.

He was his work, and Mom was cool with that. Dad was what people used to call a "company man," completely loyal and dedicated to his employer and clients. Back when we lived in Pleasant Hill, if something broke around the house, Mom had a list of repairmen in town who were clients of Dad's firm. We shopped at stores owned by clients; we ate at restaurants owned by clients. We had even ordered the flowers for Mom's funeral from a client. But all those clients he'd worked so hard to build relationships with had been left behind when we moved, so now it was like he was starting all over again. And it was my fault. He thought moving closer to Sonny would make things easier on me. No way was I going to tell him it had all been for nothing.

"It's cool," I said. "I made pot roast for supper. Want me to mix up some of that gravy you like so much?"

"Nah, I grabbed something at the office. You go ahead."

Dad went to change clothes, and I turned on the TV in the kitchen to watch *One Big, Happy Family* while I prepared dinner. Colby Summers, who played the wisecracking teenage son, was the best-looking guy I'd ever seen. He had the most beautiful hazel eyes and the smile of a mischievous little boy. He was a singer, too. His song "Are You the Girl?" was number one for eight weeks straight. I had his picture in my locker, but it wasn't just because he was so handsome. He was a really nice guy, too; you could tell from his interviews. He was the kind of guy who, if he went to your school, would be nice to you even if no one else was, and he would probably ask to read your poems and would tell you what he liked about them.

I put a few pieces of the roast on a slice of bread, threw some grated cheese on top, and placed it in the oven long enough for the cheese to melt and the edges of the bread to become toasty.

Just the way Mom used to make it.

Two

In my favorite picture of her, my mom is wearing a white turtleneck and blue jeans. She is standing in our kitchen holding a head of lettuce. Dad was messing around with the camera and caught her without her knowing. She is smiling a genuine smile, not one of those forced ones she had when was posing for a picture and ended up looking nothing like herself. Her teeth are perfectly white, and her eyes are sparkling blue—not like the ocean, but like the impossibly blue water of a swimming pool.

Sometimes when I'm dreaming, I step into that photo, and my mom, healthy and brimming with energy, is chopping up the lettuce and making supper. Sometimes I am helping; other times, I am sitting at the table doing my homework.

She is singing to herself—in her softest voice because she doesn't think she can sing well.

I'm happy just to be there with her. Then all of a sudden I realize that her body is, at that very moment, betraying her. I try to tell her that she is sick, that we have to do something now to stop the cancer. But when I try to talk, I can't make a sound. All I can do is cry silently.

So I go to her. She puts the lettuce down, and she hugs me and strokes my hair.

"What's wrong, sweetie? What's wrong?" she asks, but still I cannot speak.

I simply stand there, my face buried in her neck. I smell her and feel her warmth.

When I wake up, I keep my eyes closed and try to get back there, to force myself back into sleep. But the kitchen and my mother have faded away.

Three

No one spoke to me the day after the Coke incident. At Wright Middle, students had to wait for the first release bell in the lobby. Everyone stood around in groups—the A-list crowd at the northernmost part of the lobby, B-listers at a respectful but aspiring distance, C-listers farther down still, and so forth, and the teachers stuck with lobby duty had to stand guard to make sure not only that we didn't kill one another but also that we didn't escape and roam around the school before classes started. When I came near any group, everyone got quiet and I could feel their eyes on me as I passed. Then they'd start to whisper again. Though I couldn't make out what they were saying, I knew it was about me snitching on Heatherly and her friends.

For a while, I sat against a wall and pretended to do some homework by writing in my Cool Stuff book. It was a small green notebook I carried around with me to write down words that I liked or thoughts that interested me or unusual images that popped into my head that I might want to use in a poem sometime. Mrs. Crutchfield said writers should always have a notebook handy because you never knew when the muse would pay you a visit. Or when you'd need to pretend that you didn't mind being a pariah. I was glad I had it with me that day. I wrote about how much I wanted to go home or move back to Pleasant Hill or be hit by a giant meteor.

When I decided a respectable amount of time had passed so that the other kids wouldn't think I was running from them, I gathered my books and asked one of the teachers for permission to go to the library.

"How's my favorite patron today?" the librarian asked. She liked me because I was one of the few people who treated her with any respect. My guess was that she used to be an elementary school librarian because whenever a class would get loud in the library, she'd threaten to turn off the lights. The guys had made it a big joke—*Let's be noisy so the librarian will turn off the light. Just try to do it when I've got Kelsey Brown alone in the biography section.* Ha ha. Very funny. As if Kelsey Brown, the head cheerleader, required that much privacy. She was in Vannies with me—the Vanguard Program, first and second period English and Social Studies classes for gifted students—and she held her own in class discussions, but there was a rumor that her mom had pulled some strings to get extra points added to her IQ score. And everybody knew she'd hooked up with Chip Young at the ballpark last summer and let Tyler Olsen get to second base at the movies. I'm not exactly sure what second base even is (and you can't really ask without sounding stupid), but how would you get there at the movies, anyway? Kelsey had been the most popular girl in school until she threw her reputation away. She would have been a sure thing to win May Queen, but nobody wanted to vote for someone who got around the way she did.

The librarian was booting up her computer. *The computer!* I had completely forgotten about checking the forums last night. The thought made me feel sick. Of course they would have trashed me on the message boards; I should have checked to see how low they'd go—so at least I could be prepared.

"Would you mind if I checked something online?" I asked. "The firewall on the student computers limits access to most sites."

"Of course, Emily. I have to reshelve a few books anyway."

I tried to brace myself. *No matter what the forums say,* I told myself, *I won't cry.* One thing Mom had always told me was to never, ever cry at school. "Don't give anyone the satisfaction of knowing they've hurt you," she'd told me. She was right, of course. Crying in front of people at school was like bleeding in a shark tank. Once they smelled the blood, they'd circle for the kill.

I quickly pulled up a chat room everyone hung out in. The last post was to a thread called "RE: Emily Wood." My stomach turned. There had been fifty-three posts since nine o'clock last night.

I clicked to the beginning. I scanned the first post and the next two—they were about how I'd gone to Warren, how I was a rat, how no one would let me get away with it. But the last couple of pages. . . .

"She thinks her long hair is soooo pretty. She ought to use it to cover up her face!" one said.

"I know for a fact that Emily has never kissed a boy," someone else had posted.

"Who would want to kiss HER?" the next post said.

Of course it was true that I'd never kissed a boy, but how did people know that? Could they tell by looking at me? Some of my Pleasant Hill friends had also never been kissed—but it wasn't something we went around telling people. Maybe the Daisies had asked someone from Pleasant Hill on MySpace? Technology could really suck sometimes. It used to be that a girl who had never kissed a guy before and had pretty much zero chance of it ever happening could move to a new town and people could *assume* she'd kissed a guy or two at her old school. But no—thanks to the Internet, my whole pathetically dull life history could follow me everywhere.

Mom had always told me that kisses were special and shouldn't be given out carelessly. It wasn't so much that I was following Mom's advice as that no one had actually ever tried to kiss me, which meant that the last post was true. I'd never thought of it that way before.

Except for the librarian and Mrs. Crutchfield, my English teacher, no one at school talked to me the entire day. When I got home, I checked the forum, but the posts about me had been removed. The admin had posted a notice about how this was a positive and safe teen site and that users should not use the boards to trash people. They added that anyone abusing posting privileges in the future would be banned. Translation: when treating people like dirt, choose instant messaging, texting, email, the telephone . . . or do it in person.

Everyone at school ignored me for a full three days, and it was horrible.

But then they stopped ignoring me, and it was much worse.

Four

"Hey, Emily Wood!" a jock yelled at me from one of the cool tables as I was standing in the lunch line. "That girl with the long hair?" he said turning to Heatherly, who was sitting beside him, pointing at me and whispering in his ear. He wasn't her boyfriend, but like all the other guys, he seemed to want to keep that option open. "Hey, Emily Wood, I'm talking to you!"

I turned.

"No, no . . . stand sideways again," he said.

Not knowing what to do, I turned away from him, just as I had been, waiting in line. "Looks more like Emily *Ply*wood to me. Flat as a piece of plywood!" This brought howls of laughter from everyone in earshot, even at the table three rows away, where I'd been coexisting with three guys who were always arguing about which comic book character was the most invincible.

"Plywood," the guy with the glasses and bad acne said to the one wearing a Spiderman T-shirt. "Get it? Plywood. That's pretty funny."

Fantastic. I officially had a nickname.

Things can't get any worse, I thought.

My last class of the day was choir, where we were arranged in a three-row semicircle, standing in front of chairs we were allowed to use only when we weren't singing. I was in the second row, and the Daisies were on the third, directly behind me. Sometimes, if I came in late enough, Mrs. Stewart would shut everybody up and start playing piano, and then no one would have a chance to say anything to me.

Today's song was some crap about *I'm gonna make it on Broadway, no matter what!* Mrs. Stewart, a short woman with the energy of a hamster, was bouncing up and down as she played the piano, urging us to stand up straight and sing *with feeling!* Yeah. Like that song was something we could really relate to and get all worked up about. When we got to the part about how a dime won't shine your shoes, someone kicked me in the butt.

It hurt, but I didn't turn around.

As we kept on singing, someone kicked me again. This time, they kicked so hard that I stumbled into the first row and my songbook flew from my hands.

Mrs. Stewart stopped playing.

"Emily," she said, "what's going on?"

The Daisies were giggling.

"Nothing," I said. "I'm sorry."

Mrs. Stewart resumed playing the song. I went back to my spot, making sure not to make eye contact with anyone.

As soon as we got to the part about Broadway's bright neon lights, one of them landed a hard, swift kick right in the small of my back. I yelled before I could think. But it didn't matter; Mrs. Stewart had seen the whole thing.

"Alexa!" she shouted. "What is the meaning of this?"

I kept my eyes on the floor.

"I'm sorry, Mrs. Stewart," Alexa said. "I was just fooling around."

Mrs. Stewart began writing up a pink slip. "You can take this to Mr. Warren and explain it to him," she said. "And take your books with you. You will not come back into this class today."

Alexa gathered her books, took the pink slip, and left the room.

"Emily," Mrs. Stewart said. "I'd like to see you after class."

When the bell rang, I waited while everyone left. On her way out, Heatherly whispered, "You'd better keep that big mouth of yours shut this time, Plywood."

Once the room cleared, Mrs. Stewart motioned me over. "Come here, Emily," she said. "I want to know what's going on."

"It's no big deal," I said. "I guess Alexa was just fooling around."

"Emily, is there a problem between you and the other girls? Anything I can help with?"

"No. Everything is fine."

"I'm not so sure," she said. "To be on the safe side, I'm going to send a referral to the counselor. Maybe she can help you girls sort this out."

"Oh, no, Mrs. Stewart, that's not necessary," I said. "It's fine, really." Just what I needed: another adult getting involved, like Warren's "help" with my locker. And the counselor, of all people. What was she going to do? Give us a personality test and make us do some stupid role-playing exercise? Yeah, right.

"I'll take care of everything," Mrs. Stewart said. "Now you run along."

The next day was when they wrote on the outside of my locker in Sharpie, and then on Friday, I was called to the counselor's office during study hall.

The Daisies were already there.

Five

I had nothing to tell the counselor about anyway. The three of them hadn't really done anything to me yet. I knew it was coming—they were toying with me, the way a cat does with a bird or a mouse, letting it think it's free for a moment, then grabbing it again and chewing on its head—not enough to kill it, but just enough for the cat to enjoy knowing that the smaller animal realizes it's going to be eaten alive eventually. You wonder if it's actually the cat's teeth that deliver the death blow, or if the bird or mouse dies simply as a result of the prolonged terror.

Heatherly, Meredith, and Alexa were already there when I arrived. Mrs. Moore's office was filled with posters of kittens and puppies, all with inspirational quotes such as, "Smile: It's Contagious!" and other garbage that doesn't work in real life—or at least not in eighth grade.

"Okay, girls," Mrs. Moore said. "Now that we're all here, I think we need to talk about what's going on. Heatherly, perhaps you'd like to start."

"I don't know what you're talking about, Mrs. Moore, honest," she said. People always say *honest* when they're lying.

"Well, it seems that you three girls have an issue with Emily. Would that be a correct statement?"

"Whatever do you mean?" Meredith asked.

"Yeah, we don't have a problem," said Alexa.

"All right, then, Alexa," Mrs. Moore continued. "Then perhaps you'd like to tell me why you got detention for kicking Emily in choir."

Alexa shuffled a bit in her chair. "Gosh, I'm really sorry. I was kidding around. I didn't mean to really kick her. I feel just *terrible* about it."

"Good, Alexa!" Mrs. Moore beamed. You could tell she was thinking, *We're really making progress here! I'm making a difference in these kids' lives!* "Emily, how does that make you feel? Do you accept Alexa's apology?"

"Sure," I said, not looking up.

"Fantastic," said Mrs. Moore. "I think it's really important that we each consider how the other person feels when we act out inappropriately. So let's work on that, okay?"

"Absolutely," Heatherly said.

"Very well, then. I think we're done here. And, girls, please feel free to come to me if I can be of any further help."

When we got up to leave, Meredith put her arm around my shoulder. "Come on, Emily," she said. "Let's go see what's for lunch!" Mrs. Moore was eating it up.

Meredith walked with her arm around me all the way to the end of the hall, until the counselor went back into her office. Then she wrapped her arm tightly around my neck and shoved me into the lockers.

"I can't believe you, Plywood!" she said. "Did you really think hauling us to the counselor's office was going to work? Like we'd suddenly realize that, ▆▆▆ we haven't been acting very swell and we're awful sorry?"

"I had nothing to do with it," I said.

"Yeah," Alexa said. "And I'll bet you didn't spill your guts to Mrs. Stewart, or tell Warren about our locker either. You are such a snitch!"

"Cool it a minute," said Heatherly. "You know what? I believe her."

"What?" Meredith asked. "Are you kidding? You said she's a fink. You said—"

"I know what I said," Heatherly continued. "But people make mistakes. Don't they, Emily?"

"I guess," I said, tentatively.

"And I'm sure Emily just made a mistake or two. Let's put it all behind us. Let's be friends."

"No way!" Meredith said. "She can't get off that easy!"

Heatherly looked at Meredith. "Let's talk about it later, Meredith," she said. "Emily, we'll see you around. Everything's fine, okay?"

"Okay," I replied. But I knew it was like Meredith said: I wouldn't get off that easy.

Six

Clearly, I knew better. But how could I refuse a chance for the torment to be over, a chance to actually have friends?

Heatherly called my house that night and told me that she'd smoothed over everything with Meredith and Alexa. "I think Mrs. Moore was right," she said. "There's no reason we shouldn't all be friends. So when we go back to school Monday, we want you to hang out with us."

"Me? Why?"

"Oh, come on, Emily! You're a total sweetheart! I know you didn't mean to get us in trouble. Sure, it took some convincing, but trust me, Meredith and Alexa are over it. Really. So, we'll see you at school, okay?"

And starting that Monday at school, the Daisies were nice to me. The little torments—the nail polish spilled inside my books if I left them for even a second, the whispers, the throwing things in my path to try to trip me—all of them stopped, and the Daisies suddenly became my BFFs. Meredith and Heatherly started sitting by me in science and talking about how hot Colby Summers was, who everybody had crushes on, or telling stupid jokes, or whatever. For four days, I had friends. And not just any friends, but three of the most popular girls in school. I'm not saying it felt natural or real, because it didn't. But since I hadn't had friends in so long, I convinced myself that I was just being paranoid and I let my guard down. Just like they'd planned.

By Thursday of my Friendapalooza, the whole school was buzzing about some exciting news.

I was standing with the A-listers before school when someone shouted, "Look, everybody!"

Kelsey Brown had a copy of the local newspaper. The headline said, HOLLYWOOD MOVIE FILMING SOUTH OF BRUMBAUGH

FARM. "Remember a few weeks ago how they blocked off the old access road? Now it all makes sense," Kelsey said. "The paper says it's been super hush-hush; the movie people didn't want anyone in town to know about it before the filming. It's a big-budget blockbuster. And guess who's the star?"

"Who?" everyone asked.

"Colby Summers!" Kelsey answered. "Colby Summers is here, in our little town!"

"Wait," I said. "Why would they film a big Hollywood movie here?"

"Something about an explosion," said Kelsey. "They needed to blow up an old building with smokestacks—the director said smokestacks look cool crumbling in slow-motion or blah blah blah. Anyway, since the old mental hospital was out there empty and falling apart, they struck some sort of deal with the county. After they finish filming the other scenes, they demolish the building. The movie people get the explosion they want, and the state gets rid of that old eyesore for free. Plus, there's lots of room to drive around out there for the car chases."

"What kind of movie is it?" asked Meredith.

"Colby Summers plays a high school guy who kicks terrorist butt! The movie's called *Die, Terrorists, Die*," Kelsey said. "It's a musical."

"An action/adventure musical?" I asked.

"Yeah," Kelsey said. "Why waste a great singer like Colby Summers, right?"

When the final bell rang that day, everyone from our school—and every other middle and high school student in the surrounding area—made for the set of *Die, Terrorists, Die*. Girls were holding up signs that said WE LOVE COLBY! and MARRY ME, COLBY! The local cops had set up barricades to keep the crowd back. Nobody was getting through. I saw Uncle Sonny standing by a patrol car, talking to some other police officers. I waved, and he walked over.

"I guess I don't have to ask what you're doing here," Sonny said. While we were chatting, Meredith, Heatherly, and Alexa came over.

Heatherly pulled me aside.

"You know the hot cop?" she asked.

Girls always went nuts for Sonny; he was twenty-seven, an athletic six foot two, and had the same swimming-pool blue eyes as my mom. But it was his personality that made him a real catch—he was absolutely the sweetest guy in the world, and even if he hadn't been my only uncle, he still would've been my favorite.

"He's my uncle," I said.

"Your uncle?" Heatherly said. "This is great! Get us in!"

"What? I can't do that. He'd get fired."

"Come on, Emily! Do it! Ask him!" she said.

We walked back to where Alexa and Meredith were drooling over Sonny. "Hey, Sonny," I began. "Any chance you could—"

"No way, Emily," Sonny replied. "You know better than to ask."

"Oh, come on, Emily's Hot Uncle Guy," Heatherly said flirtatiously. "Do a favor for your little niece and her very best friends."

Sonny looked at Heatherly as though he thought it was a shame that the mental institution behind him was no longer operational. "Not going to happen," he said. "You girls might as well go on home. Security around here is tighter than a drum. Nobody's getting past this perimeter."

"Wow," Meredith said as they walked off. "Lucky for us that we know you, *Emily*."

"Those are your very best friends?" Sonny asked.

"In a manner of speaking."

Sonny nodded his head a moment, then said, "Do better, Emily." He looked around and asked, "Did you ride your bike here?"

"It's over there," I said, gesturing.

"My shift's almost finished. We can put your bike in the trunk of the squad car, and I'll drop you off at home."

"Okay, I'll wait in the car."

I opened the door to the passenger side. On the seat was a black zippered notebook with the police department's seal. The notebook was half unzipped, and when I moved it out of the way, a white piece of paper shifted so that it was partially sticking out. I saw the words

terrorist and *Summers*. I knew I shouldn't, but I took the memo out
of Sonny's notebook.

INTRADEPARTMENTAL MEMORANDUM

To: All Officers and Support Personnel

From: Chief Scolpino

RE: Die, Terrorists, Die location filming

Attached you will find a detailed map of the secure perimeter
around Brumbaugh Farm during the filming of the motion picture *Die, Terrorists, Die*. As you have been briefed, the Governor
himself has requested the utmost level of security for the set
and for all persons associated with filming. Besides uniformed
officers of our department and state troopers, no one other
than those with official passes is allowed onto the set, with
the exception of credentialed journalists who have confirmed
appointments with Mr. Summers's publicist, Brynn Sterling. Ms.
Sterling will meet members of the media at the south entrance
and escort them onto the set. Questions regarding media access
should be directed to Ms. Sterling at 917-555-8993. Any journalists not cleared by Ms. Sterling are to be escorted off the
premises at once.

All officers are reminded that their level of professionalism
will reflect not only on the department but on the great state
of Ohio as a whole.

---

*Credentialed journalists who have appointments scheduled with
Mr. Summers's publicist*, I read again. Without really knowing why, I
pulled a clean sheet of paper out of Sonny's notebook, jotted down
the publicist's name and number, folded it up, and put it in my pocket.
I wasn't sure what I was going to do with it, but it was potentially
valuable information.

Seven

I hadn't really paid attention to the fact that the Daisies had been particularly interested in hanging out with me whenever I was putting books in my locker. It didn't take long before they'd memorized the combination and stopped pretending to be my friends.

They were waiting for me at the lockers early Friday morning. Heatherly was holding my Cool Stuff book. She had it flipped open to the back pages. That was where I kept first drafts of poems.

I never showed my first drafts and unedited ideas to anyone. That stuff was too personal.

"Check this out, everybody!" Heatherly said. "She labeled this notebook, 'Cool Stuff.' It's a bunch of quotes and vocabulary words. What is *that* about?" She laughed. A crowd had gathered, and they were all laughing, too. "Wow, that is really, really cool, all right. Plywood is so cool, she collects words! Look, she even has stars by the ones she likes best!"

Heatherly started reading loudly. "A sacred space between us / A chasm reaching farther than an eternity / Will I touch your hand again before I've forgotten your face?" Heatherly giggled. "Sounds like a crush to me! Who's your secret crush, Plywood? One of the nerds at your lunch table? Which one?"

I didn't say anything.

"Come on," she continued. "Who's the lucky guy? The pizza face or the one with the greasy hair? Oh, wait—that could be any of them!" Everyone laughed, and she kept reading.

I could feel my face getting hot. The poem was about my mom. I'd written it because sometimes I can't picture her face without looking at a photo of her, and that bothers me. I would quiz myself by closing my eyes and trying to visualize her as she really had been, but I could produce only the blurred face of someone you might casually glance at in a grocery store or dentist's office. You're not supposed to forget what your own mother looked like, and it worried me that maybe I hadn't loved her enough, that maybe one day my memories of her would fade away altogether. It was bad enough that Heatherly was reading my poems out loud to everybody, but of all of them, she had to choose the one that was the most painful to me: she had to expose to the whole school the feeling that caused me the most shame. They could laugh at it like it was a poem about some stupid crush, but I knew better.

My eyes welled up. I told myself to stop it, but the more I tried not to, the more I wanted to cry.

"Oh, look!" Meredith said. "She's going to cry! She's actually going to cry! Too funny!"

"What a baby!" Heatherly snapped. And then she did it. In a baby-talk voice, she said, "Does Plywood want her mama?"

That was it. My mother was a beautiful angel, and I couldn't let an evil rodent like Heatherly Hamilton say anything about her.

The next thing I knew, I had thrown all of my ninety pounds at her, knocked her down, and grabbed her by the throat.

She was pretty surprised, which is probably why it took her as long as it did to react. Then, she was on top of me, pulling my hair and slapping me in the face until some teachers pulled her off. One of them was Mrs. Crutchfield.

"Break it up! Break it up!" she shouted.

Within seconds, Warren was bustling down the hall. "My office! Both of you! NOW!"

While Warren did his song and dance, my face was stinging from Heatherly's scratches. He gave us both five days' suspension and then assigned us ten days of work detail. Mrs. Crutchfield came in during the sentencing and asked to speak to Warren outside. They took Heatherly away to call her mom so we wouldn't be left alone in the room together.

When Warren came back in, he said, "Miss Wood, in light of the fact that you inflicted very little damage on the other perpetrator,

I'm going to allow Mrs. Crutchfield's request to supervise your work detail. She has also suggested that I move your locker to a part of the building that is closer to her classroom. That will be in effect as of the day you return to school. You may go with Mrs. Crutchfield now until your parent picks you up."

As Mrs. Crutchfield and I walked out of the office, I saw Heatherly sitting by the front desk. She kept her eyes on me the whole time. If there'd ever been any question as to whether she could take me on, I'd removed any doubt. Well played, Emily. Attack and get your butt kicked. Nice.

Mrs. Crutchfield's classroom was empty. "This is my prep period," she said. "Emily, do you want to talk?"

"Not really," I said. I held tightly to my Cool Stuff book. I was glad to have it back in my hands.

"Look, I don't know what's going on, exactly. But it seems the other kids have been doing a number on you for a while now. And you've been through a lot already. You're nice kid, and a fine writer, too. That's why I want to help you."

"No one can help me," I said.

"I know it seems that way," Mrs. Crutchfield said. "But this will pass. And until it does, I'm going to make a deal with you. I've been thinking about ramping up the school literary magazine—doing one at the end of the year in addition to the one we put out last fall. But I haven't had the time. I've always compiled the student work myself and photocopied it. Never really put into it the attention it deserves. To make it really good, I need an editor. I'd like you to take the job."

"No offense, Mrs. C, but I don't think that's going to propel me to new heights of popularity among my peers," I said. "I mean, I love writing, but I don't see how that's going to help."

"It will require extreme dedication to edit this journal. You will have to work on it before school, during break time . . . it might even be a good idea if you dropped choir for the rest of the year. I checked your file, and you don't need the elective credit. You could work in here during seventh period instead," she said. "I also think that I might need you to work through lunch. I could give you the room key and let you bring a sack lunch in here." She smiled.

I realized that Mrs. Crutchfield's offer wasn't so much about the literary magazine: she was offering me a sanctuary.

"I think I could definitely do that," I said.

"Emily, you have the soul of a poet," she said. "You see things differently. You feel more deeply. It's kind of a drawback in eighth grade, but one day you'll see that it's a gift."

Mrs. Crutchfield walked me back to the principal's office, where I waited for Dad to pick me up and wondered what he was going to say. I'd never gotten into trouble before, not even a reprimand for talking in class or a note sent home for not turning in an assignment.

My first-ever act of subversion.

If it hadn't involved suffering a humiliating beat down, it might have been a pretty stellar debut.

Eight

Dad didn't come to pick me up. He was out of town on an important audit, one his office wouldn't interrupt unless it was a matter of life or death. Instead, Sonny came to get me in the squad car. Everyone probably thought Warren was having me arrested.

"Emily!" Sonny said, rushing into the office's reception area. He sat next to me on the sofa and put his arm around my shoulders. "Are you all right? You're pretty scratched up. What happened? They said you'd been fighting."

"You must be Emily's father," Warren said, approaching Sonny.

"Actually, I'm her uncle."

"I was told her father would be picking her up."

"He's not available," Sonny said, "but I assure you that—"

"Sir, are you a parent or legal guardian?" Warren had a scorching Napoleon Complex. Barely five foot six, he couldn't pass up a chance to bully a buff cop like Sonny.

"Well, technically, no," Sonny said. "But as her uncle, I can act on her father's behalf in his absence."

"This is unacceptable!" Warren said. "If the girl's father can't come, then I want to speak to this young lady's mother. Young lady," he said to me, "I want to see your mother!"

"So do I," I said.

Sonny stood up, towering above Warren. "Her mother is dead."

Even Warren couldn't argue with that one. "I see," he said, shaken. It was weird how someone as sweet and gentle as Sonny could flip a switch and become so intimidating. I think even if he'd been half Warren's size, he still would've had him running scared. It was just how he carried himself. "Well, then, if you'll step into my office, I have some papers for you to sign."

When we got in the car, Sonny asked, "You want to talk?"

"Do I have to?"

"Nope."

He took me to his apartment. "I'll leave word for your dad that I picked you up," Sonny said. "You can explain things to him. Help yourself to anything in the kitchen. I'll see you after my shift, okay?"

Sonny hugged me, and I started to cry.

"It's all right, sweetheart," he said, kissing the top of my head. "Everything's going to be okay." He held me away and raised my chin so our eyes met. "Your dad's working late, so tonight I'll make my famous spaghetti, and we'll hang out. You don't have to talk about anything unless you want to."

After Sonny left, I tried watching TV, but I couldn't relax. I was filled with nervous energy, wondering what Dad would say and what would happen to me when I went back to school. It was as if the fighting had tapped something buried. I was tired of sitting back and letting the Daisies have their way. I had to do something. I just didn't know what.

I poured a glass of orange juice from Sonny's fridge and sat down at the bar that separated the kitchen from the den.

I thought for a while. Then I remembered the memo I'd found in Sonny's squad car.

Where had I stashed that number? After rifling through my backpack, I found it.

I picked up the phone and dialed.

"Brynn Sterling," a woman's voice said.

"Yes, hello, Ms. Sterling," I said, trying to sound professional. "My name is Emily Wood. I'm editor in chief of the *Saber*, and I'd like to request an interview with Colby Summers."

"What's the *Saber*? I've never heard of it. And how old are you?"

"It's the Wright Middle School paper," I said. Thanks to funding cuts and the fact that our school was way over maximum enrollment, Wright hadn't had a school paper in years. But I figured literary magazine, newspaper, close enough. "I'm fourteen." I crossed my fingers and hoped for the best. It was unlikely I could convince Mrs. Crutchfield to put a celebrity interview in the lit mag, but it was the best excuse I could come up with for meeting Colby. I don't know exactly what I thought I'd gain from meeting him—maybe I hoped he'd fall desperately in love with me at first sight and take me away from all my problems. As if. Okay, so maybe it wasn't the best plan, but at least I was taking some kind of positive action.

"We appreciate your interest, but Colby Summers doesn't have time for small media outlets," she said.

"But we're his primary fan base," I said. "The teen market is responsible for taking his album platinum, and his show is a favorite among the twelve-to-eighteen demographic." I was totally shooting from the hip, but one thing I love about words is that if you use them right, sometimes they come in pretty handy.

"Is that so?"

I thought about how I usually come across better on paper. "How about I fax you a detailed proposal, with stats about the number of students at my school and how many movie seats would be filled should, say, 85 percent of my readers see the movie based on reading my article? Plus, let's not underestimate the importance of word of mouth among teens. Assuming each of my readers in that 85 percent mentions the movie to five friends—"

"What did you say your name was again?" she asked.

"Emily Wood."

"Well, Emily, you're certainly persistent," she replied. "That counts for a lot in the entertainment industry. All right, then. You've got yourself an appointment. Five o'clock this evening, south entrance of the set. And, by the way, how did you manage to get this number?"

I hadn't planned on being asked that question. I didn't want to get Sonny in trouble. "A good journalist never reveals her sources, right?" I said.

The woman laughed gently. "Good answer," she said. "No recording devices, by the way. You'll have to rely on your notes. See you at five."

Nine

Five o'clock was perfect. Sonny's shift would be over before then, so I wouldn't run into him on the set. I left him a note that I was walking to my house and would catch up with him tomorrow. When I got home, I changed into a pair of black pants instead of jeans, guessing that this would give me more of that "professional journalist" look, and I rode my bike to the south entrance of Brumbaugh Farm.

Lucky for me, the officer at that entrance wasn't one of Sonny's buddies, so I didn't have to worry about being recognized. "Sorry, no teenyboppers allowed," the police officer said.

"I'm not a teenybopper," I said. How old *was* this guy, anyway? "I'm with the press."

"Sure you are. And I'm the Easter Bunny."

"I have a five o'clock with Brynn Sterling," I said, trying to sound official.

Then a pretty young woman pulled up in a white golf cart. "You must be Emily," she said. "Colby's looking forward to meeting you." She shook my hand and said, "Come with me."

We got into the golf cart and started driving through the set. There were groups of people standing everywhere, most of them wearing baseball caps and T-shirts. Not exactly glamorous. Men were lifting big, heavy lights and props and moving them from one place to another. "Who are they?" I asked.

"That's the crew," the publicist said. Next I saw several tables filled with all kinds of junk food—chips, french fries, the works. "And that's why the guys on the crew don't have six-pack abs, in spite of all the heavy lifting. It's called craft services."

"How do all these movie stars stay so thin?"

"They avoid craft services," she replied. "See over there? That's the catering truck. It's where the real meals are cooked. It's got fridges, stoves, everything. They make two meals a day. The first one we call 'breakfast,' even if it's served at three P.M.; then, six hours after breakfast, no matter what time it is, the second meal is served. Is this your first time on a movie set?"

"How did you guess?"

The woman smiled. She pointed back toward an area near craft services. "That over there is called Video Village. It's where the director, script supervisor, and cinematographer have a TV monitor set up so they can see exactly what the camera sees."

Lots of people were standing around in groups, just like at school before the first bell. It was funny—I could kind of tell who was more important or what their job was just by what group they were standing with. Brynn Sterling labeled them for me: "Gaffers and grips, set dressers, hair and makeup. Each group works at different times, so they just stand around and wait until it's time for them to do their thing. You'll notice there aren't many chairs. Only the top dogs get to sit down."

"So the chairs are kind of like the cool kids' lunch table," I said.

She smiled. "I guess you could say that."

"A lot of people here," I said. "Are they shooting the whole movie today?"

"Hardly. Today's shooting will take up maybe 30 seconds of the entire film."

"You're kidding me! Why does it take so long?"

"Because in this business, it's all got to be perfect."

As we continued to ride through the lot, Brynn Sterling asked, "What happened to your face?"

"Oh, yeah," I said. "My cat—had to get him into the pet carrier to take him to the vet. He resisted."

"I'll say." She handed me a piece of paper. "This is the list of off-limit questions," she said. I quickly scanned the page. I was not allowed to ask Colby about schools he'd attended, girlfriends, or earnings. "Keep it light. Your readership will want the basic favorite-this-and-that type of questions anyway," she said.

"Ms. Sterling—"

"Call me Brynn, please."

"Okay, Brynn. The thing is, I thought reporters were supposed to ask hard questions, find out what the person is really like."

"Look, Emily," Brynn said, "I know you're new to this, but this is how it works. My job is to control the public persona of my client. Because Colby is such a big star and so many reporters want to interview him, we leverage access to him with a certain understanding of how we expect the interviews to be conducted. It's good business on our part. You understand."

"So what happens if somebody asks one of the off-limits questions?"

"Then the interview is over," Brynn said. "And so is that entertainment journalist's career, if we have any say about it. Given our client list, we have a pretty wide reach. If we choose not to work with a particular writer again, it would be difficult for them to get the interviews they need to make a living."

"You freeze them out if they don't do what you want," I said.

"I wouldn't put it in exactly those terms, but I think you have the general idea," she said. "Your phone, please."

"My phone?"

"Yes. And any other cameras or recording equipment. You'll have to rely on written notes, and we'll require final approval of your copy before it's printed."

"I didn't know celebrities got to see stories about themselves before the articles went to press."

"Depends on the celebrity. And the publication. And, of course, how good the publicist is," she said. "Your phone, please."

I handed it over.

"Here we are." Brynn pulled up to a trailer with Colby Summers's name on the door. I couldn't believe I was so close to him, that he and I were separated by only a few inches of door and wall. I felt this burst of excitement shoot through my body, and I kind of wanted to jump up and squeal, "I can't believe I'm about to meet Colby Summers in person!" Really professional, I'm sure. I took a deep breath and pulled myself together. Brynn knocked, and a man's voice yelled, "Yeah, come on in!"

Colby Summers was sitting on a small couch, playing a video game. He moved from side to side in tandem with a character on a motorcycle while orange and red explosions blazed across the screen. Colby furiously clicked the controller over and over while his tongue curled tightly around his upper lip. "Oh! Denied!" he shouted as his cyber alter ego exploded. "I almost made it to the next level, too. Oh, well. Better luck next time." He stood up and put down the controller, then smoothed his gray Led Zeppelin T-shirt. His jeans had holes in the knees and hung loosely below his waist. "You must be here for the interview," he said as he brushed the hair out of his eyes with his hand. Then his expression changed to puzzlement.

"She got on the wrong side of a vicious attack cat," Brynn said.

"Yikes," said Colby. "Sorry to hear that."

Awkwardly, I extended my hand. "I'm Emily."

"Nice to meet you, Emily," he replied, gently shaking my hand. "Would you like to have a seat?"

Colby gestured for me to sit down next to him on the couch. I couldn't believe how gorgeous he was in real life. Up close, his hazel eyes were a beautiful labyrinth—green, yellow, and brown. I guess I must have been staring at him, because he sort of grinned at me and said, "So . . . do you have some questions for me?"

You're so hot, I thought—then I realized I'd said it out loud.

Colby laughed. "Well, thanks," he said. "I appreciate that."

Brynn said, "Emily's with her middle school's paper. This is her first celebrity interview."

"No way!" Colby said teasingly. "You're kidding me!" Then he put his hand over mine and said, "Relax, Emily. We're just two regular people having a conversation. What do you want to talk about?"

His hand was touching mine!

"You do have a list of prepared questions, right?" Brynn asked.

"Of course," I said. How could I not have thought of that? I'd been so excited about the whole thing that I'd completely forgotten to plan what I'd say when I actually met him. I took my Cool Stuff notebook out of my backpack and pretended to read from a blank page. "First question: What's your new movie about?"

Colby shifted, putting his arm on the back of the couch and his right foot on his left knee. "Well, it's called *Die, Terrorists, Die,* and it's about terrorists and how my character wants them to . . . um . . . die, I guess."

It was weird—it was as though Colby was the one nervous now.

"And you sing in this movie, too?" I asked.

"Yes." He didn't elaborate.

"So, you're after a bunch of terrorists, trying to kill them, and then sometimes you're singing and dancing, too? How's that work?"

Colby looked at Brynn. "It's kind of interspersed," he said. "The director's vision is difficult to explain." He hesitated, and when he began talking again, his tone of voice and facial expression had changed to a sort of programmed bliss. "But it's going to be a great movie. You should totally see it. I'm really happy to be involved in this project."

Sing/Dance, I wrote. *:) 2B N-volved w/proj.*

"Okay," I said. I tried to think of what sort of things I'd always wondered about him. "Hey—I mean, next question: Are you dating Jill Tatum from *One Big, Happy Family*?"

"That pertains to relationships," Brynn said. "It's on the list of off-limits questions."

"Oh, right," I said. "Sorry." Then I thought of a good one that wasn't on the off-limits list. "What do you do for fun?"

Colby smiled. "I don't have much time for fun. But I like to play video games."

"Your typical teenage guy," Brynn added.

For the next ten minutes, I asked Colby about his favorite food (pizza), when his next album would be coming out (he wasn't sure yet), his biggest pet peeve (rude drivers), and if he liked working on a sitcom (yes). Except for the obvious fact that anything Colby

Summers said was interesting, it was probably the most boring interview ever. But it wasn't entirely my fault—there were too many questions I wasn't allowed to ask.

When my time was up, Brynn gave me a folder with three approved photographs that we would be allowed to run in my imaginary school paper. It seemed a shame that I couldn't actually print them. "Can I take a picture with him? Just one?" I asked.

Brynn shook her head.

"Oh, come on, Brynn," Colby said. "Just one. What's the harm? We do it for fans all the time."

"Well, I guess it's okay," she said. She took my phone out of her jacket pocket, and Colby put his arm around my shoulder. I could have died right then and there. I'd seen him shirtless on TV and in pictures, but I still couldn't get over how solid his perfectly toned arm felt against me. His skin was flawless, the color of gingerbread, and he was warm and smelled kind of citrusy. Everything about him was so perfect; it was like he'd been grown in a lab as the ideal specimen of a human male.

"Take care, Emily," Colby said. "It was nice meeting you."

"You, too," I said, still feeling dazed from the whole encounter.

"Since you're a member of the media, we'd prefer that you not publish that photo on the net or in print media without our prior approval, as a courtesy to us for granting the interview," Brynn said. "Of course, the paparazzi take candid shots all the time, as do fans, but we always appreciate the opportunity to have Colby photographed according to our specifications about angles and lighting, that sort of thing. And, of course, trying to stay ahead of media saturation is close to impossible these days, but we do what we can." She handed me her business card: NOREEN J. WOLFE PUBLICITY, INC. "You can send me the edited draft at this email address. I'll get back to you with any changes as soon as possible. And, once again, we appreciate your interest in Colby." Brynn's BlackBerry started beeping. "Colby, we need to get you over to makeup. Emily, I'm sorry I can't walk out with you, but I'll page one of the police officers to pick you up."

We walked outside, and a few minutes after Brynn and Colby left, the Easter Bunny cop came to get me in one of those carts. He drove me back to where I'd parked my bicycle. "Hope your interview went well, Lois Lane," he said. "You're probably too young to get that. Lois Lane was Superman's girlfriend. She was a reporter."

"I'm familiar with the reference," I said. After almost an entire school year sitting at the nerd boys' table, I was well versed in Superman trivia.

"Stay out of trouble, now! Heh heh! Good-bye, young lady!" he said.

"Good-bye, man with one foot in the grave," I muttered.

"What?"

"Oh, what I said was, 'Good-bye—if I can, I'll be good and behave.'"

He chuckled. "You do that!"

He went back to sitting in his squad car with the driver's side door open as I got on my bike and rode away. I'd gone about half a mile when I realized I'd left my interview notes—in my Cool Stuff notebook!—in Colby Summers's trailer.

When I got back, the Easter Bunny Cop was still sitting in the squad car, engrossed in a conversation with someone on his police radio. His back was to me, so he didn't even realize I was there. I waited for what seemed like forever for him to turn around, but he never did. It was getting late, and I knew Dad would freak about me riding my bike alone after dark, so I needed to get home before he did. I decided I'd ride back to Colby's trailer, grab my notebook, and be on my way before anyone even noticed. It wasn't like I was sneaking onto the set or anything.

I left my bike by the side of Colby's trailer and knocked on the door. No answer. There was no telling when he'd get back; I tried the doorknob. It wasn't locked. I'd grabbed my notebook and was about to leave when I heard someone coming. I don't know why, but I instinctively felt the need to hide, so I quickly crawled under a table that had a tablecloth that went nearly to the floor. I could see three pairs of feet: two women's and one man's.

"I don't see why this one bothers you so much more than any of the others," Brynn was saying. "We do this all the time."

"Come on, Brynn," Colby said. "She was so young, with her middle school paper. Such a cute little thing. So sweet."

Was Colby Summers talking about me? Colby Summers thought I was cute? I nearly screamed.

"The majority of your fans are cute little girls," said Brynn. "I don't see what you're getting at."

"Amy, you understand, don't you?" Colby asked. "You should have seen her. She was so nervous. I think she had a crush on me."

"Of course she had a crush on you," the other woman said. "You're adorable!"

"I felt so bad lying to such a sweet kid," he said.

Lying? What could he have lied about? What, he didn't really like pizza?

"What else could you do?" Brynn asked. "Tell her the truth?"

"Yeah, right." Colby sort of laughed. "Hi, Emily. It's so nice to meet you. I'm not really seventeen. I'm twenty-eight. Would you like to meet my wife Amy?"

WHAT???

"Yes, I'm sure Noreen would have loved that," Brynn said. "Look, I know it's difficult, but there's no turning back now. It was Noreen's decision to sell you as a teen heartthrob, and in all fairness, her strategy has made you a star."

Then I heard a baby—not crying, but making those drooly, babbling noises they make.

"How's Daddy's big boy? Has Daniel been good while Daddy was working?" Colby said in a soft voice.

DADDY?

"You're right, Brynn," Colby continued. "I shouldn't complain. Let's go get something to eat. I'm sure I'll shake this off."

I waited until they'd been gone a few minutes before slipping out and jumping on my bike. Instead of going back the way I'd come, I ducked the barricade and rode off into the surrounding woods. It took longer to get home that way, but I wanted to make sure no one saw me, and the long ride was a good way to clear my head. I couldn't believe that Colby Summers was a twenty-eight-year-old father. No way.

I thought about calling up one of my old friends in Pleasant Hill and dishing—I mean, I was dying to tell *someone*. But even though we'd said we'd stay in touch and all that stuff you say when somebody moves, I hadn't really been in contact with them much, and it would be weird to call up out of the blue and tell them something this bizarre. They'd think I was making it up. Still, what a strange piece of information to find myself with. It wasn't like I was going to write an exposé in our imaginary school paper. I could've emailed a tip to a tabloid or something, but what would have been the point in that? I didn't know much about how all this Hollywood stuff worked, but I did have enough common sense to realize that this type of thing could damage someone's career. And Colby really was as nice as I always thought he'd be—nicer, even. As I turned the key in our front door, I vowed that I would be a true and loyal fan and never let anyone know what I'd found out.

I was sort of congratulating myself on being such a good person, and imagining how beautifully literary it was that I would carry Colby's secret to the grave without his ever knowing, when I heard Dad's car. As soon as he opened the door, he yelled, "EMILY!"

I guess he'd heard about the suspension.

Ten

"*First question,*" Dad said, "are you okay?"

"I'm okay," I said. "A few scratches on my face, that's all."

Dad pulled me toward the middle of the kitchen and gently tilted my head so the overhead light illuminated the damage. "Nothing a little cortisone cream won't fix," he said. He hugged me tight. "I had a message to call Sonny when I got out of the audit. He kept telling me you were fine, but I drove like a maniac coming home. I had to see for myself. You're really okay?" Dad and I walked into the den and sat down. "What's going on, Emily? It's not like you've ever gotten into trouble at school before. Is somebody picking on you?"

I nodded.

"Why didn't you tell me? Maybe I could have helped. Did this other girl attack you today?"

"No. I attacked her. She said something about Mom."

"What did she say?"

"Nothing specific—some crack about me wanting my mommy. I don't even know if she knows Mom's gone, or if she'd care if she did, or if she knows and meant it that way because she's the evil spawn of Satan. But she said it, and I lost it."

"What happened with these girls? And why didn't you come to me?" Dad asked.

"It's all so stupid. I thought it would blow over, and I didn't want to bother you. You're busy trying to make partner."

"Emily, I'm never too busy for you."

"It's hard to explain. I'm sorry I got suspended, but my grades are all really good. I can still keep my average up," I said.

"That's not my primary concern," Dad replied. "I don't like the other kids messing with you like this. Maybe if I had a talk with the administration and asked if they could step in? Or maybe the school counselor could help?"

"No, Dad!" I said. "That will make it worse. Please, let me handle it."

"How are you going to handle it?"

"I'm not sure yet," I said. "But I've got five days off to figure it out. Lucky me, huh?"

Dad looked skeptical. "All right, Emily. But I want to be kept in the loop from now on. I'll stay out of it for the moment, but if these kids keep it up, I'm going to get involved and demand that the administration put a stop to this. Fair enough?"

"Okay," I said.

"You know, it's kind of funny . . . ," Dad said.

"What?"

"I was going to take you out of school for a few days this week anyway. One of the partners was supposed to give a presentation on estate planning at a big CPA convention in New York. He's not going to be able to get away, so he asked me to fill in. I thought I'd take you with me—unless, of course, you'd like to stay here and have your uncle babysit."

"And miss New York City?" I said. "Not likely! When do we go?"

"Tuesday morning," Dad said. "But keep in mind that you'll have to stay in the hotel room while I'm in meetings all day. We won't be able to do any sightseeing until the evenings. I can't have you running around the big city all by yourself."

"I've got to pack!"

"I question the wisdom of rewarding your suspension with a trip," Dad said. "But given the circumstances, maybe a little time away is just what you need."

So many things were going on in my head: the fight with Heatherly, what they'd have in store for me when I came back to school, the trip to New York, the truth about Colby. Before I went to bed that night, I took another look at Brynn's card. I typed "Noreen J. Wolfe Publicity, Inc." into my computer's search engine. "Results 1–10 of 27,890 for Noreen J. Wolfe Publicity, Inc.," the screen read. I scanned the first several pages and saw that nearly every major celebrity was listed in connection with that agency. They must've represented dozens of A-listers. One of the results was an article from two years ago about the woman the company was named for. I clicked on it.

WHO'S AFRAID OF THE BIG, BAD WOLFE? EVERYONE

If you visited the homes of every major actor or singer in the United States, you'd find that 9 out of 10 of them have one thing in common: Noreen J. Wolfe is number one on their speed dial.

Wolfe has made a name for herself—and plenty of enemies along the way—by structuring the universe to suit her clients' needs. "She's the most powerful publicist in the industry," one insider told us on condition of anonymity. "Everyone plays by her rules because we're all terrified of crossing her. She's that invincible."

Most aspiring stars would sell their grandmothers to get on Wolfe's client list, and with good reason: Wolfe's track record is impeccable. She creates public opinion on a global scale, crafting her clients into the most adored and sought-after entertainers in the world. No public relations debacle has thus far proven too difficult for her to spin: she's taken actors who were overwhelmingly reviled for bad behavior and flipped their image completely.

To read the rest of this article, subscribe now for a low monthly price!

Brynn's card said that Noreen J. Wolfe Publicity, Inc., had offices in Los Angeles and New York. The New York address was below Brynn's name.

I was going to need some money.

Eleven

I tossed and turned all night, excited that I had a plan but worried about how I'd fund it. I owned one valuable thing, and I was reluctant to part with it. But I couldn't think of any other option.

It was an heirloom bracelet Mom had left me. Total carat weight of 2.36, with seventy-nine diamonds in platinum settings. Mom had never been much of a jewelry person. She'd said that she felt bad wearing thousands of dollars on her wrist when there were people in the world who went to bed hungry. Besides, Mom was practical, and there was absolutely nothing practical about a diamond bracelet. She'd kept it, though, because it had been her great, great grandmother's. Apparently, our ancestors had been pretty loaded at one time, but they'd lost it all during the Great Depression. Still, they'd managed to hold on to one sweet piece of ice.

There's an old saying about desperate times calling for desperate measures.

Mom would understand. Especially since she never cared that much for bling in the first place. She'd probably have been proud that I was doing something practical with it. At least, that's what I told myself.

There was only one jeweler in our town, and he was in Lions Club with Dad, so I couldn't go to him. There were pawn shops in a neighboring city, but I wasn't sure how I could get there. Sonny would never drive me to a place like that—he'd always said they were armed robberies waiting to happen. Besides, I'd have to lie to him about my reason for going.

I went back to my computer and typed in "buy sell jewelry." I found a place, researched them to make sure they were legit, uploaded a photo of the bracelet along with a copy of the old appraisal, and waited. They were interested and emailed me, saying I should overnight the bracelet using their account number. The FedEx guy showed up early the next morning, right after Dad left for work. Lucky for me it was tax season or Dad wouldn't have been at the office on a Saturday . . . at least not that early.

I got an email from the company Monday morning. They offered me three thousand dollars. I'd never sold anything before, but since my dad had taught me something about money, I felt compelled to haggle over the price. Thirty-five hundred, I told them, and I'd need it sent to the Western Union at the grocery store in town that night. Thirty-two fifty, they said.

Sold.

I had Dad drive me to the grocery store to pick up a quart of milk when he got home. While he waited in the car, I showed my student ID to the lady at the Western Union counter and got the $3,250.

I ran through a mental checklist: a trip to New York, $3,250, an address, and Dad stuck in meetings all day.

All systems go.

Twelve

We got to the airport in Cincinnati at an obscenely early hour and arrived in New York before ten A.M. that Tuesday. Dad had a few minutes to put his things away before it was time to register at the conference. "I'll be only a block away," he told me. "Call me if you have an emergency. You can catch up on some homework or read or watch TV until I get back around five, and we'll get some dinner and look around the city. Stay here in the room and keep the door locked. Don't go anywhere, all right?"

"I think it could be potentially dangerous for a girl my age, who's never been to New York in her life, to wander around the city by herself," I said.

Notice how I didn't say I wasn't going to do it, though.

I propped a couple of pillows behind me and clicked on the TV. As soon as Dad was gone, I changed into a skirt and sweater, fixed my hair, and put on a little lip gloss. I grabbed Brynn's business card, the key card to the hotel room, the cash, plus a little extra I had from my allowance that I figured I'd need for expenses.

One cool thing I already loved about New York was how nobody paid any attention to you at all. No one seemed to care that I was unaccompanied by a parent or guardian as I breezed past the front desk and out the door of the hotel. I was afraid I'd get lost if I took the subway, so I decided to catch a cab. The doorman was getting them for people outside our hotel, but I didn't want to risk drawing attention, since he'd seen me come in with Dad. I watched how he hailed them, and then I walked to the next block. When I saw a cab coming, I stepped slightly off the curb and raised my hand like the doorman had done. It worked! I climbed into the back and gave the driver the address. He let me out at a skyscraper on Madison Avenue.

I took the elevator to the thirty-ninth floor. A young man whose dramatic sideburns seemed at odds with his professional necktie sat at the front desk. "I'd like to see Noreen J. Wolfe, please," I told him.

He looked at me with an amused sort of pity. "What time is your appointment?" he asked.

"I don't have one," I said. "But I need to talk business with her."

"Of course you do," he said smugly. "I'm afraid that Ms. Wolfe is all booked up today. She's in a staff meeting right now and has client appointments for the rest of the day. Is there something I could help you with? You want me to buy some cookies for your Girl Scout troop?"

"No—real business. I want to hire Ms. Wolfe."

"Do you have any idea what that would cost?" he asked.

"I've recently come into an inheritance," I said. "I have money."

"All right, then. Perhaps I could book an appointment for you with one of her assistants. Let's see . . . I could work you in . . . the third week of October?"

"That's seven months from now!" I said. "I need to see Ms. Wolfe today. Before five o'clock."

"I'm afraid that's impossible," he said. "Excuse me." He pushed a button and began answering calls. "Noreen J. Wolfe Publicity. How may I direct your call?"

What this guy didn't understand was that I had a very small window of time in which to operate, and I wasn't giving up that easily. I had one shot at this before I went back to Ohio and the Daisies and whatever new persecution they'd had time to cook up during Heatherly's five-day suspension.

"Hi, it's Robert," I heard the guy at the desk say. "Noreen's got twenty-five for lunch today. Are you ready?" Then he began placing an order, with all sorts of specifics about which salads required dressing on the side and that kind of thing. One of the types of sandwiches he ordered was called the Joe Namath. I recognized the name because Sonny had a book about him on his coffee table. He had been some big-deal football player for the New York Jets a zillion years ago. "Put it on the account and send it over as soon as it's ready," Robert the desk guy said to the person on the phone.

I went back outside and flagged down another cab. "Where can I get the Joe Namath sandwich?" I asked the driver.

When I got to the deli, I went up to the counter and told the man at the register, "I'm here to pick up the order for Noreen J. Wolfe Publicity." The man wrinkled his eyebrows at me like he didn't believe me. "Robert sent me."

"I thought we were delivering," he said.

"Change of plans. You know Noreen," I said. Apparently, he did, because he shook his head.

"You're a kid. I thought they only used college students as runners."

"I *am* a college student," I said. "Skipped a bunch of grades. My IQ scores are completely whack—ask me to multiply something."

Thank goodness he didn't take me up on that, because I actually pretty much suck at math.

"It'll be a few minutes," he said.

Now I just had to figure out a way to get past Robert again without being recognized. "You guys sell those hats, Frank?" He was wearing a name tag.

"Why would you want to buy one of those?"

"Are you kidding me? Logo caps are so in they're almost out!" Yeah, like a few years ago. But I figured he didn't know that.

He took a cap from under the counter and looked it over. "Fifteen bucks," he said.

I figured I'd better seem like I knew my way around. If I jumped at it, he'd know I wasn't from the city, and it might tip him off that I wasn't really working for the publicity firm. "Get outta here!" I said.

Frank grinned. "All right, twelve. But that's my final offer."

I handed over the cash and tucked the cap into my purse.

When the order was ready, there was no way I could carry the bags all by myself. "They should've known better than to send one kid to pick up all of this," Frank said. "Mickey, take her over in the van and help her get the stuff upstairs."

Right before we got off the elevator with the food, I slipped the cap on, tucking my hair under it, and followed behind Mickey with stacks of bags obscuring my face. Robert waved us through as he worked the phone, never even noticing me. We set the food on tables outside a conference room with glass doors and walls. "Thanks for your help," I told Mickey. "I can take it from here." Brynn was sitting at the end of the table, and at the other end was a middle-aged woman who was standing up, speaking. I'd have to make sure Brynn didn't recognize me. I pulled down the bill of the cap as far as I could.

I separated salads from subs while the people in the meeting tried to pretend they were focused on the speaker instead of the food. The woman addressing the meeting gestured for me to bring the food in as she spoke, so I went in. "Cobb salads?" I said, and began distributing them around the table to those with raised hands. The speaker continued going over some boring percentages.

After I'd distributed everyone's lunch, I hung around the back of the room, waiting for the lady to finish talking.

"And by the way, I wasn't pleased with the way that event came off," she was saying. "So you tell the planners that if they expect our clients to show up to their next little fete, we'd better be talking private jet, deluxe accommodations for the client and a guest, and some serious swag—the gifts at these past few events have been pathetic. We won't waste our clients' time for a watch and a handbag or two. If they want our people to make the scene, it had better be worth their while." She noticed me standing there. "I think we have everything we need. You can go now."

I almost lost my nerve when she spoke to me, but I took a deep breath and said, "I was waiting until you were finished. I wanted to talk to Noreen J. Wolfe for a quick second after your meeting."

"I am Noreen J. Wolfe, and that was a quick second. Now get out. We have work to do."

"But I'm not really a deli employee," I said. "I want to hire you."

Noreen J. Wolfe looked at the people seated around the table and snickered. "You want to hire me? That's rich. Is this some sort of practical joke? Did one of you put her up to this?" Then the smile left her face. "I hate practical jokes. Whoever did this is fired."

"It's not a joke," I said. "I have money—three thousand two hundred fifty dollars!"

"Well, since you have three thousand two hundred fifty dollars, then I guess that's a different story," she said. "That should almost cover the five minutes of my time you've just wasted. Pay at the desk on your way out."

Brynn was hiding her face behind her hands.

"But I really need your services," I said. "You create public opinion. I read about you. You're like magic—you can do anything. I need your help . . . desperately." Noreen stared at me a moment and then smiled strangely.

"All right, young lady," she said. "I'll tell you what. If you can answer one question correctly for me, I'll take you on." Glancing at the group behind her, she pulled me toward a window, tapped on the glass, and gestured at Rockefeller Center. "Who was the man responsible for that structure?"

"John D. Rockefeller, the rich philanthropist. He gave away tons of money to help people."

"Wrong," she said. "The man responsible for the Rockefeller Center was Ivy Lee, Rockefeller's publicist. If you knew your history, perhaps you'd be familiar with the term 'robber baron.' John D. Rockefeller was widely condemned by his contemporaries because they perceived him as someone who made his fortune at the expense of the common man. After a little incident called the Ludlow Massacre, where twenty people were killed during a riot over the horrible conditions at one of Rockefeller's coal mining camps, Ivy Lee developed what we now call crisis communication. He advised Rockefeller to give away substantial sums so that the public would change their view of him from rich fat cat to someone who actually cared about them. It was Lee's idea to name it Rockefeller Center—in so doing, the name Rockefeller came to be associated with wealth, stability, charity, and civic mindedness—not murderous riots. The majority of the American public today has no idea what happened in Ludlow, Colorado, in 1914, but any fool can tell me exactly what you just did.

"The point of this little history lesson, my dear, is simply this: It's not what really happens, it's what I can make you *think* happened. For all practical purposes, perception is reality. I create perception; therefore, I create reality. I make the world what I want it to be.

"And I don't do it for three thousand two hundred fifty dollars.

"Now, get out of my conference room before I call security."

I was almost speechless.

Notice I said almost. I couldn't give up just yet, not after getting so close.

"I'm sorry, Ms. Wolfe," I said. "I didn't mean to offend you. I want you to know that I have complete respect for what you do."

"You don't have the first clue what I do," she replied.

"No, really, I mean it," I said.

She stared at me, and there was an awkward silence. Like I said before, awkward silences freak me out, so I started talking to fill the space. "I read about how powerful you are. You're a total genius at this stuff. That's why I went to all this trouble to try to talk to you— you're amazing! I mean, I totally bought that Colby Summers was seventeen! I never would have guessed that—"

"What did you just say?" Noreen snapped.

Uh-oh. So much for taking it to the grave. "Nothing," I said. "I'm so sorry. I'll get out of your conference room now."

"Everyone out!" Noreen yelled. As everyone made a dash for the door, Noreen called, "Not you, Sterling." Brynn turned around. "Explain this," said Noreen.

"Hi, Brynn," I said. "Sorry."

"Lovely. So you know each other," Noreen said. "You complete imbecile!" she yelled at Brynn.

"Noreen, believe me—I have no idea how this got out. I granted her request for an interview with Colby for her school paper—"

"You did *what*?" Noreen said. "Why would you waste his time on a school paper? What were you *thinking*?"

"You're always telling us to think outside the box," Brynn explained. "I was hoping for a viral marketing sort of result—we give an interview to an unlikely source, a girl in his primary fan base. The mainstream media picks up the story that a major celeb grants an interview to a middle school paper, and Colby then comes across as a down-to-earth guy in touch with the teens who love him. Plus, Emily tells all her friends at school—"

"Not likely," I said, more to myself than anyone else. They both looked at me. "I mean, I'd have to have friends first before I could tell them anything. That's pretty much why I'm here."

"Look, Ms. Wolfe, this is all my fault. Please don't blame Brynn. She was super nice to me, and I really appreciate it. I didn't mean to spy, but I left my interview notes in Colby's trailer, and when I went back to get them, Brynn and Colby came in with his wife and baby, and before I had a chance to think about what I was doing, I was hiding behind the furniture, overhearing everything they said."

Noreen said to Brynn, "I repeatedly stressed to you the importance of security on the set! This is a complete fiasco! I've fired people for far less than this."

"Please, Ms. Wolfe," I said. "It's not her fault. I won't tell anyone. I promise."

Noreen laughed. "Oh, that's good news. She's not going to tell anyone! What a relief! Teenage girls are renowned for their ability to keep secrets!"

"Have you told anyone about this?" Brynn asked. "Anyone at all?"

"Not a soul," I replied. "I told you I don't have any friends to tell."

"Perfect! The juiciest piece of Hollywood gossip this decade in the hands of a social misfit—naturally, she's going to use it as social currency!" said Noreen.

"Maybe we could have her sign a confidentiality agreement?" Brynn offered.

Noreen looked at her, disgusted. "She's a *child*, you twit! Her signature's not worth the crayon it's written in." She squinted her eyes at me. "What's all this really about? Come on—cards on the table. You came here to blackmail me, didn't you? All right, name your price. Let's begin the negotiation."

"I'm not trying to blackmail anybody," I said. "I would never do anything to hurt anyone on purpose—especially not Colby. He may be eleven years older than I thought, but he's still a great person."

Noreen scoffed. "We're ruined," she said to Brynn.

"Emily," Brynn said, "you said something about wanting to hire our agency. Why don't you tell us exactly why you came here."

"Everyone at school hates me," I said. "I need someone to do for me what that guy Ms. Wolfe was telling me about did for Rockefeller. I want people to see me differently. If things don't change, I don't know how I can ever get through middle school. It's too awful. I can't take it anymore."

Noreen paced the floor, thinking. Then she spun around. "Welcome to our agency, Emily," she said.

Brynn said, "What are you talking about, Noreen?"

"Crisis management," Noreen said. "Colby's fans find out he's twenty-eight, and his career tanks, along with our commission and our reputation. Emily needs us, and we need her. Emily, we'll represent you, and in exchange, you keep your mouth shut about Colby. Brynn, from now on, your top client is Emily . . . what's your last name?"

"Wood," I said.

"And you live in the little town where Colby's filming in Iowa?"

"Ohio."

"Ohio, Iowa . . . some place where they grow corn. What's the difference? All right, then, Emily Wood from Ohio," Noreen said. "Brynn, make her a star. Make her own that little school of hers. I want this girl to be the biggest thing her classmates have ever seen. You do that, and she won't need any dirt on Colby to carve out a place on the popularity totem pole."

"But, Noreen! You can't be serious!" Brynn said. "I worked so hard to be assigned to Colby. I earned handling his publicity during this film!"

"And you promptly blew it," Noreen said. "But I'll give you a chance to redeem yourself. I'll keep you on Colby, but now you have two big clients instead of one. You keep this girl busy. You keep her happy. You want to prove to me that you can make a celebrity's career, then you show me what you can do for one kid in a little Ohio town. Do it right, I'll promote you. Screw it up, you'll never even fetch coffee in another PR firm." Noreen stood right in front of Brynn, but Brynn didn't flinch. If she was intimidated, she hid it well. "You sweet young things always think you can walk right into my job and fill my shoes. Well, sister, if you want to get where I am, you're going to pay some dues. So, do you think you can handle this assignment?"

"Of course. In fact, it's insultingly easy," Brynn replied. "I could do it in my sleep."

"Good," Noreen said. "In that case, let's make it a little more interesting. Your budget for this campaign is . . . how much money did you offer me again?"

"Three thousand two hundred and fifty," I replied.

"You expect me to launch an entire campaign on three thousand two hundred and fifty dollars?" Brynn protested.

"I'm sure you can dream up something. After all, you'll be doing this in your sleep, right?" Noreen said. "Colby's filming schedule has him in Ohio until early May. That gives you . . . let's see . . . roughly two months, start to finish. Brynn, get to work." With that, Noreen walked out of the conference room.

"Four years at the most prestigious university communications program in the country, three years working my butt off here, and now I'm a glorified babysitter!" Brynn said.

"I am really, really sorry," I said. "I didn't mean to get you in trouble."

"It's not your fault," she said halfheartedly. "Well, I mean, it *is*, but . . . whatever."

"You really think you can make people at school stop hating me? Even when three of the most popular girls have made it their mission in life to destroy me?"

"Oh, please," Brynn said. "As I said, it's insultingly easy. Those little witches won't know what hit them." She sat down and put her head in her hands. Then she looked up at me resolutely. "You're not exactly the first major launch I had in mind, but if Noreen wants to see a campaign, I'll show her a campaign."

"Campaign?" I asked.

"It's a P.R. term for an entire communications plan. I'm not sure yet how the campaign will take shape or how I'll pull it off with this pathetic budget, but it will happen. I'll need some information—I want to know everything about these girls and what they've been doing to you at school; then I'll do some analysis. After that, I'll develop tactics. In the meantime, you don't say anything to anyone unless I tell you to. Don't let anyone know you have a publicist. Understand?"

"I'll do whatever you say."

II.
BENCHMARKS AND SWOT ANALYSIS

Thirteen

Brynn met me at my hotel room the next morning after Dad left for his conference.

"I've got to get some data from you about our target market. I'm well versed in youth and how they negotiate their buying power, but I'll need to verify some things for your particular geographic area, and of course, I'll need to know your specific situation so I can decide how best to proceed."

We sat down at a table, and Brynn took notes on her laptop while I told her the whole story about the Daisies and everything they'd done to me and why.

"So what did your mom say when you got suspended for fighting?" she asked.

"My mom died right before I turned twelve," I said. "Cancer."

Her expression softened. "I'm sorry."

I nodded.

She seemed uncomfortable for a moment, then said. "All right, let's focus." She ran through several questions about what was popular at my school and things I liked. But it was funny—she didn't have to ask me which bands were cool and which TV shows people watched and the magazines they read—she would tell me the answer, with a sort of question mark at the end, just to make sure she was correct.

"How did you know all that?" I asked.

"Our agency knows what teenagers will like before they do. It's our job," Brynn explained.

"I don't get it. How can you know what's popular before it's popular?"

"Try to keep up." She turned her computer so I could see the screen too, and created a document called GOALS. "All right, then. Let's decide what we're shooting for. First, what does every girl on the planet want?"

"What do you mean?" I asked.

"I mean, what does any girl your age—regardless of where she lives, what she looks like, who her family is, whatever—what does she want?"

"I don't know. World peace?"

"This isn't a beauty pageant, Emily."

"Okay, well, I guess most girls my age want to be pretty and have great clothes."

"Exactly." Brynn typed CLOTHES/LOOK on the first line. "What else?"

"Gosh, it sounds so shallow, but . . ."

"Say it."

"A hot boyfriend?" I said.

HOT BOYFRIEND, she typed on the next line. "Moving on to the specific," she said. "In your town, what thing, position, or state of being does most every girl covet?" I thought for a moment, and then Brynn said, "This May Queen thing seems to be pretty important to that Heatherly you were telling me about."

"Well, yeah," I said. "May Queen is the pinnacle of popularity for girls at my school."

MAY QUEEN, she typed.

"You're putting May Queen as a goal for me? That could never happen."

"Brainstorming sessions are supposed to be free from linear thinking," she said. Then she asked, "What else? What's the primary vehicle for social status at your school?" She snapped her fingers. "Cheerleading—of course! Do a cheer for me."

"You're not serious," I said.

"I'm completely serious. It's a universally known fact that in any American school, cheerleaders are popular. Get up." She moved the chairs back to give me room. "Come on. Do a cheer you're familiar with from school, and then end with that sort of flourish they do."

"Flourish?"

"You know—the flourish. Big fake smile, some interjections coupled with kicks and arm motions, and an encouragement for the team to defeat the other team. Like this." Brynn's expression changed from serious to frighteningly ecstatic, like an evil monkey that had consumed a dozen espressos. "WOO! YEAH!" she yelled, smiling painfully. She kicked her right leg, touching it with her right hand. "Go, Tigers! Defense!" Then, as immediately as she had begun, she was serious again, as though the whole incident had never occurred. "Your turn," she said.

"No way. I'm not the cheerleader type."

"You have exactly five seconds to perform a cheer," she said sternly.

"All right," I replied, "but I'm warning you, I stink." I put on a big, fake smile like the one she had modeled and ran through a cheer I knew from pep rallies: "Hey, Jets! . . . Yeah. . . . Are you hot? . . . No. . . . You know why? . . . Why? . . . 'Cause we're too, too COOL!" For my flourish, I yelled, "All right! Woo! Make a touchdown!" and tried to kick the way Brynn had done. But my leg bent like the letter *L*, and I nearly kicked her in the face.

Brynn looked at me in silence.

"I have lousy hamstrings," I said. "Never been much of a kicker."

"Promise me that, no matter what I say in the future, you will never, ever do that again."

"I told you! Didn't I tell you?" I said.

"It's probably for the best. Cheerleading tryouts tend to be toward the end of a school year anyway, and it would take time we don't have. We need something more immediate. A crowd you can hang with that has serious social clout. Some sort of organization everyone wants to be in. All towns have them. What's the network of the social elite?"

"Well, there's Delts, but you might as well try to get me a seat on the next space shuttle. I'd never get in."

DELTS, she typed. "What's that?"

"Short for Delta Something Something. I can't remember the rest. It's a sorority at Wright High. They take about fifteen new girls every year, mostly from the high school and only two from eighth grade, to represent the following year's high school freshman class. Total popularity contest. If a Delt sister decides you have 'potential,' she'll let you hang out with them for a few weeks—they call that 'rush'—which I guess means they hurry up and see if they like you. If they do, they name you a 'pledge,' which means you get a tentative membership. During your pledge period, you kiss up to your 'big sister,' which is what they call the girl who rushed you, and her Delt friends until you're an official member. They basically try to see how much crap you're willing to take to become one of them. I think all they do is have parties and do fund-raisers for the end-of-the-year debutante presentation at the country club. But getting into Delts, especially at the end of eighth-grade year, is popularity gold."

"You seem to know a lot about it for someone who can't even remember the official name," Brynn said.

"Even though it's repugnant, it's culturally fascinating."

"Stop talking like that," Brynn said.

"Like what?"

"Like a comparative lit professor. It's creepy. You're only fourteen."

"So I'm supposed to sound like an empty-headed moron?" I asked.

"A moron, by definition, would be empty-headed, so that's redundant," Brynn said. "Don't get sassy with me. I'm trying to help you."

"Sorry," I said.

"Back to this Delts thing. You said only two get in from your grade?"

"Right. Most girls, if they get in at all, don't make it in until the end of ninth or tenth grade."

"Good. We'll need to get you in as soon as possible."

I laughed. "Sorry, Brynn. Not gonna happen. I can't even get anyone to sit with me at lunch. I'm certainly not going to get into Delts."

"Oh, you'll get in," she said. "And thank heaven there's no athletic ability involved."

"Would you let that go? It was embarrassing enough in the first place!" I looked at the computer screen. "So do we choose our goal from this list now?" I asked.

"Choose?" Brynn said. "We're going to do them all."

"No way! Why?"

"Because we can. Now then," she said, "let's begin our SWOT analysis."

"Our what?"

"SWOT," she said. "Strengths, Weaknesses, Opportunities, Threats. Public Relations 101. Here, take notes for me." She slid the laptop over to me and began inspecting me as though I were a horse at auction.

"Strengths and Weaknesses. Hair: a weakness at the moment, but nothing that can't be fixed. Eyes: strength—nice color, but make a note for more definition. Skin: strength—mostly clear, but note slight patchiness. Teeth: strength—nice alignment, good jaw structure. You wore braces, right? Money well spent. Moving on. . . . Body. Hmmm." Brynn had me get up and turn around three times, while she put her hands on my hips, inspected my ankles, and made me stand up straight. "Body—definitely a strength."

My body? A strength?

"You're kidding, right?" I asked. "I have no body."

"Neither do fashion models, and if I play my cards right, we might be able to snag some of those designer pieces," Brynn said. "All the major models our agency represents were wormy little things like you when they were your age. The other kids would call them the Flatlands or Pretzel Stick or something stupid like—"

"Plywood?" I offered.

"Plywood? That's yours, huh? You left that part out," she said.

"You mean you think I can be a model?"

"You're tall for your age, and thin, and you certainly have the gigantic feet they all seem to have—no offense. But there's more to it than the body. A lot of it is in the eyes, the attitude. You're cute and have potential to be stunning, but I don't see you as the modeling type."

"Fair enough," I said. Cute and potentially stunning worked for me.

"In any case," she continued, "the samples come in size two, so we're in business."

"Samples?" I asked.

"Patience. We'll get to them in time. Now then . . . opportunities. Opportunities are generally considered to be things you've got but haven't been using. You said you write poetry and that you're the editor of the school literary magazine. That means you're a creative thinker and you're good with words. That holds potential if we handle this campaign correctly. Okay . . . threats."

"That one's easy enough," I said. "The Daisies are my threat."

"Wrong," said Brynn. "First of all, you have me as your publicist, and they haven't seen the day they were a match for me. Second, threats aren't external. They're the barriers to success that come from within the brand. The only threat here is that you may not be able to sell it. I can create the brand, but you have to make the target audience believe in it. Think you can pull it off?"

"I'm not sure I understand. What brand?" I asked.

"In a manner of speaking, Emily, you're the brand. Only it's not the real you—it's the image we're going to create. It's how we publicists sell celebrities. We assign them a brand—sexy, macho, girl next door, romantic, humanitarian, whatever—and that's the way we sell them. Product development is consumer driven: we give people what they want. Become the brand that Wright Middle School wants, and they'll all line up to buy it."

"I'll do my best," I promised.

"That's all I can ask for. Now, obviously, the first thing we'll have to take care of is this awful hair."

"What's wrong with my hair?" I asked.

"You're not serious, right? When do you fly back to Ohio?"

"Tomorrow," I said.

"That's Thursday. And you're suspended until Monday?"

"Right."

"Splendid," Brynn said. "That will give us a little preparation time. I'll fly out Thursday as well; I need to get back to Colby anyway. Can you meet me at the set Friday morning?"

"Sure. I'll head over as soon as Dad leaves for work."

"You could have him drop you off."

"He'd ask too many questions," I said.

"Your call." She shut down her laptop. "In the meantime, I've got some details to take care of here in the city. No time to lose. We've got just a few days to lay the groundwork—and only a little over two months to pull off this entire campaign."

III.
PACKAGING

Fourteen

When we got back from New York, I had to tell Dad something to keep him from asking questions. If he knew what I'd done, he'd surely give me a lecture about how I shouldn't go around hatching zany schemes to try to deal with my problems when instead the thing to do would be to approach a conflict head-on with honesty and integrity. Yeah, and then at the end, I nobly shoot my own beloved dog because he has rabies or, hey, maybe Heatherly and I sit down and have a genuine talk and realize that we're both just two girls trying to make it in this crazy, mixed-up world, and we suddenly share a big hug and an orchestra starts playing.

Dad had no idea what I was dealing with.

Plus, if I explained what was going on, there'd be the matter of how I went around New York by myself and how I had hocked Mom's bracelet. I was still feeling kind of bad about selling it, and I knew Dad would flip out if he knew.

So, when he asked the obligatory "What are your plans for the day?" question before he left for work Friday morning, I replied, "Busy. I've actually got a project to work on."

"Really? What sort of project?"

I had to think for a minute. "Sort of a career project."

"Oh. I don't suppose you'd need to interview a CPA, because I happen to know a very smart fellow who'd be more than happy to assist."

"Thanks anyway, Dad, but you know I'm never going to be an accountant."

"I know—so, you're doing your project on becoming poet laureate?"

"Not exactly. Public relations."

"PR? What got you interested in that?"

"Well, I just read up on it a little bit. It's a career that requires good communication skills."

"True. I just figured you'd go for something more artistic. PR isn't exactly a creative field."

"Oh, you might be surprised," I said.

"Very well, then. Good luck on your project."

As soon as his car was out of sight, I biked over to the set to meet Brynn. "I'm taking you to see Patrick," she said. "If you wanted to get an appointment with him, you'd have to sell your soul, and even then you'd have to wait two years."

"I'm not so sure about this. It took me forever to grow my hair this long."

"Perhaps you're familiar with a little movie from last summer called *The Sexy Six*?" Brynn asked.

"Duh! Everybody knows that movie."

"As you may recall, the actress playing one of the spies had part of her hair torched on the set when an explosion had more bang than anticipated."

"I read about that!" I said. "She refused to wear extensions or wigs, so they had to come up with a completely new cut to compensate for the damage. When the movie came out, everyone wanted that haircut because it was so different and cool."

"Very good. Patrick, the man you're about to meet, is the one who created that cut. Whatever he wants to do with your hair, go with it," Brynn said.

When we got to the hair and makeup trailer, a man hugged Brynn and kissed her on the cheek. "Brynn, honey! Look at you! I could gobble you up with a spoon!" he said.

"Thanks," she replied. "Patrick, this is Emily."

"Sit, darling, and let's assess," Patrick told me, gesturing to a chair in front of three mirrors. He ran his hands through my hair for a moment and then sucked air noisily between his clenched teeth. "It's horrific," he said. "It's so wrong! Who would do this to hair? Obviously a stylist with no sense of composition. Everything is symmetrical!

Why doesn't someone tell the people who wield scissors that human beings have unique faces? Not to worry, though. I'm a professional; I can handle this." He composed himself and ran his hands through my hair in different ways, pulling parts of it back or pushing some forward as he spoke. "Okay, hmmm. I'm loving the cheekbones. I'm thinking, a layer to hit right here, and then some longer layers for a wispy look. And of course we'll razor instead of cut. The idea of scissors on this hair! As for color, we'll warm it up with some low lights, and then just around the face, we'll go with towheaded, dazzling highlights that scream, 'Youth, now!'"

"Be sure to show her how to style it, so she can re-create the magic—as much as anyone can without you there," Brynn said.

"Ooh, you're flattering me!" Patrick said. "You know how I love it!" He poked her playfully. After he finished the cut and color, Patrick showed me how to use the brush with the blow-dryer and how to seal my hair's cuticle with a flatiron. I didn't know my hair even had a cuticle, but the technique plus the highlights made my hair look super shiny, and the cut itself was nothing short of rocking. It was like something out of a music video.

After Patrick finished, Brynn said, "Next is makeup. You've never met the makeup artist before, but you've seen her feet."

It took me a minute to figure that one out. "Colby's wife is the makeup artist?"

"Yes," said Brynn. "So just make sure you don't say anything about how dumb this movie is in front of her."

"You know it's a dumb movie?" I asked. Brynn nodded. "Then why are you guys letting him do it? Why didn't you tell him to turn it down?"

"Noreen doesn't foresee Colby as having a long career. Teen idols are quick, big money, but they have a short shelf life. A savvy publicist takes the money and runs before the fan base grows up and the client's career tanks." She must've seen the look of disappointment on my face. "It's simply good business, nothing personal." She took me to another chair for makeup.

"Amy, this is the girl I told you about," Brynn said.

"Oh, hi—it's so nice to meet you. Colby said you were really sweet."

"I'm...I'm so sorry about...." I felt like I should apologize, but I didn't know what to say.

Amy said, "Don't be embarrassed. Brynn brought us up to speed on everything. Colby and I really appreciate your discretion. I'm glad to have the opportunity to help you out in return."

As Amy applied my makeup, she patiently walked me through the process so I could learn how to do it myself. Even though she spent a long time and used lots of different products, everything looked really natural: sheer pink on my lips and cheeks, and browns and beiges on my eyes. She even plucked my eyebrows, giving them a perfect arch. When she was finished, I barely recognized myself. Then she handed me a little bag filled with the same makeup she'd used on me. "Keep it. I have a great relationsip with Bonne Bell," she said.

It was getting late, and I needed to get home before Dad returned from the office and started worrying about me. "So what do we do next?" I asked Brynn.

"We need to continue to work on repackaging you," she replied.

"Repackaging me?" I asked. "Isn't that what we just did?"

"Hair and makeup are only part of it. You're not planning on wearing those clothes with this new look, are you?" Brynn said. "Since you don't want your dad to know, can you arrange some way to get him out of the house this weekend, at least for a few hours?"

"Not a problem. He always works all day on Saturdays during tax season."

"Perfect! Call me tomorrow when he leaves for work. I'll come to your house and we can go through your closet to see what we have to work with. Then we'll do some shopping."

Fifteen

Dad was gone before seven thirty that Saturday, and Brynn was there by seven forty-five—with contraband.

"These are proofs of the fashion spreads that will run in the May issue of *Flirt*," she said.

"How'd you get them?"

"My housemate's an assistant editor there," she explained.

"You have a roommate? But you're out of college and you work for a big-deal publicity firm."

"Have you priced housing lately in Manhattan?" Brynn asked. "Anyway, here's what we're going to do. This would be much easier if Noreen had given me a real budget to work with, but since she didn't, we're going to have to rework your existing wardrobe by adding a few key pieces. We can spend only about a thousand dollars or less from your budget. Incidentally, how does a kid your age come into $3K in discretionary funds?"

"My mom left me a diamond bracelet. Really old and beautiful. I sold it online."

"Seriously?"

"I know . . . I'm trying not to think about it. I'd probably never have worn it—Mom didn't—but still. It was hers, you know?"

Brynn looked sad. "In that case, let's be sure we make every penny count," she said. "Is there a thrift store around here?"

"Yeah," I said. "A big one, south of town. It's a whole warehouse of stuff."

"Good. Take a look at these spreads," she said, arranging the pages on the kitchen table. "There's a lot of retro feel going on. If we're really lucky, somebody's well-dressed grandma just cleaned out her closet for the first time in forty years. What we can't find there, we'll have to buy online. Look here. Two major themes for spring: they're calling them 'Flirty Florals' and 'Heavy Metal Glam.' I hope you realize what my roommate is risking by lending us these. Her EIC would kill her if she found out."

"EIC?" I asked.

"Editor in chief," she said.

"Why are we risking your roommate's job for this?"

"The idea, Emily, is to be ahead of the fashion curve," Brynn said. "But not too far ahead. You'll wear these looks before the magazine hits newsstands, before everyone else sees the fashion spreads and these styles become trends. You'll have worn them first. You'll be an early adopter."

"What's that?"

Brynn leaned her head back and rolled her eyes. "It's like I'm a walking dictionary," she said. "Early adopters are the people who are in on the fads first. They wear the new styles before everyone else does. They know about the hottest bands before they become mainstream. They use new slang before everyone else knows what it means. They're trendsetters. They're the ones advertisers and marketing people spend a fortune trying to capture: every hip brand needs them because they're the people consumers aspire to be. What they buy, everyone else will buy in six months to a year. Luckily for us, magazines work pretty far in advance. And since my roommate gave us these spreads before everyone else at your school will see them, making you an early adopter of the next big fashion trends won't be a problem. Now let's focus. Since these clothes aren't in stores yet, we'll have to improvise based on the general ideas.

"Flirty florals are definitely all about a free-flowing silhouette. Nothing tight. Very laid-back yet feminine. This heavy metal glam look is a tip of the hat to the over-the-top, ostentatious style of eighties glam rock. But they make it new by pairing it with traditional pieces. It's all about adding something unexpected and irreverent—giving it an edge. Do you own a black jacket?"

"Yeah." I took Brynn to my room and she started sorting through my closet.

"We'll make two piles," she said. "Stuff we can work with and stuff that's got to go." She tossed clothing into one pile or the other with comments such as "Burn this," or "Passable," or "What were you thinking?" When she got to the black jacket, she picked up one of the magazine pages and said, "See, right here. All we need to make this work is some flashy jewelry."

When Brynn finished with my closet, the "toss" pile was much bigger than the "keep" pile. We drove to the thrift store and purchased three bags full of stuff I never would have picked out on my own: a lime mini skirt; a pink dress from the eighties with a pattern of tiny green purses and shoes; a couple of belts with funky designs; a denim skirt with a frayed hem; a black camisole; an art deco blouse with little pictures of geishas; a burgundy blazer with giant lapels; side-zip jeans; a black, beaded cardigan; a navy blue hoodie from a high school I'd never heard of; a classic pair of jeans with faded-out knees; a faux-fur-lined denim jacket; a brown dress with a frilly collar and Western-style belt; a four-inch-wide rhinestone bracelet; and finally, a gigantic 1970s belt buckle, which Brynn said was meant to be because it was the only one in the whole store and just happened to be my actual zodiac sign, Scorpio.

"That was really fun," I said when we got home. "I don't usually enjoy shopping, but that was awesome."

"We need more stuff," Brynn said.

"Look at all we've got!" I said.

"But you've got a lot of days to fill with cool outfits. Too bad you're an only child. I'd love to raid your sister's closet right about now."

Then I remembered. "Some of my mom's stuff is packed away in boxes on the top shelf of my dad's closet," I said.

"Let's see what we've got," said Brynn. We took down three big boxes and began digging through them. "Dig the funky shoes!" she said, holding up a pair of strappy brown suede heels I'd never seen Mom actually wear. "Can you fit into them?" I slipped them on. Perfect. She sorted through a few more things and came upon a solid forest green silk brocade vest. "This one's a keeper," she said, "if we pair it correctly." Next, she found Mom's jewelry box. When Brynn opened it, a ballerina began dancing.

"I bought this for her birthday when I was six," I said. "Dad took me out shopping, and when I saw this, I thought the ballerina was so beautiful—graceful and willowy with light brown hair, like Mom. I had to get it for her. Dad tried to talk me out of it, but I was so determined." The ballerina had spun slower and slower until the music faded and she finally stopped. I met Brynn's eyes; they looked gentler than I'd ever seen before. "Probably the lamest present ever for a grown woman," I said, "but Mom seemed to like it."

"Of course she did," Brynn said.

I pulled out a necklace. "I always loved this one." It had a watch pendant, with light blue rhinestones on the back.

"Well, you're in luck," Brynn replied. "Last year, no way. This year, it could definitely work."

Brynn spent the next hour going through the clothes with me, putting together different variations on outfits and showing me how to pair each piece. I took notes and Brynn even took photographs of me and downloaded the files onto my computer: there were certain details that had to be just so in order to make each outfit work. For example, I had to roll up the sleeves on a certain shirt or leave a button open or pull a collar out exactly right so everything appeared effortless and captured the spirit of the fashion spreads. We spent the last of the money ordering some things from online specialty boutiques I'd never heard of. "The girls in this town will never know where you found these pieces," she said. "It will drive them crazy."

Brynn checked over the magazine pages again. "I wish we'd been able to find a tunic," she said. She looked at the silvery blue pillows on my bed. "Ever seen *The Sound of Music*?" She took off a pillowcase and held it against me. "Perfect. Do you sew?"

"I took home ec last semester. We made duffel bags."

"When I took home ec, we made collared shirts with buttons. Mine was a mess, but between the two of us, I think we can pull something together." We found Mom's old sewing machine in the basement. Brynn cut the top seam off the pillowcase, sewed a hem and armholes, added some ribbon detailing, and I had a tunic. Then Brynn pulled out a stack of magazines from her bag. "Reading material," she said.

"What do I need these for? I already have the wardrobe."

"Stylish girls don't simply *wear* the right outfit; they understand why it's the right outfit. Study these. Read what the fashion editors have to say about each trend. Analyze why you feel drawn to some looks and not others. Pay attention to how the models with your body type and coloring play up their features."

"I don't want to be shallow," I said.

"Then think of it as art—a personal extension of your visual aesthetic."

I nodded. "When you put it that way, it might be cool."

"Next item of business," said Brynn. "We've worked on the outside packaging, but that will take us only so far. You have to deliver on the brand promise."

"You're going to explain that, right?"

"Okay, let's say you have this product that comes in a snazzy box. All the ads say how great it is. The dazzled consumer forks over the money to buy it, but upon using said product, finds that there's nothing to it."

"But the manufacturer already has the consumer's money, so what do they care?"

"Because the consumer knows other consumers. And he or she might decide to tell those other consumers that the product was a rip-off. By and by, word gets around, and nobody else is buying. All that packaging and advertising have gone to waste as the product dies on the shelf," she said. "But, if that product lives up to the hype once purchased, the satisfied consumer tells others, who are influenced to make the same purchase. See what I mean?"

"Popularity," I said.

"Precisely." Brynn pulled out a notebook, where she'd jotted down a sort of outline. She checked off "Style/Fashion" and circled "Posture/

Body Language." Then she said, "Stand up straight. Shoulders back, head up. Now walk up and down the hall."

I did.

"Nope," she said.

"But I kept my head up and my shoulders back," I said.

"Yes, but you lack the attitude. Try it again, and this time, own the room."

"Own the room?"

"Keep your gait easy and relaxed, not too fast, not too slow. Put a little bit of your hips into it. Your walk has to say, 'I own this place. This is my world, and you just live in it.'"

I tried again.

Brynn shouted, "Hips, baby! You're not returning your books about stamp collecting to the library! You're working the room! The world is your catwalk!" After my fourth or fifth try, I could see what she meant. It really was all in the hips.

"That's weird," I told her. "It's kind of like your whole body walks, not just your legs."

"Kind of," she said. "Now practice that about twenty more times." After all that practicing, it felt pretty normal. Then Brynn went over body language with me—stuff like how to stand when you're talking to someone (not with your arms folded, which indicates you're emotionally closed off), how to sit (once in a while, letting your butt slouch down in the chair is okay because it indicates you're bored and too cool to be there), and what's an appropriate amount of personal space (you don't want to get close enough to count people's pores).

Next on Brynn's list were "Eye Contact," "Hallway Greetings," "Conversation Starters," and "Crisis Management." She looked at me the way a psychiatrist might a patient. "You're pretty good with adults, but it sounds like you don't make friends easily with kids your own age," she said.

I laughed. "You think not?"

"But *why* not?"

"Because I'm a freak?"

"When you're walking in the halls, do you make eye contact with people?"

"No."

"Do you talk to people before they talk to you?"

"No."

"And why don't you do either of these things?"

"I don't know."

"Yes, you do."

"Because everybody already hates me. The Daisies have turned everyone against me!" I said.

"The Daisies have seized upon a weakness, not created it," Brynn said. "Eye contact and initiating conversation are indicators of self-confidence, something you clearly lack when it comes to your peer group. What I want to know is why."

"Maybe it's just easier with grown-ups because they're probably going to at least be polite to you whether they like you or not. Or maybe it has nothing to do with self-confidence," I said. "Maybe people at my school are a bunch of fascists I don't want to be friends with anyway." Brynn didn't say anything, but the way she looked at me told me she wasn't buying it. "What if I did try to make eye contact, or start talking to somebody first . . . and it didn't work? I mean, why would anyone want to talk to me?"

"Because you're a nice and smart person?" Brynn said.

"Bor-ing!" I sang.

"All right," Brynn said. "As much as I'd love to psychoanalyze you and get to the bottom of this, we simply don't have the time. You think Emily is a freak, or boring, or whatever. I disagree, but fine. This campaign isn't about selling Emily; it's about selling the brand we're creating. That brand is confident and sparkling with positive energy. To sell this brand, you'll have to make eye contact, be the first to say hello . . . and have zero qualms about walking right up to someone and starting a conversation."

I groaned. "I don't know if I can do that."

Brynn said, "Think of it as playing a part, or as an experiment.

When you're afraid or it feels too hard, dig down deep and channel the brand. Forget scared little Emily and become the brand. This could be really good for you. The great thing about self-confidence is that, like any skill, it improves with practice. Fake it till you make it, as they say. Now, first, you're going to have to learn to look people in the eye. You'll have to do this in the hallways when you pass the other students. If it's difficult at first, look at the bridge of their nose, but never for more than a couple of seconds. They won't notice the difference. And here's a list of age-appropriate greetings. Familiarize yourself with them and vary as much as possible." She handed me a typed list:

TEENAGE GREETINGS
'Sup?
Wazzup?
What up?
How's it goin'?
[Person's Name]! (Draw out for effect. Ex: Bryyyyn!)
Hi.
Hey.
Yo.
Dude!
What's goin' on?
(*Note: Avoid old people salutations such as "good morning.")

"And try to use the person's name whenever possible along with these," she said. "For example, not merely, 'Hey,' but 'Hey, Brynn.' People love to hear their names—it implies that they're important. Speaking of which, close your eyes."

I closed them.

"Picture a bunch of kids at your school, maybe in the lunchroom or the auditorium."

"Okay."

"They're all wearing T-shirts. What color are the T-shirts?"

"What difference does it make?" I asked.

Brynn huffed. "Focus! What color?"

"Um, yellow?"

"They're all wearing yellow T-shirts," she said. "And these T-shirts have a slogan. You know what the slogan is?"

"No idea."

"'Value me,'" she said. "All the shirts say 'Value me.' Sit there a minute and envision it. Take a mental picture. Now open your eyes."

"What was that all about?" I asked.

"If you want people to like you, fulfill this need. Everyone wants to be valued, to feel like they matter. That's why knowing their names is important. Get last year's yearbook from your school library and add it to your required reading material," she said, gesturing to the stack of magazines. "Learn the faces and the names of everyone you can. It makes a difference."

"Looking people in the eye and saying 'Hey' is one thing, but how do I actually start talking to somebody I don't really know? I don't want to come across as desperate and weird."

"Try it with me," she said. "I'm a stranger. Strike up a conversation."

I took a deep breath. "I'm Emily. My dad's an accountant, and my mom died."

Brynn shook her head. "No, no, no—all wrong," she said.

"See? I suck at this!"

"Now you be the stranger," Brynn said, "and *I'll* strike up the conversation." She sat up straight and got into character, looking away and then pretending to suddenly notice me. "I love your haircut!" she said enthusiastically.

"Thanks," I said.

"I would kill for straight hair like that—mine is way too curly to wear it that way, but yours is *so* cute. Is it naturally straight, or do you have to style it a lot?"

"Well, it's kind of wavy, so I use a flatiron on the top and a curling iron right here," I said, pantomiming my routine.

"Yeah, I see," Brynn said. "I'm Brynn, by the way. I don't think we've met. Do you go to Wright Middle?"

"Yeah, I'm Emily." Then I stopped. "This is goofy—you already know me."

"We just carried on a friendly conversation as two complete strangers," she said. "Let's review: notice how I opened with a compliment? That's a good ice breaker, but the way to keep it going is to ask a question related to the compliment, because people love to talk about themselves."

"So I should tell everyone I like their hair and then ask how they fix it?"

"That was an example," Brynn said. "The compliment must be sincere—that's key. Remember when Noreen was talking about Ivy Lee, Rockefeller's publicist? One thing she didn't tell you was that Lee encouraged his clients to think about what people needed and then fulfill that need, not simply pretend. He didn't advise Rockefeller to *trick* people into thinking he'd done good things—Rockefeller really did do an awful lot of good things with his money, but it was Lee who crafted his public image based on that. So for you, I want you to pay more attention to people and find things about them you truly admire, whether it's their hairstyle or a funny joke they made in class, and then tell them so. Be genuine—and be specific. Don't just say 'Oh, you're so pretty.' Say 'You have fantastic bone structure!' There's a world of difference between 'You have pretty eyes' and 'Your eyes are such a pretty shade of green.' The first is okay, because it starts a conversation in a friendly way, but the second shows you've paid real attention.

"And don't forget the follow-up question. Got it?"

"I think so," I said. "Does it really work?"

"After you try it for a couple of weeks, you'll see for yourself," Brynn said. "Now, last but not least: Crisis Management. It's going to be hard to start up friendships when the Daisies have already turned people against you, so first you're going to have to learn how to gracefully dodge their little tricks."

"How do I do that?" I asked.

"It's kind of hard to explain. You have to be zen," she said. "You know what zen means?"

"It's like being enlightened," I said.

"Yeah. It's like existing on a different plane, sort of above it all. Whatever the Daisies throw at you never quite reaches you."

"That swift kick in the butt in choir reached me pretty well," I said. "Heatherly's beating the crap out of me reached me."

"But they're not going to resort to physical violence again," Brynn said. "Heatherly doesn't want to get expelled; she just wants to torment you. Girls are much better at psychological torment anyway, and they enjoy it a whole lot more, too. They'll keep coming after you, but they'll do it with mind games. So you have to deflect masterfully."

"I've tried the sticks-and-stones bit, Brynn. I'm not good at it. They *do* get to me, and they know it. I don't know how I can pretend any better than I have been."

She thought for a moment. "Do you have TiVo?"

I took her to the den and gave her the remote. She typed in "G-O-M-E" and was given the choice "GOMER PYLE, USMC," on some nostalgia channel. She found all episodes and programmed it to record. "Ever seen this?"

"Is it one of those boot camp reality shows?"

"It's an old comedy," she said. "Way before my time, but I've seen it once or twice with my dad. Kindhearted simpleton joins the Marines and hilarity ensues."

"What's so hilarious about the Marines?" I asked.

"This guy Gomer enlists, and he's too dense to realize that the sergeant is being mean to him. In fact, he thinks the sergeant is his best friend. This drives the sergeant bonkers—he *hates* this guy, but nothing the sergeant does breaks his spirit. I'm not suggesting you fake a low IQ, but watch a couple of these and see what I mean. Then apply the basic principle to your situation. Nothing is more frustrating than watching your best insults have zero effect. Pretend you can't even fathom the petty behavior of the Daisies. It will *infuriate* them.

Think of it as the zen of Gomer. In a sense, it's a form of poise. Ooh! You know who wrote the book on poise? Pageant girls!" She set the TiVo to record some beauty pageants. "Watch these, too. You can skip to the interview portion. They have this marvelous plastered smile on their faces, no matter what they're talking about—war, famine, poverty—it's all good, all fixable. Someone could throw a grenade on stage and they'd never lose that smile. Anyone messes with you, go all-out pageant girl on them. Practice it.

"Oh, and one last thing: when all this begins to work, and you begin to become a threat to the Daisies, they'll try to trick you. They'll bait you, then use whatever you say against you, even if they have to twist it or use it out of context. No matter what they tell you some-one else said about you, do *not* lose your poise. The press does this all the time with our clients—they try to get them to say something inflammatory about another celebrity because conflict sells. You have to know how to handle it."

"I'm listening."

"There's a standard line we have our clients use to respond to mean-spirited attacks from other celebrities. It varies according to the situation, but it's usually something like this: 'I regret that so-and-so feels compelled to make such hurtful remarks about me. However, I continue to respect her talent and hope she will get the help she needs. I wish her all the best.'"

"Hey, that's pretty smooth!" I said.

"I know, it's awesome!" said Brynn. "It's got that zen quality—you're so able to rise above the triviality—*plus,* you get to throw in the suggestion that the other person is mental and you feel sorry for her. Deliciously enraging passive-aggressive behavior at its finest. That's why it's a classic."

"I can work with that," I said.

By then it was after one, so we took a break for lunch. I made turkey sandwiches. Dad had left the paper on the kitchen table.

"I love small-town newspapers," said Brynn. "They're so charm-ing. Look, your school's baseball coach is on the front page, and the story is about how they're preparing for the big tournament. Isn't that adorable? Front page! Oh, and look, someone's stepping down from some municipal office. And I see that the local police are going to hire a new deputy this year."

"My uncle's a cop," I said. "In fact, he's only slightly older than you. All the girls think he's hot. You should meet him."

Brynn smiled. "I'm not easily swept off my feet, but thanks anyway."

"What do you mean?"

"Well, you know . . . that stuff about love at first sight and all. I'm a little cynical. New York's dating scene will do that to you."

"So you don't believe in love at first sight?" I asked.

"My parents have been married for thirty years," Brynn said, "and my mom is still gaga over my dad. I tell her that's what I want, but she says I'm too analytical and that it makes things difficult for me. I can always come up with reasons why a relationship won't work—all the ways it's impractical. She says the right guy will make me lose my head. So I suppose I'll have met 'the one' when I turn into a blithering idiot."

It was hard to imagine Brynn having any trouble with guys; she was definitely on the beautiful side. She wore her brown hair pulled back, but little tendrils escaped around her face in perfect curls. Below her left eye, she had a birthmark a couple of shades darker than the rest of her skin. It was about the size of a dime, and it was shaped like Australia.

"You're pretty, though," I said. "I bet lots of guys are after you."

She shrugged. "Not so much."

"Your birthmark is cool. I wish I had something like that."

"Oh, the birthmark!" Brynn laughed. "Really sexy. And no, you don't wish that. Trust me." She flipped to the back of the newspaper. "What's this?" she asked, pointing to an ad for Distinctive Furs's spring clearance sale.

"Cruelty to animals?"

"I mean, who's the model?" she asked.

I groaned. "Caroline Sanford. She lives a couple of blocks over. Her dad's a plumber. He fixed the pipes when we bought this house."

"So what's the problem?" she asked.

"Nothing, I guess. Caroline's just beautiful, and perfect, and a sophomore, and everyone at my school thinks she's the greatest thing ever. She wouldn't speak to me if her life depended on it. Dad and I saw their family out at dinner one night before Christmas. Her father said hi and shook my dad's hand and introduced me to Caroline. She gave me that snotty vertical once-over and then rolled her eyes. Wouldn't even say hello. Since she's signed with the local modeling agency and gotten this fur job, I'm sure her head is so big she can hardly walk through the door."

"Hmmm . . . ," Brynn said. "In spite of the poor photography, she's captivating."

"Oh, great. You too?"

"So this girl, Caroline. She's in that high school sorority you were telling me about, right?"

"Yeah. How'd you know?"

"Because she's gorgeous, in high school, and according to you, completely stuck up. Who can't do the math?"

"Good point," I said.

"And she'll be just the person to get you in—what was it?— Delts?"

"Caroline Sanford helping me get into Delts? What would ever make her want to do that?" I asked.

"Leave that to me," Brynn said.

IV.
REPUTATION SEGMENTATION AND COMPETITIVE ANALYSIS

Sixteen

The next day was Sunday. Mom had made Dad promise to take me to church after she was gone, but she hadn't specified anything about which service, so during tax season, Dad always dragged me out of bed for the early one that only about five people went to, and then as soon as it was over, we'd race out the door so he could get to the office before ten. Props to the Internal Revenue Service, because that gave me almost the whole day to continue to work with Brynn, who arrived ten minutes after Dad left. She was on her cell as she walked in.

"Brynn Sterling," she answered. "Oh, yes. Thank you for returning my call so promptly. Yes, I'm in town for the filming of Colby Summers's movie. Our firm represents him. Uh-huh, right. I was having brunch with a friend when I saw your client's photograph in the newspaper. Beautiful girl. Caroline Sanford? Okay. Let me make a note of that. Well, I think she has real potential. I mentioned her to a contact of mine at Ford—yes, the Ford modeling agency. If you could give me a copy of her portfolio, I'd be glad to pass it along when the movie wraps up and I'm back in New York. Lovely. No trouble at all. What's that? Who's my friend in town?" Brynn gave me the eye and silently pretended to laugh. "The Woods. You know"—she snapped her fingers at me and mimed writing something down.

Quickly, I wrote "Louis" on a scrap of paper.

"Louis Wood. Right, the CPA. Old family friends. His wife was my babysitter when I was a child, and of course, my family adored her and Louis. Laugh-a-Minute Louis, we call him."

I shook my head violently.

"Well, when you get to know him, that is." Brynn shrugged her shoulders and grimaced. "Oh, but please, don't mention my close personal friendship with the Wood family to anyone." She gave a thumbs up. "I wouldn't want it to get around. It might make it awkward for their teenage daughter. The kids at school might pester her about meeting celebrities and such. You know how it is in our business." She stuck out her tongue and pretended to gag. "Yes, I appreciate your discretion. You can messenger the portfolio to the police department, and one of their officers will see that it gets delivered to me on the set. No unauthorized personnel allowed on the lot, you know. Oh, you're most welcome. Bye, now." She hung up and turned to me. "Operation Delts successfully launched."

"What was that all about?" I asked.

"That was Caroline Sanford's self-important little modeling agent. He nearly wet himself when I told him I was Colby Summers's publicist. Especially when I said I'd like to mention Caroline to a contact of mine at Ford."

"You totally lied to the guy?"

"I never lie," she said.

"You told him my mom was your babysitter," I said.

"Most of the time I never lie. I simply let people come to their own conclusions. Besides, Caroline does have potential."

"Yeah, she is pretty, I have to admit it," I said.

"Pretty is only part of it. You can get pretty anywhere, but modeling is more than that. Remember how I told you that I didn't see you as the modeling type? It's not because you aren't pretty. It's that models—the big names—they have something else. Look," she gestured at a mirror. "Look at your eyes. That's your problem."

"My eyes aren't pretty?"

"No, get over pretty already. Look behind your eyes."

"Behind my eyes?" I asked.

"Emily, when a person looks at your eyes, they see you, Emily Wood. They don't see a product. Everyone thinks modeling is easy, but those girls have chameleon eyes. They can make you think that what's going on behind them is whatever the marketing team behind the product wants it to be." She paused. "Caroline Sanford's got the eyes. Not to mention the skin, the hair, the body. She's perfect."

"Trust me," I said. "She'd be the first to agree with you."

"Exactly. And attitude is a big part of it. She could be big."

"You mean you're really going to get her in at Ford Modeling? Even *I've* heard of them."

"I'll mention her to my contact there—eventually. But first Caroline's going to do something for us," Brynn said.

"I don't understand."

"A little something we in the PR business call reputation segmentation. You identify influential people in the social network, and you court their opinion of your brand—by making it worth their while or rewarding them. If they buy the brand, everyone else buys the brand, even if it means switching brand loyalties. Do you follow?"

I didn't.

Brynn explained, "I let it slip, quite on purpose, that your mom and dad were dear old friends. But, by making the agent promise to keep that information confidential, I introduced a caveat that makes repeating it absolutely irresistible. So as soon as Caroline's agent talks to her, he'll immediately spill it that someone from our agency—someone who's tight with people at Ford—is a friend of Louis Wood, her neighbor. Caroline, recognizing that Louis Wood is your father, will seize the opportunity to have her lips glued to your butt. The kids at your school then see that Caroline, an opinion leader, is buying your brand. Caroline gets you in this little Delts thing before you can say 'sorority,' and suddenly everyone at your school is all overstocked on yesterday's Heatherly and Company, and they're ready to trade up to Emily Wood."

I thought for a moment. "That's brilliant," I said. "But I feel sort of bad, using someone that way, even if it is Caroline Sanford."

"Who's using whom?" Brynn asked. "We specifically told the agent that we didn't want anything personal coming into play, right? So when Caroline starts suddenly getting friendly with you, who's the one trying to manipulate the situation?"

"Well, that's true," I said. "Wow—I've never had anyone try to use me for anything before, except maybe homework."

"Listen carefully, Emily. It's crucial that you make her work for it. When she calls, don't answer, and don't call her back until she's tried you three or four times. She doesn't have a cell number or IM address for you, does she?"

I raised my eyebrows.

"Of course not," she said. "Perfect. Now then, if my calculations are correct, Caroline should be calling any minute."

Like magic, the phone rang.

The caller ID said SANFORD CAROLINE J.

Seventeen

Brynn turned the volume all the way down on the answering machine. "No time for distractions. Let's get back to work."

"But aren't you dying to hear what she says?" I asked.

"Of course not. I could write you a word-for-word script of what she's saying, and what she'll say the next couple of times she calls. Forget about her for now." We moved into the den and sat down on the couch. "Your next lesson in PR is competitive analysis—in this case, we might call it 'knowing your enemy.' Right now, the Daisies are the dominant brand. We want to replace them with you, the brand alternative. So let's analyze our consumers, your peers. What do they think about Brand Daisy? Do they like them?"

It was something I'd never considered. "I don't know. I mean, it doesn't make sense, but I don't think anybody really likes them. Guys want to date them, and girls want to hang out with them, but I don't think it's because anyone really enjoys the Daisies's company. The Daisies are just cool, and if you cross them, then you're not cool. I don't know how to explain it. It's like everyone's drawn to them."

"So whatever it is about the Daisies, they've solidified their power to the point that they're no longer questioned," Brynn said. "What we need to do, then, is identify their vulnerability. What weakness can we exploit to take their market share?" She lay back against the sofa, then sat up again almost immediately. "The other two. The non-Heatherlys. What are their names?"

"Meredith and Alexa," I said.

"Yes. Hangers-on. They're the weakness. All we have to do is make a big splash early on with our campaign, and they'll begin to consider defecting to your brand. I'm not sure how long it will take, but eventually, they'll ditch her and try to glom on to you. Divide and conquer. I wish I could be there when you go back to school Monday.

You're going to make quite an impression with the hair, the makeup, the clothes . . . oh, which reminds me," she said, pulling a plastic bag from her satchel. "After assessing your wardrobe situation yesterday, I had my roommate overnight this. She couldn't believe it was still in the magazine's closet. She swiped it for you—but only for a couple of days." She held up a floral dress. "This is the *pièce de résistance*—the exact dress from the first page of the Flirty Florals layout, complete with coordinating scarf. It's a sample garment made especially for fashion shows or photo shoots before the line is available. Wear this Monday and then bring it by after school so I can overnight it back. I know it's not exactly seasonal yet, but it's close enough to official spring. And, Em, try not to get anything on it."

"Brynn, nobody at school wears stuff like this. It's kind of weird looking."

"You'll have to wear it around the house today until it feels normal. That's key. If the dress is wearing you, it will never work. Remember, to sell the brand, you have to believe in the brand. You've got to pull it off with confidence. So, are you ready, Em? Got a big day at school Monday, right, Em?"

"Okay, what's up with the nickname?" I asked.

"I'm glad you asked, Em," Brynn said. "As you probably know, lots of celebrities adopt stage names. Usually it's done to compensate for a ridiculously difficult or embarrassing real name, as in Colby's case."

"His real name's not Colby Summers?" I asked.

Brynn giggled. "It's Butts. Colby Butts!"

"Get out!"

"Nope. Dead serious. How many teen girls would swoon over a guy named Butts? Not many. That's why Noreen had him change it. A good move."

"Definitely," I said. "But what's wrong with my name?"

"Nothing, but I like the concept—a stage name can be a means of remembering that your image is not the real you. Remember how I keep talking about brands? If Emily Wood shows up for school Monday, she's a prime target for humiliation—I believe the term you used was, 'dead meat.' Right?"

"I've been trying not to think about it, but yeah. Right."

"So Emily Wood doesn't show up. Em does." I looked at Brynn, confused. "Let me try to explain this again. New look, new clothes, new attitude, new persona. You're not selling Emily Wood; you're selling Em, the brand. When you get back to school, I want you write 'Em' on your papers, in your class notes, use it when you talk to yourself. All the time. Become the brand. I want you to go by Em. Not Emily. Make the consumer believe in Brand Em," she said. "Remember that when you replace the Daisies' brand, you're offering a superior product—a hellaciously hip girl who isn't mean. You have what's called a USP, or Unique Selling Proposition: unlike the Daisies, you're a nice person. So Brand Em offers cool without the torment. A socially responsible new market leader. That's giving the consumer a terrific value, if you ask me.

"And one last thing to keep in mind before your launch: remember that this is sort of a game we're playing. We're creating a product, not a real person. Play your part, but don't lose sight of who you really are."

"Don't worry," I said. "I've got it covered."

I tried on the dress and some of my new outfits for a while, and Brynn coached me a little more on how to carry myself in them. We watched an episode of Gomer Pyle and the interview segment of a teen beauty pageant. She looked up Wright Middle on Facebook groups and helped me memorize names and faces. I'd have to learn the rest from old yearbooks. Then, when she decided we were finished for the day, we played the message Caroline had left that morning:

"Um, Emily, hi. It's Caroline Sanford. I thought I'd give you a quick call this weekend. I was just thinking, you seem so sweet, and I thought that since you're sort of new in town and we're, like, practically neighbors, maybe we should get together and hang out sometime. You know? So, anyway, call me, okay? Thanks!" She left her number.

"Whatever you do," Brynn said, "do not call her back."

V.
LAUNCHING THE BRAND ALTERNATIVE

Eighteen

I really didn't want to wear the dress from *Flirt* on Monday. It was my first day back at school after the suspension, and on top of everything else, showing up in Flirty Florals made me feel more vulnerable. Plus, the weather in Ohio wasn't exactly conducive to a breezy cotton/rayon blend—the high for the day was forty-seven degrees! But I had to trust Brynn, who had urged beauty before comfort, reminding me that swimsuit models frequently had to shoot their spreads in the cold thanks to magazine lead times. I was to think of myself as an actress suffering for my art, throwing myself into the role of Em. That morning, after I'd fixed my hair and makeup the way Patrick and Amy had taught me, I took out the photo Brynn had taken of me in the Flirt dress. I slipped on the loose-fitting white dress with purple and blue flowers and draped the blue scarf across my shoulders the way I had it in the picture. "Hello, Grandma," I said to the mirror. "Brynn, I hope you know what you're doing." I threw on a long coat to keep myself from freezing—and to leave on in case I lost my nerve—and I headed for the school bus stop.

I sat at the front of the bus like always, and no one talked to me. As we jostled past the stoplight downtown, I started to get really nervous. My hands felt cold but sweaty. When the bus stopped in front of Wright Middle, it let out its customary sigh, and the driver creaked open the hydraulic door. People filed past me, but I just sat there, wishing I could curl up and hide in one of the seats until the school day was over.

I was the last person off. I left my coat on while I waited in the lobby, off by myself, for the first bell. When the bell rang and everyone started filing outside to their first class, I thought seriously about just leaving the coat on all day.

Then I thought about Brynn. *Become the brand,* she'd said.

I took a deep breath and focused.

I took off the coat.

It was freezing, but I pinched my shoulder blades together, stuck out my chin, and strutted as though I were on the catwalk at a Paris fashion show.

The people I passed giggled, whispered, or pointed, but I looked right at them, using the bridge-of-the-nose trick.

Em is in the house, I told myself. Somehow, the idea that I was a creation, a character—a brand—made it manageable.

Keep walking, I told myself. *Own it. Sell the brand. Become the brand,* I kept repeating in my head. *You are Em. You're a trendsetter. You're wearing a dress from* Flirt *magazine; your hair was done by a top Hollywood stylist. Your makeup is impeccable. You're cooler than anyone in this whole school. This is your world and they just live in it.* The more I concentrated on seeing myself as Em, the straighter I stood, the more I put my hips into my walk. In my head, the people around me became nothing more than my audience, and I could almost feel the transformation start to radiate outward.

Then the Daisies stepped onto my catwalk, and my background music scratched like an old vinyl record. "What'd you do, Plywood, rob a funeral home?" Heatherly asked.

"I didn't think you could be any more of a nerd," Meredith said, "but you're working on it."

"Oh, she thinks she's cool now because she got a haircut," Alexa said.

"Who cares about her stupid hair? Nobody's going to notice anything but that ridiculous dress. That's the ugliest thing I've ever seen," said Heatherly.

Suddenly, I was back to being Emily, and I felt like a total idiot. Then I reminded myself, *Don't let them get to you.* "Thanks for noticing my new dress. Your outfit is nice, too. I think it's great that you are thrifty enough to keep wearing stuff even after it goes out of style! It's very economical!" I said. "It's been great chatting, girls, but I have to get to class. I wish you could join me, but there is that pesky IQ requirement. Sorry!"

I pushed past the three of them and walked to Mrs. Crutchfield's class for first period. Did I get in a major burn on Heatherly Hamilton and her crew? I could scarcely believe it.

Kelsey Brown caught me by the door. "Emily, I love your haircut! And what a great dress!" she said. I wasn't sure how to respond. Kelsey was one of those girls Brynn had mentioned—an "early adopter" who, even without advance copies of a fashion spread, had an intuition about upcoming styles. Whenever Kelsey wore something different and new, the rest of the girls were wearing the same thing within a week. Maybe she really did like my dress—or maybe she was just being sarcastic. Either way, zen of Gomer, I told myself.

"Thanks, Kelsey," I said.

We started the roll. "Em's here," I called when we got to the Ws. Mrs. Crutchfield looked up, and the rest of the class turned to look, too. I said it again: "Em's here." And I said it like I meant it.

When I left first period, though, my mojo quickly began to wane. Some jock ran into me in the hall the minute I walked out Mrs. Crutchfield's door.

"Excuse me," I said.

Why was I apologizing to him? He was the klutz, not me.

But by the time the second, third, and twenty-seventh person knocked into me, I figured out that the Daisies had officially designated a Bump into Plywood Day. Ah, the bump: an old standby, but nevertheless effective. Since getting constantly run into gets old superfast, and if you say anything about it, they act like you're crazy because, *Hey, what's your problem? It was just an accident.* And even though you know that they know that you know it wasn't an accident, you still feel like maybe they're right and you are the crazy one after all. A total head trip.

I wondered if they'd come up with it during first period, after my super Gomer burn, or if they'd planned it to begin as soon as I'd gotten to school but had been thrown off by my new look. Either way, being a human pinball sucked. And it wasn't just the humiliation: I was terrified that the dress would get torn or that I'd get knocked down and dirty it. I waited in third period until the last possible second before racing to fourth, hoping that the halls would be clear. Pretty nerve-racking, but necessary. Luckily, I'd brought my lunch, so I wouldn't have to go through the line. I'd have to go to the cafeteria though, to check in with Mrs. Crutchfield before I went to work on the literary magazine.

I estimated when everyone would be sitting down with their trays before I entered. I had Mrs. Crutchfield sign my pass as the Daisies watched me from the cool tables. Not much they could do to bump into me while they were sitting down, and they'd have to come all the way over to the teachers' table to pull anything, which would be too risky. I couldn't help but feel a little proud of myself. They'd underestimated me once again. Stupid Daisies.

"Hey, Coach," I heard a voice say behind me. "I was thinking, what if I held my curveball kind of like this?"

And when I turned around, Chip Young's curveball, in the form of an open bottle, came flying across the front of my dress, sending a vertical splash of cranberry juice cocktail from my neck to just below my rib cage.

The teachers gasped, and the lunchroom went silent.

"Oh, man!" Chip said. "Sorry about that—my hand must've slipped."

I looked over at the cool tables, where the Daisies were looking very pleased with themselves.

"Oh, Emily," Mrs. Crutchfield said. "Your dress!"

I looked down at the stain and thought about how Brynn was going to kill me. *Zen of Gomer,* I reminded myself. I looked up at Chip—not at the bridge of his nose but dead in the eye.

And I smiled like a pageant girl for all I was worth.

"No harm done," I said, maintaining my best I-hope-to-use-my-position-to-bring-about-world-peace expression. "Accidents happen! I'm sure this will wash right out. Excuse me."

I walked out of the lunchroom with my head up and my shoulders back. Everyone was still silent; they hadn't expected that.

I hung onto my zen until I got to the bathroom. *No, no, no,* I kept whispering over and over as I tried to wash the stain away with those rough, brown bathroom paper towels and that pink squirty soap. It wasn't working.

Then I heard one of the toilets flush and Kelsey Brown came out.

"You okay?" she asked as she began washing her hands.

"Feeling groovy," I said.

"Oh, no—did you spill something on your new dress?"

I knew her Little Miss Friendly routine in first period had been too good to be true. *I'm going to get suspended twice,* I thought. *Or do they expel you the second time you fight?* Not only did the Daisies have their Neanderthal jock-toy throw cranberry juice on my dress from *Flirt* magazine, they'd even arranged for the head cheerleader to wait for me in the bathroom and taunt me about it.

"Yeah, Kelsey," I said. "That's right. *I* spilled something on my new dress. Imagine that."

The venom in my voice seemed lost on her. "That's not going to get it out," she said. "Turn around."

"What?"

"Turn around so I can check the fabric content."

Kelsey spun me around gently by the shoulders and pulled the tag out of the back and inspected it. "No, it's got rayon in it, so you're going to damage the fibers if you keep rubbing it like that. Soak it in some dishwashing liquid and vinegar when you get home. After that, hand wash it. It might work."

Then it occurred to me that maybe Kelsey *didn't* know what had happened in the lunchroom. Either that or she really did belong in Vannies, because if this was a mind game, she had me fooled.

I looked in the mirror. "Well, this is attractive," I said.

She studied me a moment. "Let me see that scarf." She began untying it and then held it up over the stain at a couple of different angles. "How about this?" She tied the scarf so that the ends hung down the center of my chest, perfectly camouflaging the red stain. "Yeah, I like," she said, nodding her head. She glanced at her watch. "I'd better get to lunch!"

And that was how Kelsey Brown, the head cheerleader, kept me from having to either (a) call my dad for a change of clothes, potentially creating a scene that would draw attention to my unfortunate situation, which the Daisies would have loved, (b) wear gym clothes the rest of the day, or (c) walk around with a the equivalent of a giant LOSER sign around my neck. Go figure.

Thanks to Mrs. Crutchfield's deal with Warren regarding my work detail, I got to drop seventh-period choir with the Daisies and instead work on the literary magazine. The administration had Mrs. C team-teaching that period in another classroom on Tuesdays and Thursdays, so I'd have the room to myself those days—Mrs. Crutchfield trusted me to work unsupervised, and Mr. Warren hadn't noticed the scheduling conflict. Cool.

"Here are the submissions," Mrs. C told me. She handed me a folder with five poems, a couple of short stories, and maybe four drawings.

"Not much to choose from," I said. "Is this all we have?"

"You might want to work on publicizing the magazine," she said. "Try to drum up more submissions?"

"I'll say." I spent the rest of the period reading the short stories and poems, which were pretty terrible. "Can I reject all of these?" I asked just before the last bell rang.

"They can't be that bad," said Mrs. C.

"This story about skateboarding uses the word *penultimate* to mean 'better than ultimate.'"

She laughed a little and shook her head. "Each of the students who submitted gave me at least two pieces," she said. "I encourage that, so I can choose the lesser of two or three evils. Remember, we want to encourage creative expression, not crush dreams."

"I guess you're right," I said.

"Besides, we don't have time to work miracles here. We've got to have this magazine to the printer by the last week of April. You think you can whip these submissions into shape and have the layouts completed by then?"

"Done and done!"

"By the way, I like your new haircut," she said. "Very trendy."

"Thanks."

"Glad to have you back, too."

"I really appreciate your letting me edit this magazine, Mrs. C," I said. "I'll try to do a good job."

As soon as I got home, I changed out of the floral dress and soaked it the way Kelsey had said to, praying she knew what she was talking about. As I watched the stain disappear in the bathroom sink, I finally started to breathe normally again for the first time since noon. I rinsed out the vinegar, then soaked the dress in the sink again with some shampoo, agitating the water with my hands, and then rinsing with cool water. I ran it through the dryer on a gentle setting. When it came out, it looked okay but slightly wrinkly, so I ironed it under an old T-shirt to protect the fabric. To me, it looked perfectly new, but I couldn't remember if it looked exactly the way it had when I'd gotten it. What if Brynn was furious when she found out? She'd told me not to get anything on it. I put the dress in a box and rode my bike to the movie set.

Sonny was one of two cops at the barricades. "Emily, what are you doing here? You know I can't let you in."

"It's okay. I'm meeting a friend," I said. I called Brynn's cell, and she rode over in her cart. As she stepped out, she took a look at Sonny and stumbled.

"Brynn, this is my Uncle Sonny, the one I mentioned to you."

Brynn and Sonny looked at each other, wide-eyed.

"It's nice to meet you," Sonny said. "I'm Sonny Anderson."

Brynn blinked as though she were just waking up. "Synn Brerling," she said. "I mean, Brynn Sterling."

"That's an unusually beautiful name," Sonny said, gently shaking Brynn's outstretched hand.

"Brynn," I said, "I brought that package you wanted."

"Oh, yes," she said. "The package. Right."

"Brynn's helping me with a project," I told Sonny. "We have to shadow someone for a career exercise. Brynn's a publicist. I'm thinking about going into public relations." Sonny didn't take his eyes off Brynn. "So, we'd better get to work." I practically had to pull her away.

"You're going to kill me," I said. "Well, you might not actually kill me. Because the stain came out."

"What stain?" she asked.

"The Daisies got to the dress," I said. "Cranberry juice. I'm sorry! I tried so hard to stay out of their path. I really did!" The more I talked, the more rapid and shrill my voice grew. "I washed it out, and I don't think anyone could ever tell. I think it's as good as new. . . . I used vinegar and dishwashing—"

"Emily!" Brynn said. "Get ahold of yourself! Let me see it."

I gave her the box, and she took out the dress and inspected it. "Good job, Susie Homemaker. I don't see any sign of a stain." I must have still looked worried because she said, "It's okay. Really."

"It is?"

"Yeah, calm down."

"But the dress—your friend will get in trouble if they can tell something got on it. I don't want to get her fired."

"It's okay. Really. Even if the stain didn't come out, it's not the end of the world. They have insurance."

"Insurance? On clothes?" I asked.

"Of course. You think nobody's ever borrowed something from a photo shoot and spilled a drink on it before? Of course they have insurance."

I nearly collapsed into a heap. I was relieved, but frustrated, too. "You mean I've been panicking since lunchtime about this dress, and all the time there was nothing to worry about? Why didn't you tell me there was insurance?"

"Because, best case scenario, insurance of any kind is a big waste of money—you don't want to use it unless you have to. My friend wouldn't have gotten fired, but it might have made things a little awkward for her. Borrowing from the closet is to fashion magazine editors what Botox is to wealthy socialites: you do it; you just don't talk about it. So how old is your uncle?"

"Twenty-seven," I said. "And I told you he was hot."

"I didn't really notice," Brynn said.

"Yeah, right."

"What?" Brynn asked. "Honestly, you teenage girls and your romance fantasies. But I guess it's appropriate, since you are about to have your first date."

"What? When?"

"This Friday night."

"A date with whom?"

"You do realize that you just used the word *whom* correctly, right? And you wonder why you don't fit in with your peers?"

"Simple objective case. I have a good English teacher. But that's beside the point. My dad doesn't let me date, not that anyone's ever asked. Not until I'm fifteen."

"So don't tell him," Brynn said. "What're you, Mother Teresa? Haven't you ever broken a rule in your life?"

"I did disguise myself as a deli employee once to sneak into a meeting at a top publicity firm."

"Touché," Brynn replied.

"So who's my date?"

"Colby Summers, of course . . . but you can call him Mr. Butts, if you like."

"Hell-o! Twenty-eight-year-old-married-father-of-one Colby Summers?"

"You know that, and I know that," Brynn said. "But the kids at your school don't know that. And if I recall correctly, HOT BOYFRIEND is on our list of goals."

Nineteen

"*I feel absolutely ridiculous,*" Colby said as he and I were getting ready for our "date" that Friday afternoon at his trailer. Brynn was choosing his outfit, and Amy was fixing my makeup. "It's downright creepy is what it is." Then, turning to me, he said, "No offense."

Brynn said, "All you have to do is get your picture snapped together. I tipped off a freelance photog that Colby Summers would be having coffee with a mystery girl this afternoon at a place downtown. Your fans are a little suspicious that you never go on dates with teenage girls. This will help sell you as a teenager."

"And I'm using this poor girl for that?" he asked.

"Are you kidding me?" I asked. "The girls at my school will die when they hear I went out with Colby Summers!"

"She's right, Colby. You're doing Emily a huge favor. It's called competitive benefit," Brynn said. "If we want our target consumer, the kids at Emily's school, to switch brands, we have to give them a better alternative. When these pictures hit the press, it will create brand synergy: you each help the other. Her classmates will believe that Emily's dating a celebrity, and she'll be the coolest girl in school, and a quiet rendezvous with a mystery girl will put your name on everyone's lips again, which will help sales of your CD."

"Why don't you buy advertisements to sell his CD?" I asked.

"Because ads are less interesting and not as cost-effective. A juicy story about a celebrity's personal life is the best buzz you can get—and it's free. You know how rumors work in middle school? How one minute nobody notices you're alive and then the next, everyone's dying to know all about you? Rumors in the entertainment industry work the exact same way."

"All you're doing is getting a cup of coffee," Amy said. "It's no big."

Normally, it might be awkward for your date's wife to fix your makeup before you go out with her husband, but Amy clearly didn't feel threatened.

"All right," said Colby. "Emily, you seem like pretty good company, anyway."

"Thanks," I said. "But, Brynn, what if the kids at school don't buy the idea that Colby and I are a couple? They might think I won some 'Win a Date with Colby Summers' contest or something."

"That's why you'll be wearing this for the next few weeks." Brynn unfastened from Colby's neck a short leather necklace with a brass medallion that said, "GETTONE TELEFONICO."

"Hey!" Colby protested. "That has sentimental value!"

"That's your signature necklace," I said. "I read that you made it from an old Italian telephone token when you went to Italy to shoot your first video. The article said you wear it to remind you of your first big break. Is that true?"

"Actually, I wear it because I was in Italy when Amy found out we were having a baby."

Amy smiled, and he hugged her gently.

"I didn't know that," Brynn said. "Noreen said she wanted you to wear it all the time because it calls attention to your collarbone."

"He does have a great collarbone," Amy said.

"Anyway, it's yours for a while," Brynn said, handing me the necklace. "Don't actually show it to anyone. Wear it nonchalantly. They'll notice when it's time."

"Take good care of it, okay?" Colby said.

"What time will your dad be home tonight?" Brynn asked.

"Not sure, but definitely not before seven."

"Plenty of time, then," she said. "Have fun, you crazy teenagers!"

Colby drove the two us to a little coffeehouse a few miles from the set. As soon as we'd gotten in the car, he'd pointed out the photographer following us. "Right on time," he said. When we stopped, the photographer leapt from his car and began taking pictures before we even got inside.

"Who's the girl, Colby?" he asked.

"A friend," Colby replied. "Could we have a little privacy, please?"

"Depends. You go ahead and give me a good picture, and I'll be on my way. You two want to make out for me?"

"Anyone ever tell you you're a real classy guy?" Colby said. We walked into the coffee shop, which was nothing more than a narrow little storefront crammed with overpriced, cutesy gift items. The photographer continued snapping pictures through the window after the manager kicked him out. "He's got a good lens," Colby said, "so we can sit at that table in the back. Here we go," he said. We sat down, and he put his arm around my shoulder, leaned in, and whispered in my ear, "This is the kind of shot they want. Perfectly innocent, but they'll caption it like it's a big deal."

It must have done the trick, because the photographer soon left.

"Oh, Mr. Summers," the manager said, "we're so honored to have you here. Anything you want, on the house."

Colby and I both ordered the same thing. Normally, a decaf vanilla cappuccino with extra whipped cream and caramel would make me forget all my troubles, but I couldn't help feeling nervous. I was, after all, having coffee with a famous actor. And twenty-eight or not, he was still disorientingly attractive. I had to think of something to say, but what? Complimenting him on his hair seemed the wrong way to go in this case. I remembered how Brynn had said that a good way to start a conversation was to ask people a question about themselves. And since I no longer had a list of what was off limits, I could go for something a little more interesting than his favorite snack.

"Is it always like this when you go somewhere?" I asked.

"I wish!" he said. "In New York or L.A., there'd be a lot more than one guy sticking a camera in my face."

"I mean, are people always either acting like they own you or bending over backward for you?"

"Pretty much," Colby replied. "It's a drag sometimes, but it beats being unemployed. Still, this wasn't the career I had in mind."

"How so?"

"I don't know . . . this whole business of pretending I'm a teenager. It wasn't my idea, exactly. I was going to get the audition that way, and then, once they saw what I could do, tell them the truth. But Noreen signed me before I had the chance and took over from there. She told me I should trust her, that she could make my career take off. I was scared to say no, I guess—I mean, she's Noreen Wolfe, and I was nobody, had nothing. Amy and I were on the verge of being evicted from our apartment. It all happened so fast. I guess Noreen knows what she's doing, though. We've made a lot of money. But I sort of wish I had more control."

"In what way?" Keeping the conversation going by asking more questions wasn't a ploy—I really wanted to hear what he had to say.

"Well, for instance, this movie. It's an action/adventure *musical.* One minute, I'm doing a fight scene, and the next, I'm singing about it. It's so dumb. But Noreen said if I didn't take this role, I might not get another chance to jump to the big screen. She said my fans would love it. And I'm grateful for my fans—really, I mean that—but I wish I could choose my own projects based on my real identity. You know, instead of pretending to be a teenager, be who I really am."

"If it would make you feel any better," I said, "I could call you Mr. Butts." I blushed.

"Ha, ha," Colby said. "If you think that's funny, you should've seen my brother's wedding announcement in the local paper. They always run the headline with the wife's maiden name, followed by the groom's last name. Well, my sister-in-law is Chinese-American, and when they got married, the big headline was TAN BUTTS TO WED."

I almost spit cappuccino all over the table. When I was able to stop laughing, I said, "You are making that up!"

"I'm dead serious! Everybody told my sister-in-law that she must truly love my brother. I can't really blame her for not taking his last name, though!" We both laughed so hard we were nearly in tears. "Oh, and hey, remind me to thank Brynn for sharing that bit of information with you."

When I caught my breath again, I said, "Honestly, I think your fans would still like you, even if you used your real last name."

"I wonder. It's hard being someone else. I'm grateful for my career, but sometimes I get tired of the illusion."

"Hang on a sec." I took my Cool Stuff book from my purse.

"What are you doing?" Colby asked.

"Sorry. A little eccentricity of mine."

"Okay, I'm intrigued. Tell me about it."

I shook my head. "You'll just think I'm weird."

"Oh, come on . . . I already think that," he said, nudging my arm and laughing. "If you can't trust a man named Butts, who can you trust?"

"You have a point," I said. "All right. Here's the thing: I keep this notebook with me all the time, and whenever I get an idea for a poem or hear a word I like or a phrase I think sounds cool or an image I may want to use sometime, I write it down"

"So what are you writing down now?"

"See, while you were talking—this is going to sound so crazy—I glanced down at the small print on this coffee cup and saw the word *liquid*. Then you said the word illusion, and I liked the way they sounded together because of the assonance."

"What's assonance?"

"Well, in this case, it's the short *i* in both *liquid* and *illusion—ih, ih*. It's pleasing to the ear."

"Liquid *i*llusion. Liquid *i*llusion," he repeated, stressing the vowel. "You're right."

"Assonance is one of my favorite poetic devices. Like even when someone says 'shut up,' it sounds right, the way the *uh* sound is repeated."

"Okay, then. If you call me Mr. Butts, I'll tell you to shut up, and then we'll both be happy." We laughed.

"I just mean that I love the musicality of language, the way certain words go together. I love it when people say that bad news is a *bitter pill*—not only because it's a good metaphor, but because the assonance makes it kind of beautiful.

"I'm sorry," I said. "This is why I don't have any friends. Nobody talks about assonance in a normal conversation. I'm such a freak!"

"Emily! No way! It's cool to be passionate about something. The way you feel about poetry is exactly how I feel about music. I totally understand. Like with music, it's always been who I am. I don't remember ever deciding I'd get into music as a career; it was just something I always did and always had to keep doing. It's a part of me. I can't *not* create music. I love it," he said. "The only difference is that you're all about the words, the lyrics—I usually work with a cowriter on the words to my songs, but the music—it's straight from me. I can feel it, hear the melody in my head. I even wake up a lot of times with a riff on the brain, like it came to me in my sleep."

"Wow," I said. "You *do* get it."

"So now will you tell me more about poetry?"

"Really?"

"Yes, really. What other, um, 'poetic devices,' do you like to use?"

It was nice to have someone understand. I could feel myself relax again. "Well, there's meter," I said.

"Meter?"

"The pattern of stressed and unstressed syllables in a line of poetry—or even in lyrics, I guess. You studied meter, right?"

"I may have missed that class," Colby said. "One reason this teenage thing is so easy to pull off is because my family moved around a lot and I never stayed in one school very long—never got to know anyone much."

"That's funny. I assumed you chose your stage name because it was trochaic." Colby looked confused. "You know . . . stressed, unstressed, stressed, unstressed: COLby SUMmers. Kind of has that zip to it, you know?"

"I pay people to consider every little detail about my image, but you're the first person to tell me my name's trochaic. I'd bet you anything that even Noreen doesn't know what that means. How'd you get to be so smart?"

"I picked up a lot of it from studying my favorite poet, Robert Frost. Everybody likes him because he wrote these nature poems, but there's so much more going on. He was such a craftsman. Most people read his work without even noticing the form—perfect meter and rhyme patterns so subtle they don't call attention to themselves. My English teacher pointed it out to us, and I was so into it, I kept reading more of his poetry. Why are you looking at me like that?"

"Are you going to let me see some of your poems, or what?"

I smiled. "Maybe."

"May I?" He gestured toward my notebook.

Since the incident with Heatherly, I was kind of afraid to let it out of my hands again, but after what he'd said about music, I thought I could trust Colby not to laugh at me. I handed him the notebook.

He flipped through the pages and read for an agonizing few minutes while I tried to pretend I wasn't worried about what he was thinking. He was perfectly silent and still—no nods or "hmms." I wondered if he was stalling, trying to think of something nice to say. Finally he looked up, straight into my eyes. "Wow—there's a great rhythm and sound to what you've written in here. Some of this would make killer song lyrics."

"Hey, if you see something you like, feel free to use it," I said, relieved. Then, before I even realized what I was saying, I heard the words, "You can borrow the book and give it back when you're done."

Had that really just come out of my mouth? *Erase, erase, erase. Tell him you've changed your mind.*

"No kidding? You know, with a little change here and there, with some of the lyrics I've already been working on . . . you never know," he said. "Maybe there's something I could use. If I do, I'll give you a cowriting credit. Deal?"

How cool would it be to have my poems turned into song lyrics for Colby Summers? I decided not to ask for the notebook back after all. "Deal!" I said.

He smiled at me. "Emily, if you learn nothing else from me, learn this: be who you are. If the kids at your school don't get you, forget them. You're smart and a talented writer. No matter what anyone thinks, be yourself." He took a drink from his cup. "I wish I could."

"So why can't you?" I asked.

"I don't belong to just myself," he said. "I have to think about making a living for Amy and Daniel. I've waited too long already, and I can't turn back now. So many people are depending on me—not only my family but my agent, the studio, my record label. All of them took a chance on me, and if my reputation goes, so do theirs." He seemed uncomfortable thinking about it. "But, hey, no pressure, right?"

"Now you really do seem like a grown-up," I said.

We finished our coffee and drove back to the set. I played with Daniel for a little while, and then Brynn drove me home.

Later that night, I got to spend time with another dedicated dad: mine. He got home around eight while I was studying Gomer. He looked tired but seemed to perk up when he saw what I was doing. "You're watching *Gomer Pyle*?" he asked. "I love that old show!" He took off his jacket and tie, kicked off his shoes, and sank into the recliner.

"Can I make you something to eat?" I asked.

"You know what? I completely forgot to eat tonight," he said. "What've we got?"

"How about one of those ham and cheese sandwiches that you pop in the microwave?"

Dad sighed. "That sounds like heaven, actually."

"You relax," I said. "I'll get it for you." I made the sandwich and poured a Coke (caffeine free, of course—he needed a good night's sleep), and I even put a couple of pickle spears on his plate because he totally loves those gross things.

"Ooh, pickles!" Dad said when I brought him his plate. "You braved the smell of the pickle jar just for your old dad, huh?" He smiled. "What did I do to deserve such a wonderful daughter?"

"Feel free to raise my allowance any time," I replied.

"Nice try. So how's school going?" he asked.

"Fine," I said.

"Did you and those girls patch things up?"

"To patch things up, we'd have to have been friends before-hand."

"But are they leaving you alone, at least?"

"Pretty much."

"Anything I can do to help?"

"No, I think it's probably one of those typical kid things that will just take care of itself eventually, but thanks for asking."

Dad looked at me funny. "Did you get a haircut?"

"Last week, actually," I said.

He grimaced. "Guess I should have noticed before now," he said. "It looks cute, though. Different."

"Thanks. I figured I could use a change."

While Dad ate his dinner, we watched Gomer together, not really saying much but kind of enjoying being in the same room, doing the same thing. The goofier the show got, the more Dad liked it. He was laughing his butt off.

The room was dark, but every so often, when he wouldn't notice, I'd look back at Dad in the glow of the television. I thought of what Colby had said about how Amy and Daniel depended on him, and for the first time, I realized that Dad didn't spend all those hours at the office trying to make partner just for himself.

Twenty

Dad waited to go to work until I woke up that Saturday morning. "Good morning, sunshine," he said. "I've been missing my girl. Thought we could have a quick breakfast together before I head for the office. Sorry I had to work so late all last week."

"No big," I said. "I'm staying pretty busy myself."

Dad kissed my head. "Oh, by the way, I checked the messages this morning. Did you hear the ones from that plumber's daughter? What's her name? Carolyn?"

"Caroline Sanford?" I asked. I'd been so busy the past couple of days, what with my big "date" and all, that I'd totally forgotten to check the machine. I pushed the Play button.

"You have two new messages," the robotic voice said. "Thursday, four-seventeen, p.m."

"Emily! Hi! It's Caroline Sanford again. Just checking back with you. I know you're probably busy studying and stuff, but give me a call when you can, okay? Thanks!"

"Friday, six-twenty-one, p.m."

"Um, yeah, this is Caroline Sanford. I've left a couple of messages, but I'm not sure I have the right number. I'm trying to reach Emily Wood. If this is the correct number, would you please have her call me? Thanks."

"That's certainly thoughtful of her to call you," Dad said. "You know, I hate to say it because her father was such a nice guy, but she didn't strike me as the friendly type when we met her that time."

"I know; go figure."

When Dad went to work, I called Brynn.

"All systems go on this end," she said. "In exchange for the tip, I made the photographer promise to sit on the pictures of you and Colby for one week so they'll run at an opportune time. How many messages from Caroline?"

"How'd you know?" I asked. "Two more since the first one."

"Call her back," Brynn instructed me. "She'll invite you to meet up with her. Do it."

VI.
TARGETED ADVERTISING

Twenty-One

Caroline picked up on the first ring. "Hi, Emily! How's it going?" she asked.

"Great. Thanks for asking."

"Listen, what are you doing today? I'm going to the mall with a couple of friends, and we'd love to have you along."

"Sure, I guess so."

"Awesome! How about I swing by and pick you up in about an hour?"

"Okay."

"See you then!"

Unbelievable.

I called Dad's office and made sure he was cool with my going to the mall with Caroline. He seemed thrilled that I was making friends. It took nearly the entire hour to style my hair and fix my makeup the way Patrick and Amy had shown me. Of course it didn't look quite as good when I did it myself, but it still looked very hip. I wore the black cami with the beaded black cardigan and the jeans with the worn knees.

Caroline showed up right on time. Her black hair was as shiny as the tires on her just-washed red sports car, and her milky skin contrasted with all that dark hair in a way that was distinctly gorgeous. Two of her friends were in the backseat. "Emily," Caroline said, "this is Laura and MK. It's short for Mary Kate, but no one important calls her anything but MK."

"What a coincidence," I said. "No one important calls me anything but Em."

"Well, come on, Em!" Caroline said. "Let's go!"

In the car, Laura said, "I love your outfit! Where'd you get it?"

"I picked it up at a vintage boutique," I said casually. It was sort of true, after all.

"I love vintage!" MK said. "It's so cool to have clothes that aren't like everyone else's."

I said, "If you really like this, you could borrow it sometime." I imagined Brynn holding up a score as though I were participating in some sort of gymnastics tournament. Definitely a ten for that one.

As we walked around the mall, they talked about which purse would go with the shoes Laura had gotten last week and whether MK should wear plain opaque or a shimmery pearl nail polish to prom. In a clearly labored effort to pull me into the conversation, Caroline would occasionally point to an outfit of some sort and say, "Em, that would look so smokin' on you!"

Then we sat down at the food court with our soft Parmesan pretzels and strawberry smoothies, and I experienced the true meaning of the Delt sisterhood.

"You guys, look!" Caroline said. "It's Allison." Caroline stood up and waved. "Al!" she called to a girl near the Chick-fil-A. Allison flashed a huge grin and waved back enthusiastically. "You look so cute!" Caroline mouthed with exaggeration so Allison could read her lips. Allison looked down at her outfit and mouthed back a pleased "Thanks!" Caroline blew a kiss, which Allison promptly returned before going on her way.

"Can you believe what she's wearing?" Caroline said to the rest of us when she sat down again. "It's hideous!"

"I know!" MK said. "What is she thinking?"

"Ugh! I can't stand her. She makes me sick," Laura added.

"Isn't she a Delt?" I asked.

"Yeah. So?" Caroline asked.

"I thought you guys were all 'sisters,' or whatever," I said.

"Oh, we are," Caroline explained. "But Allison got picked because her family is rich and their house is great for parties. Nobody really likes *her*."

"But most of the time we just take the girls we really, really like," MK said.

"Like you, of course!" Caroline quickly added.

Uh-huh. Because she liked me so much and, *oh, by the way*, thought I could get her a contract at Ford. Before she could say more, a guy approached our table.

"What's up, Caroline?" he said. He was thin and had sandy blond hair and freckles. Really cute freckles.

"Hi, Ryan," Caroline purred. "Just hanging out with my girls. What are you up to?"

"Nothing much. Had to pick up a present for my mom's birthday." He looked at me. "Hi. I don't think we've met. I'm Ryan Shelton."

Before I could answer, Caroline said, "This is Em. Em Wood. She's going to be a freshman next year and maybe even a Delt, too."

"Wright Middle?" he asked. I nodded. "Are you on any of the teams—volleyball, softball, cheerleading?"

"I'm not much of an athlete," I said.

"So what are you much of?" he asked.

"Well, I'm the editor of the literary magazine." *Wrong answer! Lame!* I wished I could take it back as soon as I'd said it.

"Cool," he said. "I used to draw stuff for the lit mag last year when I was at Wright. One of my pictures was on the cover."

"I've seen it," I said. "The old barn? You drew that? It was really good."

"Thanks. How about you? Do you draw or write?"

"I write," I said. "Kind of."

"Stories or poems?" he asked.

"Poems." I felt less embarrassed once I realized the Delts weren't even listening. They were busy discussing their carb intakes.

"Maybe you could send me a few sometime?" he said. "What's your IM address?" He handed me his phone, and I entered my info. "Cool," he said. "I'll be in touch. Laura, MK, Caroline, see you at school."

"Bye, Ryan," the three of them chorused.

"Check it out!" Laura said. "He was into you, Em!"

"Way into you!" MK agreed.

"If I dated freshmen, which of course I don't," Caroline said,

"I would totally go out with Ryan. He's on the baseball team, and he's seriously hot. Em, he'd be perfect for you. Especially if you become a Delt. Delts always date older guys."

"He seems sweet, but I don't really know anything about him," I said.

"He's hot and he's on the baseball team! What else matters?" asked Laura.

I shrugged my shoulders and began gathering the pretzel wrappers.

"Em, what are you doing?" Caroline asked.

"Picking up our trash," I said.

"They pay people to do that. Delts don't pick up trash," Laura said.

"But you're supposed to throw your paper away. Everyone does," I said.

"Everyone who's nobody, maybe," said MK. "Leave it. Give the cleaning people something to do."

As we walked away from the table, I had to fight the urge to turn around and throw the papers into the garbage can. I mean, it was *right there*; it wouldn't have been any trouble.

When we reached the food court's doors, we ran straight into Heatherly Hamilton and her mom.

The other girls stepped around them, but I stopped in my tracks. Heatherly did, too. Neither of us said anything. We just looked at each other.

"Em! Come on!" Caroline called, already several steps ahead.

I followed Caroline and the other two, looking back only once to see Heatherly staring after me in disbelief, as though she'd just witnessed a two-headed woman giving birth to a litter of puppies.

Twenty-Two

The next day, Ryan IM'd me. I was typing a science paper when my computer chimed.

Hi, Em. Remember me?

Yeah, I'm always forgetting gorgeous high school guys who ask me about poetry.

Of course, Ryan. How's it going?

Pretty good. Working on some bio hw. Thought I'd see if this address was fake or not.

LOL. Guess now U know.

So, RU writing a poem or what?

Hardly. Paper for science about continental drift. *yawn*

Xciting. :p

A few seconds went by before Ryan typed anything else, like he was trying to think of what to say next.

OK—new topic: fave poet?

Robert Frost. Yours?

Don't really have 1. Read Frost in English, tho. Not bad.

Mrs. C calls him "deceptively simple." All his stuff has layers of meaning.

Crutchfield?

Yeah.

Had her last year. Pretty cool lady.

Best teacher ever!!!!

A minute or so went by without either one of us saying anything, so I wrote

I really did ❤ that pic you drew in the lit mag. U draw a lot?

I wish. I'm so busy with baseball that I don't have much time to draw. I miss it, tho.

UR gr8 at it.

Thx. I like arty stuff—pics, lit...would ❤ 2C poems by U. :)

I'd ❤ 2C more pics by U. :)

So when will U B hanging with Caroline? Catch U again sometime?

I felt my whole body tense with excitement. Hot Ryan wanted to see me—or was it Em he wanted to see?

Not sure.

OK then. Whenever's cool. Talk l8r?

He typed his cell number and wrote

Call me if ur out and want 2 get 2gether.

OK.

I went back to work on my science paper:

Although German geologist/meteorologist Alfred Wegner first proposed the theory of continental drift in 1915, let me just say that

it's extremely hard to concentrate on drifting land masses and plate tectonics when you're completely distracted by the fact that freshman baseball player Ryan Insanely Hot Freckle-icious Cutie Shelton has just IM flirted with you!!!! WOO-HOO!!!!!

I decided it would probably be best to delete everything past "1915" before I turned it in.

I also wondered if a guy like Ryan would ever have asked me about poetry if I hadn't had the new haircut and makeup and clothes and been at the mall with the Delts. *Don't analyze it—just enjoy it,* I told myself.

The May issue of *Flirt* arrived in everyone's mailbox and on newsstands over the weekend. I'd been wearing the outfits inspired by the spreads for two and a half weeks. The tunic had been especially well received—Kelsey had even asked where to get one. Unfortunately, it was a one-of-a-kind, I'd said. On Monday, I showed up at school wearing the black jacket with white shirttails sticking out beneath and the lime green miniskirt. The chunky rhinestone bracelet, some garish silver and rhinestone pins, and a pair of fuchsia cat's eye glasses Brynn and I'd gotten for a dollar at the drugstore—fake, of course, since my vision is perfect—completed the outfit. And I made sure Colby's necklace was clearly visible around my neck. At first, I'd thought the whole ensemble looked ridiculous, but my new style had begun to feel natural to me—I was kind of into it. My outfit looked a lot like one the magazine's fashion editor had put together for the Heavy Metal Glam spread.

Heatherly, Meredith, and Alexa were actually looking through a copy of *Flirt* when I saw them that morning in the lobby. "How did you do it?" Heatherly demanded.

"Do what?" I asked, trying to sound bored.

"All these clothes you've been wearing. They're in this magazine. How did you get them? I haven't seen any of this stuff at the mall."

Kelsey Brown came up to me before I could answer. "Em! Love your look!" she said.

"Thanks."

"Hey, I heard the Delts are rushing you!" Kelsey almost shrieked. "Me too! Who's your contact?"

"Caroline Sanford," I said.

"Caroline Sanford is getting you into Delts?" Alexa asked. "I don't believe it."

"Why don't you ask Heatherly?" I said. "Caroline and I ran into her at the mall Saturday."

Meredith and Alexa turned to Heatherly with accusing eyes. "Heatherly, you didn't tell us you saw Plywood with Caroline Sanford," Meredith said. She sounded annoyed. "You said they were going to rush you and me, but I haven't heard from any of them yet."

"You will," Heatherly answered. "They'll call us."

"Well, see you in class, Em!" Kelsey said as she walked away.

"I don't know what you're up to, but you're not fooling me," Heatherly said. "Don't think for one minute that you're ever going to be anything at this school, because I'll make sure that doesn't happen. I'm going to be May Queen, and if anybody from eighth grade gets into Delts, it's going to be me. I'll make sure they all know what a loser you are. You don't stand a chance."

"Really? That's funny," I said, staring her straight in the eye with a Gomer-esque expression of confusion, "because Caroline seems to think I do."

Heatherly tried to grab my wrist, but I jerked it away from her with a vengeance. The fact that she was bigger than I was didn't scare me anymore. I felt tough suddenly, as though I could've wrestled a bear.

"Nice seeing you, girls, but I've gotta run," I said.

"Yeah, you'd better run. Because I'm still going to get you, Emily!" Heatherly called after me, her voice tinged with desperation.

Within a week of the new issue of *Flirt,* all the girls at school—even the Daisies—were wearing flirty florals and heavy metal glam, even though the real fashionistas, like Kelsey, opted to wear leggings under the dresses since it was still cold in Ohio in March (why hadn't I thought of that?). And they wore the scarves vertically—as though to hide a cranberry juice stain down the front.

"The brand totally works!" I told Brynn the next day when I visited her on the set. "You wouldn't believe the way I've been standing up to the three Daisies. I'm totally pulling off the brand. Instead of doing what I would normally do in a situation, I think of what Em would do, and then I remember, hey, I'm Em, and I do it! And the Daisies are running scared!"

"Just as I expected," Brynn replied. "Bullies go after the weak. You stand up to them and they don't know what to do with themselves. But they haven't seen anything yet. The photographer sold the pictures of Colby and his mystery girl to the number-one celeb weekly. They should run in the new issue, which is on stands"—she looked at her calendar—"tomorrow!" Then she smiled wryly and said, "Strap in, baby!"

VII.
MEDIA BLITZ

Twenty-Three

Our doorbell rang before seven o'clock the next morning. It was Sonny. I was in the bathroom getting ready for school, so I couldn't hear what he and Dad were talking about, but it didn't sound good.

"There you are!" Sonny said when I came into the kitchen. "Explain to me why I'm holding a copy of the *Informer* with your picture on it!"

There it was. COLBY SUMMERS DATING MYSTERY GIRL. As Colby had predicted, they'd gone with the shot of his arm around my shoulder.

"It's kind of a long story," I began. "You guys trust me, right?"

"Emily, you are not allowed to date. Period," Dad said. "And you're certainly not allowed to date without my knowledge. And absolutely not a boy who's seventeen!"

"I agree completely," I said. Sonny and Dad seemed at a loss. They hadn't anticipated winning so easily. "You're right—Colby's definitely too old for me. But it wasn't a date. My friend, Brynn, works for his publicity firm. She's helping me with that career project I told you about."

"The one you mentioned about public relations and marketing?" Dad asked.

"Yeah. Remember? I went out to the movie set, to her office there, to work on my project. Sonny, you were guarding the gates that night."

Sonny looked nervously at Dad.

"Yes," he said. "And I met the young woman. She seemed very responsible."

"Yeah. So I got to meet Colby Summers, see? Which was awesome because, hey, he's a movie star. He came by Brynn's trailer while we were working and said he wanted to get out for a while, so he was going to pick up some coffee in town and bring it back to the crew. He needed help carrying all those cups, and it was cool to get to run an errand with a movie star. No big deal. We were gone all of thirty minutes, tops. Besides, Colby's hot and heavy with his makeup artist; he's not interested in me at all. The tabloids just made it look that way."

"His arm is around your shoulder!" Dad said.

"Would you guys relax?" I said. "It's nothing. He was playing mind games with the photographer because he kept bugging us. Come on, if it weren't for that headline, couldn't that just as easily be a picture of me with, oh, I don't know . . . my uncle or my dad?"

"Well," Dad said, seeming disappointed. "I suppose it could be a platonic gesture. But, on the other hand—"

"If you don't believe me, you can ask Brynn," I said. "You can call her right now and ask her if Colby isn't completely devoted to Amy, the makeup artist. She'll tell you."

"That's a good idea. I'll call her," Sonny said a little too quickly. "What's her number?"

"That's not necessary. I trust you to tell me the truth, Emily," Dad said. "But the fact of the matter is that you *did* go off by yourself with a teenage boy, without getting permission from me or your uncle. That is enough to warrant some consequences."

"I concur," Sonny said, nodding. "Although I'm still willing to call and double-check her story with this Brynn person if it would make you feel better, Louis."

"I'm sorry, Dad. I didn't think of it like that. It was a once-in-a-lifetime thing. Come on, what girl wouldn't want to run an errand with a movie star? He was a perfect gentleman."

"You're still grounded," Dad said.

"Dad! For how long?"

Dad looked at Sonny. This was new territory; I'd always been a model daughter. (Well, as far as Dad knew, since he hadn't found out about my New York escapade.) "Two weeks," he said. "You don't go anywhere but school and home, unless you're with your uncle or me."

"Two weeks? Come on! What if, when you were fourteen, you'd gotten to run an errand with . . ." I tried to think of some old woman who was hot when Dad was young.

"Farrah Fawcett?" Sonny offered.

"Exactly." Whoever that was.

"My parents would have grounded me," Dad said. Then he smiled a little bit. "But I probably would have done the exact same thing you did. A week and a half."

"But what about my project?" I asked. "I can't work on it without seeing Brynn."

"That's a good point," Sonny said. "It is a school project. I could drive her to and from the set to see Brynn, you know, so she's chaperoned."

"All right," Dad said. "But if you have to work on your project, your uncle takes you. You can't go on your own. And nowhere else besides school and to work on your project for one week. Understood?"

"Understood," I said.

"And just so we're clear, no more going anywhere with boys without permission," Dad said. "I don't care if it's Elvis himself."

Sonny and Dad weren't the only ones who'd seen the *Informer*. Kelsey, accompanied by most of the cheerleading squad, pounced on me when I got to the lobby. "Em! Look what I saw when I stopped at the gas station this morning to buy a slushy! Is that you?" She held up a copy of the magazine.

Heatherly walked up. "Of course it's not her. What would Colby Summers be doing on a date with Plywood?"

Kelsey seemed skeptical. "It looks like her to me."

"That doesn't mean anything. She's pretty plain; a lot of people look like her," said Heatherly.

"It looks exactly like Em to me," Kelsey said. "So, come on! Spill it! Are you dating Colby Summers or aren't you? You can tell us."

I didn't know what to say. I didn't want to lie, but I really wanted to put Heatherly in her place, too. "Well . . . ," I began, not sure what I would say next.

Just then, another one of the cheerleaders noticed the necklace. "You guys! Look!" she yelled. "It's Colby's necklace! The exact same one he's wearing in the poster on my wall! She *is* dating him!"

Everyone started talking at once and clamoring to get a look at the necklace. *How did you meet him? How long have you been dating him? Is he a good kisser? Are you going to get married someday? What's he really like?* My ears were ringing with all the questions.

"It's really no big deal," I said. "It's nothing."

Kelsey hung out with me all day, in Vannies and in the halls between classes. At lunch, she insisted I sit at her table. Mrs. Crutchfield had asked me to work on the lit mag during lunch that day, but I promised her I'd catch up on it later. I couldn't pass up the opportunity to hear Kelsey say to the Daisies, "Can you guys scoot down? Em is sitting here."

You could almost see the steam coming off the three of them.

I used the formula Brynn had taught me of name plus compliment plus question to start conversations with people who'd never said jack to me before. "Hey, Victoria, cute earrings! Where'd you get them?" "Carmen, that was hilarious how you burned Mr. Rudolph at that lame assembly! Did you get in trouble for it?" "Hayden, I saw your picture for the art contest—it was awesome! Were you surprised when you won?" They ate it up.

Still, sitting at the cool table wasn't all it was cracked up to be. In fact, it was like spending an afternoon with the Delts or like one of the phone conversations I'd had recently with Caroline, who'd taken to calling me for chats. All any of them seemed to care about was who was having what party and who had hooked up with whom. The members of the cool table all wanted my take on every situation, as though I were anointed in some way and my opinion meant more than theirs. As Brynn had cautioned, I was politically savvy, making sure not to say anything that could be used against me, which no doubt made my conversation boring, though no one complained. Anytime one of the cheerleaders got up from the table for half a second, the rest of them immediately began trashing her about anything they could think of—where she'd bought her shoes or how fat she was getting—until she came back to the table and they pretended to be her best friends. I noticed, however, that Kelsey never participated. Whenever the other girls started in on someone else, she'd turn to me and start a conversation about our social studies paper or something we'd read in Mrs. Crutchfield's class. Sure, she could hold her own during conversations about stuff like pep rallies and pyramid stunts—things she and the other girls seemed to find entirely too interesting—but she didn't seem to enjoy ripping other people to shreds.

When I called Brynn that night to tell her how the tabloid pictures had gone over at school, she laughed. "Perfect! I couldn't have scripted it any better!"

"You mean I wasn't supposed to make it sound like Colby and I were madly in love or something?"

"I told you, lying isn't necessary. Telling the truth is so much better because people never believe it anyway. You told them that you and Colby were no big deal, which is true. But they're going to believe otherwise because they want to, and then your denial of any sort of passionate romance makes you seem all that much cooler. It's brilliant! Any tangible signs you've gained market share?"

"I sat at the cool table today," I told her.

"Good indicator," she said. "How is it?"

"Actually, pretty boring. They're so shallow. I guess because they don't know what it's like to have real problems."

"Everyone has problems, Emily," she said. "Those 'cool' kids are flesh and blood like the rest of us."

"Any new instructions?"

"Stay the course," said Brynn. "It's not over yet."

Later that night, Ryan IM'd me for the fourth night in a row.

So what's this every1 at school is talking about with U on some magazine cover? Is that really U?

I wished we were talking instead of typing so that I could have heard his tone of voice. I wondered if he meant was I the person in the photograph, or was the person in the photograph the "real me."

That's my picture, yeah. But it's no big deal. The press always needs something 2 write about, I guess.

Is he ur bf?

No.

U sure?

Trust me. Things aren't always what they seem.

No one was more convinced of that than Heatherly. Over the next couple of days, she continued to insist that there couldn't possibly be anything going on between Colby and me. She cast suspicion on our "date" by reminding everyone that my uncle was a cop and hypothesizing that he'd probably escorted Colby into town and let me come along. The photo, if it really was of me, was obviously nothing more than a star posing with a fan. Tabloids always made stuff up, she said. She even suggested that the necklace was a fake—a replica I'd created to try to make everyone think Colby had given me his. As the days wore on with nothing new to suggest that Colby was my boyfriend, Heatherly's conspiracy theory gained more and more ground. By Friday, no one seemed to remember or care that I'd been the first to wear the trends of floral and metal glam, and Heatherly must have worked hard to keep my association with Caroline Sanford from leaking to the masses, because no one had brought it up again since Kelsey had first asked about it.

I called Brynn and filled her in on how quickly Heatherly had begun to spin things her way again.

"She's a worthy adversary," Brynn said. "She could have a real future in PR."

Heatherly was a lot of things, but she was no slacker when it came to protecting her market share. She never took a vacation, not even over spring break.

Twenty-Four

I'd been grounded and unable to promote my brand during spring break, which Brynn said would be fine as long as I led people to assume that I'd gone on a fabulous trip. I'd made sure to jot down a few red herrings in black marker on one of my notebooks, such as the number for the Malibu Beach Inn, and "accidentally" leave it lying around so inquiring minds could fill in the blanks. I simply had to avoid being seen, which was fine with me since it provided a break from the relentless pace of the Em Campaign. It was a bit lonely, since Ryan's IMs had stopped while he was on a camping trip, but a couple of times I managed to sneak to the set and play with Daniel for a few hours.

Naturally, though, Heatherly hadn't missed the opportunity to make a power grab: she'd taken several key girls from the in crowd to her lake house, thus recapturing vital market share and consumer loyalty. When we came back to school, my vague suggestions that I'd simply relaxed and soaked up some sun over the break fell flat in comparison to the stories Heatherly and her crew told of picking up hot guys and partying at her lake house for five days. My position at the cool tables in the lunchroom symbolized my plummeting stock: at first, there was lack of conversation directed my way; next, I was edged farther and farther from the middle, and eventually, when Kelsey was out three days with strep, backpacks and purses and books started popping up in all the empty seats. Clearly, my might-have-been-in-Malibu was no match for Heatherly's five-day lake house blowout. She had the best friends money could buy.

I was back to having lunch in Mrs. Crutchfield's room, which suited Mrs. C just fine, because between my meteoric rise and now-whimpering decline, we'd gotten tons of submissions. After the tabloid picture, the lit mag enjoyed its own fifteen minutes of fame, and for a few days, submitting poems and tales of teen angst to the almost-famous editor had become kind of a fad. To be honest, I was way behind on sorting through the slush pile, not to mention the amount of editing I should have been doing. But it had been so hard to concentrate, what with everything going on with the campaign.

When I went to see Brynn, Sonny dropped me off at the set even though my punishment had ended a week before. We both knew it was an excuse to see her, but I thought it was kind of cute, so I didn't call him on it. I let him play concerned uncle. It was kind of funny to watch them together when he'd drop me off at her trailer—the way he got that goofy grin on his face and the way Brynn, normally so polished, would get all girly and giggly.

"I'm back to nobody," I told her after Sonny left. It was the first week of April. "She's convinced everyone that there was nothing to the magazine photo. Who was I kidding? I can't take on Heatherly Hamilton. She's unbeatable."

"One minor setback and you throw your hands up?" Brynn said. "You didn't think she was going to make it easy for us, did you? We have to keep pushing forward with our campaign. Our next move is a big one."

"What's that?"

"You're about to have the party of the year!"

"I don't think so," I said.

"Why not?"

"The last party I had was for my birthday in third grade," I told her. "And as I recall, that didn't go very well. My mom invited my whole class to an all-you-can-eat pizza place filled with these old arcade games. Some boy in my class had all he could eat and then some. He threw up on me while I was playing Ms. Pac-Man. My most vivid memory of turning nine is my mom peeling off my pukey sweater in the ladies' bathroom. It was awful. I haven't had a party since."

"So what's your point?" Brynn asked, barely looking up from her laptop.

"Um, that maybe I'm not exactly the party type? I don't like crowds."

"Oh, but Em does," Brynn replied. "Em is a social butterfly. She adores parties! And this one's going to be the Wright Middle School social event of the year. It had better be, because paying for the venue, the band, and the catering is going to use up the rest of our budget."

"What venue?" I asked.

"Depends on the theme we come up with," she said.

"You mean like Spiderman? Aren't I a little old for a theme party? And besides, I'm a writer. Writers don't do parties."

"I knew you were going to be difficult about this," she said. She clicked on her Internet favorites folder, and opened a page about Truman Capote. "In the 1960s in New York, acclaimed author Truman Capote threw a party that's still a legend in literary circles: the Black and White Ball—a theme party. So there. Furthermore, the guest list included the most important writers and artists of his day, so don't tell me writers don't party, thank you very much."

I scanned the page. "It says here that some considered this party to be one of Capote's major achievements, right up there with his books," I said.

"He planned it for months. Capote said that he invited five hundred friends and made fifteen thousand enemies. Now, that's what I call a party."

"All right, I'm sold," I said. "So do we copy the black and white ball idea and tell people to wear masks?"

"I'm thinking that doesn't have the right feel for a teen crowd," Brynn said. "But I do want this party to showcase what makes you different. It needs to be a party that isn't like every other middle school, hey-my-parents-are-out-of-town rager.

"I'm going to let you in on a little secret. Really cool people and nerds have one thing in common: they're different from everyone else. They're weird. The thing is, though, nerds are ashamed of being weird, while cool people celebrate it."

"That's all that separates nerds from cool people?"

"Pretty much. It's all in how you carry it off. So what we're going to do to sell your brand is to take your weird and make it a cool weird rather than a nerd weird. It's essentially your launch party. Em should be Emily without the social handicaps and awkwardness, but *with* the stuff that's special and marketable. This party has to have your unique stamp on it.

"I told you early on that your skill with words, your passion for language, could be a huge strength if we use it right. How about a party that has something to do with poetry?"

"A poetry party?" I asked.

"Not exactly," said Brynn. "But there has to be something—hasn't poetry ever been cool?"

"What about the British Romantics?" I said. "They were against the Industrial Revolution, and they wrote empassioned nature poetry."

"I'm sorry," Brynn said. "I think I dozed off for a minute."

"Hey, I'm trying!"

Brynn snapped her fingers. "Beatniks!" she said. "The nineteen fifties and sixties—they wore the cool black clothes and berets. They were like walking Gap ads! Back then, it was considered counter-cultural and rebellious to be into poetry. And they had their own little hip slang—like 'Daddy-O' and 'dullsville'! Don't you love it?"

"But didn't they take poetry seriously?" I asked. "I mean, it was kind of their way of life, their statement. Wouldn't it be crass to have a party that parodies that?"

Brynn grabbed me by the shoulders. "Trust me, Emily. They don't care about your party. . . . Most of them are probably dead! You are fourteen years old—stop overanalyzing everything!" Then she started laughing. "This confirms it: a party is just what you need."

Twenty-Five

Brynn put together an email invitation in all black and white with retro font and graphics. The headline said, "Can You Dig It, Baby?" and the text said, "All Wright Middle School cats and kits are invited to Emily Wood's Beatnik Party. Dress: You're Cool as Long as It's Black. Next Friday night at the old downtown theater. (First hundred to reply get in.) Be there or be □."

"I've scouted out potential locations. The old theater is the only place in town with enough room for all the guests and the band, and it's got that retro feel," Brynn said. "I've copied the email addresses from your school's directory; every student will receive this invitation. All we do is send it out, sit back, and wait to see what they post on the RSVP center."

"Brynn," I said, "you're not thinking like a teenager. Parties are highly political: they're all about who's giving them and who's going. The first problem is that it's my party, and I'm not cool, and the second problem is that if you invite everybody, only the nerds like me will go, and then it's a nerd party, which is just about the most pathetic thing ever. It's far better not to have a party than to have a nerd party. Trust me."

"Emily, Emily, Emily. So innocent, so naïve." Brynn patted me on the head like a puppy. "Who votes for May Queen?" she asked.

"Everybody at school," I replied.

"And of those thousand or so kids, what percentage would you estimate are in the cool crowd?"

"I don't know . . . less than ten percent? The whole point of the cool crowd is that it's elite."

Brynn nodded. "You're right. And you were also right when you said that parties are political. So we have to think politically. You'll win May Queen by running as a populist—a Girl of the People. You need the votes of those 90 percent outside the cool clique. You'll get those votes by doing something Heatherly would never dream of doing: allowing those kids to matter. 'Value me'—remember? Besides, it's the nice thing to do, and it works your USP. Remember your Unique Selling Proposition? It's that you're actually nice."

"I admit that from mathematical and moral points of view, it makes sense," I said. "But what about all that stuff about creating Brand Em as cool? The popular clique will just make fun of my sad, little nerd party. It will be a big joke."

"Not when the popular kids are standing outside, desperately trying to get in."

"Somehow, I don't see that happening."

The replies to the invitation began rolling in a few hours later. The RSVP center allowed everyone to see how the guest list was shaping up.

"Sounds like fun!" wrote Susan Eaglin, an overweight seventh-grader who'd probably never been invited to a party in her life. "I'll be there!"

"Yeah, I'll come," posted a quiet, brainy guy from my science class.

"Thanks for the invitation," Kelsey Brown wrote. "But I'll be at my dad's this weekend. Hope you have a great time, though." Sure. Like Kelsey Brown would be caught dead at my party. But at least she had the decency to make up a story.

"You've got 2B kidding," Heatherly wrote. "Social suicide, much?"

"Not in a million years," Alexa replied.

"LOSER!!!!" Meredith added. "NE1 who goes is more pathetic than Plywood."

The Daisies' comments had exactly the effect I had anticipated. The only people who were willing to sign up for the party were people who never got invited to anything.

By the next day, only thirty people had signed up—thirty people who were the social equivalent of veal at a vegetarian convention. It was humiliating. Not to mention that Heatherly and her friends got to make comments all day long—about whether we were planning to play Pin the Tail on the Donkey or hire a clown.

I called Brynn that night. "It isn't working," I told her. "Have you seen the guest list? Only thirty people. If people haven't RSVP'd by now, they're not going to."

"Patience," said Brynn. "Patience."

Twenty-Six

That Saturday, it was time for what Dad and I liked to call "Super Mondo Grocery Shopping." That's when we'd go to the giant whole-sale store across town and buy stuff in bulk, a process Dad absolutely hated. He preferred to browse the electronics section for an hour, so as part of my allowance, he kind of paid me to do all the actual shopping while he played with the TVs and stereo systems.

Normally, I wouldn't have dressed up to do something that boring, but I figured it was a good time to practice, so I did the whole hair and makeup thing and wore a pair of cool shoes Brynn and I had bought.

"You're awfully dressed up," Dad said when I came downstairs. "And don't you have makeup on? When did you start wearing makeup?"

"Dad, I'm fourteen," I said. "Lots of girls my age wear makeup."

He sighed one of those *my-baby-is-growing-up-so-fast* sighs.

"Go read some child development textbook about typical social progression and then you'll feel better about how I'm not mal-adapted."

He kind of laughed. "Okay," he said, "but we're just going to the wholesale store. Are you planning to see somebody?"

"No way," I said. "I'm simply taking pride in my appearance. It's a sign of maturity." I was half serious. Since I'd gone to the trouble, I figured it was unlikely that I'd see anyone I knew. You see people at places like wholesale stores only when you look like crap. It's one of those laws of the universe.

That's why I was so surprised when, while trying to decide between the giant boxes of raspberry or cherry Pop-Tarts, I heard someone say, "Em? Hey, it is you! What's up?" It was Ryan. For some reason, I immediately didn't want Ryan to know I ate Pop-Tarts, so I tried to pretend I'd been looking at cereal, but that was even worse, because the only thing nearby was Cap'n Crunch.

"Hey, Ryan. How's it going?"

"Okay. I'm here with my dad."

"Me too."

He looked at the boxes behind me. "Getting some Pop-Tarts, huh?"

"Yeah, sort of."

"Aw, man," Ryan said, picking up a box of peanut butter Cap'n Crunch, "I love this stuff!"

I kind of laughed. "Really?"

"What? Is that goofy?" he said. "Maybe so. But I'm telling you, I could eat this whole box in a day! Oh, look. There's a prize inside." He pointed to a picture of some sort of plastic insect toy. "Now, see, if you hadn't made fun of me, I might have given you the toy. But now I'll have to keep it for myself." His grin seemed so effortless, it made me feel like I was melting right into the floor.

"Ryan! What are you doing?" a man in jeans and a plaid shirt asked coming down the aisle.

"Nothing, Dad, just getting some cereal," Ryan said. "Dad, this is Em. Em, this is my dad."

"Nice to meet you," I said.

"Same here," his dad said. "You a classmate of Ryan's?"

"Em's in eighth grade, so she'll be at the high school next year," Ryan answered.

"Well, nice to meet you, Em. Ryan, I'm going to need some help with the varnish."

Ryan explained, "Dad has a small side business. He does woodworking and a little carpentry. He gets a lot of his supplies here."

"Woodworking," I said. "That's an excellent home business deduction." As soon as I'd said it, I felt like a dolt. *Did I really just spew some of Dad's CPA jargon to Hot Ryan and Hot Ryan's dad?*

"Home business deduction?" Ryan's dad asked.

Great, I thought. *Even middle-aged men think I'm lame.*

"I can count my woodworking on my taxes?"

"Sorry," I said. "My dad's a CPA, so I've picked up some of this stuff." Actually, I knew a lot about taxes. It was the result of making dinner conversation in the two years following Mom's death.

"Well, tell me more, Miss Em!" Ryan's dad said.

"Dad, come on," Ryan said. Now *he* seemed embarrassed, but his dad ignored him.

"I don't really know that much about it, but if you sell any of your work, you can probably go for the home-office deduction, which would make anything you buy for your woodworking tax deductible . . . such as the varnish and even the mileage for driving over here to buy it."

Ryan's dad seemed impressed. "I'd never thought of that before. I'll have to look into it. Thanks! Come on, Ryan. Let's go buy some tax-deductible varnish!"

When his dad began walking away, Ryan grinned at me again and rolled his eyes. "Now look what you've done," he said.

I blushed. "Who's the real dork?" I said. "You may like Cap'n Crunch, but I give out accounting advice at the wholesale store. Way cool, huh?"

"I wouldn't use the word *cool*," Ryan said, "but maybe *cute*." He looked at the floor and then back up at me. "I'll call you," he said, walking away with his huge box of cereal.

He called the very next day.

"Hello," he said when I answered. "Important business call for financial wizard Em Wood."

"I'm never going to live that down, am I?" I said.

"Live it down? Why, Miss Wood, you're my dad's hero! In fact, I have permission from my CEO to expense a dinner with you, so long as your tastes aren't too refined for a burger and a milk shake."

"Actually, I love burgers and milk shakes," I said. "But there's one tiny problem—"

"Let me guess. You'd rather go with my dad. This happens to me all the time. Was it the beer gut or the black socks with sneakers?"

"Believe it or not, neither one did much for me."

I had to turn him down, but I couldn't tell him why. Emily Wood might have a dad who wouldn't let her date until she was fifteen, but Em was way too cool for that, and surely that was what he liked about me, right? It had to be the persona; no guy like Ryan had ever been interested in me before. In fact, no guy *at all* had ever been interested in me before.

I couldn't blow it. I had to make up some excuse he'd believe without making him think I didn't like him: "I probably shouldn't make any plans. I stay pretty busy." That didn't come out right. It was supposed to sound nonchalant, not stuck up.

"Oh," Ryan said. "Sure. You're busy. I get it." He sounded hurt.

I couldn't let him feel that way, even if it meant I had to risk pulling back the curtain on Em a little bit. "No, wait—you don't get it," I said. "Look, here's the truth. I didn't want to tell you because it's so embarrassing. I can't date until I'm fifteen," I said. "Stupid rule my dad has." *Stupid rule that had no relevance until five seconds ago.*

Ryan seemed to perk up again. "In that case, we have no problem," he said.

"What do you mean?"

"I'm sure if we explain to your dad what a fine, upstanding young man I am, he'll change his mind immediately."

I laughed. "Yeah."

"Okay," Ryan said. "So when do you turn fifteen?"

"November," I said.

"Six months." He paused. "I guess you'll have to get the fern stand, then."

"The what?"

"Fern stand. My dad was so excited about your tax advice that he actually proposed making a fern stand and having me give it to you as a token of his thanks."

"Get out!" I said.

"I told him, 'Dad, are you nuts? I can't go around giving fern stands to pretty girls! They'll think I'm a total nerd!'"

My stomach flipped. *Ryan thinks I'm pretty!* "Tell your dad thanks, but I don't actually own a fern. In fact, I didn't even know they had their own stands."

"Well, I'll try to talk him out of it, but he's a pretty determined guy," Ryan said. "We Sheltons don't give up easily. Even if something takes us, say, six months."

"Oh, really?" I said. "Good to know."

"I'm just saying, don't be surprised if I show up at your door with a beautifully varnished, handcrafted fern stand. Hey, I know! I'll bring it to you at school so you can show everybody."

"You wouldn't!" I said.

"You think not, huh?" Ryan said. "Em, we really need to get to know each other better."

Yes, we do, I thought.

Twenty-Seven

I spent Sunday afternoon on the set with Brynn, Amy, and Daniel, while Colby shot a scene in which he seduced a terrorist spy and his irresistible sexiness made her switch allegiances to join the good guys. "I don't really want to see that," Amy said as we waited in the makeup trailer. "I need a distraction. Hey, you want a microdermabrasion treatment?"

As Amy exfoliated my dull surface cells to reveal a healthy new glow, Brynn went to change Daniel's diaper. "My job is full of glamour," she said.

"So how's everything at school?" Amy asked me. "Is it better?"

"Eh," I said. "School's school, but things are looking up in some areas."

My tone of voice must've suggested something mysterious because Amy demanded, "Dish!"

"There's this really great high school guy I met a couple of weeks ago," I said. "His name's Ryan, and he's so cute! I saw him at the store yesterday, and he called me for a date!"

"Awesome!" Amy said. "And did you say yes?"

"I would have, if I were allowed to date."

Brynn came back in with Daniel, holding him with outstretched arms as though he were roadkill. "What are you feeding this kid, Amy?" she said.

"Hang on, I'll take my little stinker back as soon as I'm finished here," Amy replied.

When my treatment was over and I'd washed my face, Brynn said, "Okay, Emily, let's check your RSVP center." She pulled it up on her laptop. Still only thirty people.

"I told you this wasn't going to work, Brynn."

"This is exactly what I'd hoped for," she replied.

"A complete lack of enthusiasm?"

"Exactly," she said. "Because it makes what I'm about to do so much more fun." She typed in a message that she wouldn't allow me to see but showed Amy.

"X, O," Amy said. "Give it a little kick."

"Good thinking," said Brynn. She typed two more letters and clicked the send button. Then she showed me the message she'd posted for everyone to see:

"Hey, Em . . . sorry it took me so long to reply. My filming schedule has been crazy the past few days. Anyway, count me in. Can't pass up a chance to hang out with you. xoColby"

Within twenty minutes, the last seventy slots were snapped up. "Colby Summers is coming to your party?" wrote one of the cheerleaders. "I'm SO there!"

"I'm in!" wrote another.

An hour later, over one hundred more people had received an email that said, "Sorry—guest list closed. Check at the door Friday night for space available."

Brynn and I analyzed the final guest list. "Perfect cross-section of every major social category," she said. "Fantastic. Colby will be a big draw for the girls, but we still need to create some major buzz about Brand Em if we want throngs of popular kids huddling outside the velvet rope."

"What exactly do you mean by 'buzz'?"

"People talking about you. Essentially, a rumor. Hollywood isn't so different from middle school and high school, you know—it's all about who's getting the most buzz. We need to get people talking about you, speculating . . . but in a good way. Let me think." Brynn drummed her fingers on the table a few minutes, then said, "I've got it!" and grabbed a book of business cards from her bag. She pulled out a card and typed the name into her computer. "Good," she said. "No picture. I'm coming to your school tomorrow. We've never met."

Twenty-Eight

When I got to my locker the next morning, Brynn was standing there with a cameraman and a guy holding one of those umbrella-looking lights and a light meter from which he repeatedly took readings. Everyone was watching, trying to figure out who they were and what they were doing.

"Oh, good—guys, she's here," Brynn shouted so everyone could hear. "Act natural," she said to me. "We're just checking the white balance and getting some b-roll. Pretend we're not here."

The Daisies marched right up to Brynn. "What are you doing?" Heatherly asked.

"I'm sorry," said Brynn. "I'm really not at liberty to discuss that right now."

"Is our school going to be on TV?" asked Meredith. "Are you with the local news?"

A crowd had gathered at this point, and Brynn made sure her voice carried. "No, not the local news. I'm sorry, but I really can't say any more. Please excuse us. We have to get these light readings, and then we'll be out of everyone's way." Then she said to the men with her, "Okay, I think we've got it. Let's get going. Em, we'll be in touch. Thanks!" As she left, Brynn made sure that an MTV business card just happened to drop to the floor.

Alexa picked it up as soon as Brynn was gone. "This says MTV!" she said. "What would MTV be doing at our school?"

"Hey!" Meredith said. "I read in a magazine the other day that they were thinking about doing a new reality series—something about inside the lives of trendsetting teenage girls."

"Then why would they be filming Plywood?" Heatherly said. "Maybe there's another reality show about wannabes." She looked at me suspiciously. "Or maybe those people weren't from MTV at all," she said. "Maybe this is some kind of setup."

"What's the deal?" Meredith asked me. "Were they really from MTV? And what were they doing here?"

"Hmm . . . ," I said. "What does the card say?"

"It says Marcita Diaz, Reality Programming Producer, MTV Networks," Alexa read.

"Very good, Alexa. I didn't realize you were actually literate."

"Shut up, Plywood," Heatherly said. "How do we know that wasn't just some random woman with an MTV person's business card?"

"I'm sure you're right," I said. "She happened to have an MTV business card. And a camera and lighting crew. That kind of stuff happens all the time."

"Well, I don't believe for a second that that was—" Heatherly stopped to read the card. "Marcita Diaz, MTV producer."

"Have you ever seen Marcita Diaz, MTV producer?" I said.

"No."

"So how do you know it *wasn't* her?"

VIII.
BRAND SYNERGY

Twenty-Nine

Brynn had wanted buzz, and she got it: the rumor that I might have a reality show in the works spread faster than a stomach virus in a preschool. With each day that passed, more of my *what ups, 'sups,* and *whazzups* were being enthusiastically returned in the halls, and people were starting conversations with *me* with compliments about my hair and clothes. I'd even become confident enough to look at actual eyes instead of bridges of the nose. I was back at the cool lunch tables again. Coupled with the curiosity about whether Colby Summers would indeed be in attendance Friday night, the MTV rumor had everyone at Wright dying to get into my party. People kept asking if there wasn't some way I could get anyone else in. *No, sorry, can't do it. Fire code.*

"Your uncle is infuriating," Brynn told me when we were working on party plans. "Two days before the party, and Sonny still hasn't asked if he can take me. I've dropped enough hints—what's his problem?"

"He thinks a big city girl like you wouldn't want to date a cop in the Midwest," I said.

"He told you that?"

"Yep," I said. "I told him he underestimates his own hotness, but he didn't believe me. To be honest, though, isn't a long-distance relationship with a guy in Ohio going to be impractical?"

"I don't see why it would be," Brynn said. "In case you hadn't heard, a few years ago, these two brothers from North Carolina invented an amazing flying machine that people now use to travel long distances in short amounts of time."

"Oh, no, you didn't just say that!"

"What?"

"First flight may have been in North Carolina, but the Wright boys were ours. Or haven't you noticed that my school is kind of named after them?"

"Huh," Brynn said. "I hadn't thought about it."

"How can people not know that?"

"If I handled your state's PR, they would," she replied. "Now can we get back to my original issue, your uncle?"

"Listen, if you're so hung up on Sonny, why don't you just ask him to be your date?"

"And make him think I'm pining away for him?"

"Brynn, you are pining away for him!"

"But I can't let him know that! It takes away the mystery, the thrill of the chase!"

"For someone who's so cutting edge when it comes to publicity, you're pretty old-fashioned," I said.

"Well, for someone who looks like James Dean, your uncle is pretty insecure!"

"Awww . . . ," I said.

"What?"

"It's your first fight!" I said. "Too bad Sonny isn't even here for it!" When I started laughing, Brynn told me to stop and then started laughing with me.

"I'll show you old-fashioned," she said, handing me her phone. "Call him." I dialed the number and gave it back to her. "Hi, Sonny, it's Brynn. Yeah, well, it's nice to hear your voice, too." She silently cheered. "I was just wondering . . . I'm having this party, ostensibly for Emily, but really to promote my client with the teen audience, of course, and Emily's learning about party promotion for her project. Yes, we are having a lot of fun with it. Anyway, I was just thinking, would you be free this Friday night to come with me? I could really use your help with security. A police officer garners so much respect, you know. Oh, yes, I really do think so! I've always had the utmost respect for law enforcement. You're heroes! You will? Oh, that will be great. I'll see you then." When she hung up, she looked at me and said, "What?"

I replied in a high-pitched voice, "Oh, Sonny! You're my hero!" She chased me around the table. "Oh, Sonny, you're so big and strong!"

Sonny was more than happy to square it with Dad about the party and drop me off at the set that Friday night. Although everyone else wanted to catch a glimpse of Colby at the party, Sonny was all about Brynn. Yeah, he was pretty much a goner. I'd never seen him so taken with anyone before. Brynn looked especially beautiful in a black cocktail dress. She told Sonny that we'd need about an hour for my styling before the party—all part of learning the ins and outs of PR, of course—so he said he'd meet us at the theater about half an hour before it started.

I wore a black A-line minidress with black tights, flat shoes, and big earrings. Patrick teased my hair high in the back, with messy fringe around my face, and Amy tricked me out with false eyelashes, tons of black eyeliner, and pale lipstick. "So, have you heard from that boy you told me about?" Amy asked as she colored in my eyebrows. Brynn had told me once that celebs sometimes had their preferred makeup artists sign confidentiality agreements, and now I understood why—it was easy to spill your guts to someone who gets that close to your face.

"Not as much in the past few days," I said. "He's got baseball practice and games almost constantly, but we've still IM'd a couple of times. I told him I was having a party tonight but that my dad would freak if I invited a high school boy. I think he bought it."

"Good thinking, since Colby's your date," Amy said.

"You're very generous with your husband," I replied.

Amy stopped for a moment and looked worried. "Hey, Brynn," she said. "What if this boy Emily likes hears about Colby coming to her party as her date? He might get upset."

"What, is she married now?" Brynn asked.

"No, but my date is!" I said. Amy and Colby laughed, but Brynn didn't.

"If you were one of our comedy clients, I'd so drop you just for that one," she said. "Look, if the boy finds out, you tell him Colby's just a friend and it wasn't a date. That's true."

"Probably he'll never even hear about it," I said. "High school people don't really talk about middle school parties."

"Of course, celebrities don't usually show up at these middle school parties, either," said Colby. Amy and I turned to look at him. "I'm just saying . . . I'm a celebrity, right?"

I felt suddenly nervous. "He's right. I hadn't thought about it that way. What if Ryan finds out?"

"Stop worrying so much and stick to the script," said Brynn. "As soon as the party is in full swing, you and Colby will come back here and hang out with Amy and Daniel for a little while," Brynn said.

"I can't," I said. "I promised my dad and Sonny I wouldn't go off by myself with a teenage boy ever again without permission."

"You see any teenage boys here?" she asked.

"Good point," I said.

"I'm putting you in the care of a responsible adult," said Brynn. "A month from now, when this campaign is over, you can explain it all to your dad and Sonny . . . and Mr. Wonderful, if you like."

"Okay," I said. "But why don't we stay at the party anyway? Then everyone will see us together."

"Because, you're too cool for your own party, of course," Brynn replied. "You can't possibly spend a fortune to throw the party of the year and then actually seem like you're enjoying it. Em is much too blasé for that.

"All right," Brynn said. "Time for Emily and me to get to the theater and make sure everything's set. The party starts in one hour. Colby, you arrive two hours from now, and make a halfhearted attempt to appear incognito—wear shades or something. The driver will bring you to the front, but make sure you go in the east entrance. I'll be waiting to let you in. We want the kids waiting out front to think they've seen you but not be 100 percent sure. The cell phones of the few cool clique kids who got in will begin ringing like crazy as the ones outside call and beg for info. And we'll have security make a big show of confiscating camera phones and the like. It's going to be great!"

We pulled up to the old theater downtown. Its retro marquee simply read PRIVATE PARTY. By the door, there were boxes of black T-shirts, printed with a white caricature of a beatnik and the words

ARE YOU EM OR OUT?

"What good is a cool party without a T-shirt to remind others they weren't there?" Brynn said.

Next to the T-shirts were baskets of little adhesive goatees for the guys and false eyelashes for the girls. "Party favors," said Brynn. The auditorium itself had two *Romeo and Juliet*–style balconies on each side of the stage and a ceiling with little twinkling lights that were supposed to be stars over the audience's heads. The band, dressed in black turtlenecks, black pants, black shoes, and black berets, was setting up on the stage. Brynn had a few little round tables and bongo drums set up in the lobby. Finally, she taped a sign next to the front doors: **NO CAMERAS OR RECORDING DEVICES ALLOWED.**

Once the band was set up and everything was ready, guests began lining up early outside the door—but I didn't recognize any of them. "Extras," Brynn explained. "We're using them in the film tomorrow—Colby's got to defuse a bomb and save these poor teenagers' lives. I hired them to wait outside the party for the first hour. They'll pretend to clamor to get in, and they'll *ooh* and *ahh* and sort of cheer as your real guests arrive—you know, give them the red carpet treatment. Peer pressure . . . the kids from your school will think that kids from other schools heard about the party, and their yearning to get in will infect the rest of the crowd."

About that time, Sonny showed up. "Thanks for coming," Brynn told him. "Having you at the door will be such a big help. And you definitely improve the scenery."

Sonny turned slightly red. "Well, anything for my niece," he said. "Maybe later we can spend some time getting to know each other."

"I'm counting on it," Brynn said. She gave Sonny a clipboard with THE LIST—the names of those who were allowed in—and instructed him to check student IDs and not allow anyone else past. Then she set up the ropes like they do for the ticket line at the movie theater. "The masses like to be herded," she joked. "It gives them a sense of security."

The extras did a phenomenal job of hyping the party they couldn't get into, and the cool clique, all except for the few who'd replied to the invitation quickly enough, had to stand outside with everyone else while members of the chess club and the marching band strode past. It was beautiful. Even the Daisies had swallowed their pride enough to stand out in the cold hoping to see Colby Summers.

I stood near the door and greeted each of my guests warmly, inviting the guys to stick on a goatee and reminding all the revelers to be sure to pick up a T-shirt on their way out. I'm not kidding: people were *loving* me! The band performed an eclectic mix of jazzy beatnik music, techno, and rock, and no one played too cool to dance.

About an hour into the festivities, Colby, wearing a black leather jacket, turtleneck, jeans, and dark sunglasses, made his entrance through the east door. I couldn't hear what anyone was saying over the band, but everyone had definitely noticed Colby. Girls were yelling questions and pointing toward him. Colby made his way over to where I was and hugged me.

"I'm going for thrilled to be here," he yelled in my ear, all the while keeping a huge smile plastered on his face.

A flash or two went off, and Sonny, who'd come inside by this time, immediately began confiscating camera phones, deleting photos, and showing offenders to the door. When those few people left, Sonny went back to the front door and let in some of the kids who were standing outside, which generated a wave of hope among the rest of the D-listers.

Brynn came over to Colby and me, and I heard someone say, "Look! There's the producer for Em's MTV show!"

"It's time to make your exit," she told me.

"One problem," I said. "My uncle's never going to let me leave with Colby—he still thinks he's a teenager."

"You don't duck out of a party by the front door," Brynn replied. "Go out the way Colby came in. If Sonny comes back inside, I'll keep him distracted."

"Let's go," I told Colby, and we slipped out the side door.

Thirty

Daniel was at that age where he thought peekaboo was the most hilarious and exciting game ever. In gleeful anticipation of the big payoff, he giggled like a fiend every time I said, "Wheeeere's Daniel?" and even more so when I finally popped my face out from behind my hands. When we'd been gone from the party about half an hour, Colby said, "Time to get Cinderella back to the ball."

He dropped me off behind the theater so no one would see us, and I sneaked into the side door. Sonny had never even noticed that I'd been gone. He was too focused on Brynn.

"Look who we let in while you were gone," Brynn said. Alexa and Meredith were out on the dance floor. They were smiling and rocking out pretty hard, as though they'd completely forgotten that this was supposed to be my pathetic nerd party.

"Why'd you let them in?" I asked.

"Because the look on Heatherly's face when her BFFs abandoned her outside was entirely too awesome!"

"Should I go talk to them?" I asked.

"No. It's your party. Enjoy yourself."

Good advice. I *did* enjoy myself. I mingled. I graciously accepted compliments on how great I looked and how cool my party was. I even danced a little bit without feeling too self-conscious. Luckily, the dance floor was pretty crowded, so a lot of gesticulation wasn't really required. No one even looked at me funny.

Shortly before eleven P.M., I went up on stage with the band and thanked all my guests for coming. "One more song, and we're totally kicking you guys out," I said. The crowd let up a collective *awww*. "Sorry, rental agreement. Thanks again for coming and have a great night!" They all actually cheered for me as I left the stage while the band cranked up the last song. I stood by the door and handed out

T-shirts as everyone left. Everyone said "Cool party, Em" or "That rocked—see you Monday!" Except for Alexa and Meredith.

"T-shirt?" I asked.

Meredith scowled. "We only came in to see if your party sucked or not," she said.

"So we could tell Heatherly," said Alexa.

"So did it?" I asked.

Meredith paused before replying, "Not entirely."

"I guess you won't need a T-shirt," I said.

"I'll take one," Alexa said.

"No, you won't," said Meredith. As she pushed Alexa out the door, I could hear her saying, "Do you want Heatherly to kill us both?"

When everyone was gone and Brynn was ready to take me home, Sonny suggested I crash at his place—but, he said, his car was a mess so why didn't Brynn just drop me off? She didn't seem to mind. Sonny must've taken a shortcut or broken the speed limit, because his car was already there when we pulled up.

"You want to come in?" I asked Brynn.

"I'd probably better get back to the set and catch up on some work."

"You're sure you won't come in? Sonny will be disappointed."

"Why? Did he say something?"

Sonny came out to the car. "Hi, Emily. Hi, Brynn. Thanks for driving her. Will you come in for some coffee?"

"Oh, I really shouldn't," Brynn replied. "I don't want to impose."

"Come on. One cup?" Sonny asked.

"Well, all right then," she said.

When we got inside I said, "Wow, look at the time! A kid my age should be in bed. Good night!"

"Emily . . . ," Brynn called as I walked out of the living room.

"Good night!" I called back.

The next morning, Sonny asked, "Have I ever told you that you're my favorite niece?"

"One, I'm your only niece, and two, all the time," I said. "I take it things went well with Brynn?"

"We talked until almost two in the morning," he said. "She's amazing. And what a knockout! That little birthmark under her eye is just about the sexiest thing I've ever seen!"

"Eww! For future reference, no teenage girl wants to hear her uncle use the word *sexy* before breakfast. Or, actually, ever," I said. "But speaking of breakfast, what are you feeding me?"

Sonny and I had Belgian waffles, and then he drove me home.

Dad said, "How'd the party go?"

"It was very enlightening. I learned a lot about event planning."

"But did you have fun?"

"Sure," I said.

"Glad to hear it," said Dad.

I checked my email before bed. Four new messages: one solicitation for a magazine subscription, one guaranteed cure for male pattern baldness, one phishing scam about my nonexistent credit card account . . . and one new message from Ryan, subject line, "hey":

Want 2 hear about your party. Pls IM me 2morrow when U get up.

Hmm. Was his tone slightly curt? He didn't sign his name or anything. Maybe I was just worrying for nothing. A lot of times people sounded brusque in email when they were really just in a hurry. He was probably tired and forgot to sign his name or write anything cute. Still, Ryan's emails usually had some sort of playful banter. Maybe something was wrong. *No, stop being ridiculous, Em. What could be wrong? It's not like he would have heard anything about the party.*

He couldn't have heard about the party—right?

Thirty-One

How was the party?

Ryan asked the next day on IM.

Pretty fun. Wish U could have come.

No older guys allowed, rt?

Rt. 'Cept my uncle was there! :)

Some1 told my ltl sis that movie guy came.

Oh, no. I'd forgotten that Ryan had a sister in sixth grade at my
school. Of course she'd heard about my party!
Start spinning, Emily.

0 Colby Summers. Yeah.

The guy from the picture with U.

Yeah.

Not 2B weird, but ???

Yikes. I had to tell Ryan something. But what if he told his sister
that there really was nothing going on with Colby and me, or what
if I let too much slip and he told someone else, and bit by bit, pieces
were put together and eventually the truth about Brynn came out?
It was a big risk, but if I didn't say something, he'd think I'd lied to
him about not being able to date. As it was, he already thought I'd
lied to him about no high school guys being allowed at my party, but
I couldn't exactly admit that Colby wasn't a high school guy. I had

to handle this just right; I didn't want Ryan to think I was playing
games with him.

Can U keep a secret?

Sure.

Colby Summers's publicist is dating my uncle!

4 real?

**Yeah. But it's top secret. He's a cop and they met when he was
guarding the set.**

That was true.

Cool. Would ur uncle get fired 4 dating her?

**Not sure. Don't think NE1 said not 2 d8 movie peeps. They prolly
didn't xpect it . . . but still . . . on the DL.**

OK. But how come movie guy was @ the party?

**His publicist came 2 the party w/ my uncle. She got Colby 2 come
2 surprise me.**

So, still not ur bf?

No! Just friends.

Just checking.

Pls don't tell NE1, OK? Not even sister?

U can trust me.

The following Monday at school, everyone who'd been able to get
in was wearing the T-shirt from my party. They were a must-have
item; I even heard that the asking price on eBay was thirty bucks—
thirty bucks to pretend you'd been to my party! Snap!

And, of course, everyone was buzzing about where Em had disappeared to with Colby—but I played coy, which drove them nuts. "We went somewhere quiet to talk," I said. Thank goodness Ryan hadn't asked about that part; maybe his sister hadn't mentioned it.

It was hard to believe that I'd once had no one to talk to. People from nearly every clique greeted me in the halls. "Hi, Em! Great party Friday night!" they'd say. Brand Em's stock was definitely up . . . a fact not lost on the Daisies.

But by Wednesday, another event had started to eclipse my bright and shining moment.

For Heatherly's upcoming birthday, her dad—an oral surgeon—was renting a limo to drive his little princess and her eleven guests to a teen dance club in Cleveland, a good two hours away. Sure, it wasn't as elaborate as my big bash, but as Brynn was quick to point out, middle school is very much like Hollywood in that you're only as hot as your latest project. Heatherly was also playing the card that Brynn would never have allowed—potential for delinquency. Dr. and Mrs. Hamilton would be driving to the party separately.

"The only chaperone is the chauffeur—like he matters!" Heatherly told everyone. Thus began much wrangling among the in crowd to garner one of the eleven coveted seats.

Heatherly was by no means a great intellect, but she was an evil genius when it came to manipulating people: May Queen voting was a one-day, one-shot deal, and it just so happened that it was the Friday after her party. Coincidence? I think not. Especially since Heatherly's birthday wasn't even in April but in late May, according to the counselor's "Growing in Mind and Body!" birthday bulletin board.

After inviting the most influential decision makers from the A-list—the people everyone else was most likely to mindlessly follow—she pretended to relent about the number of guests and begrudgingly allow other A- and B-listers to come to the party on their own. They never seemed to realize she'd just tricked them into supplying their own transportation to a venue two hours away that they'd have to enter at their own expense—something any member of the general public could do without Heatherly's permission since her family wasn't renting out the whole club for the night. And to pacify those who never for a second anticipated scoring even that kind of a pseudo-invite, she lowered herself to paying phony compliments to girls she hadn't spoken to all year and engaging in halfhearted flirting with guys who had zero chance with her.

If you think the middle school public would be savvy enough to see right through it, think again. Heatherly was back on top.

Brand loyalty: easy come, easy go.

Thirty-Two

I'd been staying over at Sonny's because it was the last couple of days before income tax filings were due, and Dad was working night and day. Brynn had come over and rented movies with us, and it had been nice to take a mini break from the campaign and worrying about Heatherly's next move. I hadn't planned any sort of coup for the next morning, but opportunity came my way anyhow.

"Mrs. Crutchfield," the secretary said through the intercom, "is Emily Wood taking a test right now?"

The secretaries in the office weren't supposed to interrupt class, but they pretty much did whatever they wanted whenever.

"No, we were writing in our journals. Do you need her?" asked Mrs. Crutchfield.

"Please send her when the bell rings. Sorry to interrupt."

Mrs. Crutchfield sighed wearily. "Emily, if you're finished writing, you can go see what they want," she told me.

I handed her my notebook and went to the office.

"You've got a package," the gray-haired secretary said. "Some young fellow dropped it off before the last bell."

"Is it a fern stand?" I asked. *Would he really do that?*

"A what?" she replied. "Here." She handed me a wrapped gift. I could tell immediately that it was a book.

"Thanks," I said.

"Get back to class," she said. "And for future reference, this is a school office, not a delivery service. If this happens again, you'll have to talk to Mr. Warren about it."

Have a nice day yourself, sunshine, I wanted to say. But then, I pictured her in a yellow **VALUE ME** T-shirt. Maybe even old people needed to feel important. "Oh, I apologize for the inconvenience," I said, oozing sincerity. I peeked at the nameplate on her desk. "I know you're awfully busy, Mrs. Snow. I hope this didn't take up too much of your time. Thank you, so much. I really appreciate it."

Her demeanor instantly softened. "That's all right, honey."

There was no card, so as soon as I got out of the office, I ripped off the paper. *The Road Not Taken: A Selection of Robert Frost's Poems.* And written on the cover page: *Em—Thought you might like this book, even though you can't sit a fern on it. You'll have to explain all these poems to me. Could take a while—maybe six months. Ryan.*

When I returned to Mrs. Crutchfield's classroom, everyone wanted to know why I'd been called to the office.

"Did you get in trouble?" one of the guys asked.

"Dude, back off!" Kelsey said.

"No, I had a package to pick up," I said.

"Ooh! What'd you get?" Kelsey asked. Everyone got up to look.

"A book of poetry," I replied, holding it up.

"Who sent it to you?" another girl asked. "Is it from Colby?"

"That's kind of personal," I said.

"Oh, wow!" she replied. "It *is* from Colby!"

Before I could respond, Mrs. Crutchfield said, "Ah, Robert Frost! May I?" I brought the book to her desk. "Very nice," she said, browsing the table of contents. "Some great ones in here. Shall I share one with the class?"

"Sure," I said. I sat down and Mrs. Crutchfield began reading aloud:

The Road Not Taken

Two roads diverged in a yellow wood,
And sorry I could not travel both
And be one traveler, long I stood
And looked down one as far as I could
To where it bent in the undergrowth;

Then took the other, as just as fair,
And having perhaps the better claim,

Because it was grassy and wanted wear;
Though as for that the passing there
Had worn them really about the same,

And both that morning equally lay
In leaves no step had trodden black.
Oh, I kept the first for another day!
Yet knowing how way leads on to way,
I doubted if I should ever come back.

I shall be telling this with a sigh
Somewhere ages and ages hence:
Two roads diverged in a wood, and I —
I took the one less traveled by,
And that has made all the difference.

"Absolutely brilliant poem," she said. "What are your thoughts on it?"

"The speaker is talking about the path you take in life," Kelsey said.

"Right," Mrs. Crutchfield said. "We each have to choose which paths to take. But what else is the poem saying?"

"That you should take the one less traveled," I said. "The one most people pass up. In the end, you'll be glad you did."

Mrs. Crutchfield smiled. "That's exactly what I thought you'd say," she said. She always got excited when we played into her hands like that, because then she had our attention.

"What? I've read that poem before. That's totally what it's about."

"Poems aren't 'about,' Emily. Poems *are*. Remember how I told you that Frost has layers of meaning? Well, this isn't merely a poem celebrating the joys of 'I Did It My Way.' It's much more complex than that. Look at the last stanza." Mrs. Crutchfield turned on the projector and laid the book on it, open to that poem. "Years from now, he'll be 'telling this with a sigh.' What does a sigh indicate?"

"Relief," I said.

"Maybe," Mrs. Crutchfield said. "But why else might someone sigh?"

"Sadness," Kelsey said.

"Exactly," Mrs. Crutchfield replied. "The sigh is ambiguous—it can mean relief or it can mean sadness, disappointment, weariness, any number of things. We all have to choose our paths, but that's a daunting task. 'Way leads on to way,' the poem's speaker says. You don't get the chance to go back, and you can never know what your life would have been like if you'd chosen the other path."

The idea made me uneasy. I'd never thought of it before, how you can't go back and undo your choices—how each choice leads to others, in an endless series you can never rewind.

The bell rang. "So, on that note, scholars," said Mrs. Crutchfield. "Choose your paths wisely. See you tomorrow."

As everyone was leaving, Mrs. Crutchfield brought the book to my desk. "You're not disappointed that the poem meant more than you first thought, are you?" she asked.

"No, no way," I answered. "I like it even more now. I'm just letting it soak in for a minute."

"Blew the top of your head off, huh?" she said. "That's what Emily Dickinson said a real poem does. Nice gift, by the way."

"It's from Ryan Shelton. He was in your class last year."

"Yeah, I remember Ryan. Good kid." She smiled at me and raised her eyebrows. "Bringing you books of poetry. Not bad. And he's a cutie, too."

"Mrs. Crutchfield, you're embarrassing me," I said. She chuckled and returned to her own desk.

"Tell him you like Auden," she said. "Then let me borrow your next gift. Oh, by the way, how are the layouts for the literary magazine coming along?"

"Fine," I said. "I'm a little behind, but I'll catch up."

"Only a week and a half until it's due to the printer. You sure you can make the deadline?"

"Consider it done," I said. "See you tomorrow, Mrs. C."

English was first period, and I *so* wanted to call Ryan and thank him for the gift, but Warren had a ban on cell phones, so I had to wait until I got home. He must have seen it was me, because he answered the phone, "Joe's Pizza."

"Hey, Ryan."

"Sorry, lady, no Ryan working here. You want a drink with that?"

"Ryan, that's so fifth grade!" I said.

"I know—but it still cracks me up. I'm not very sophisticated."

"You could've fooled me. Mrs. Crutchfield was pretty impressed with your book selection."

"Oh, really?" Ryan said. "And what about you?"

"I loved it. You knew I would."

"I hoped so. So when are you going to explain all the deep, hidden meanings to me?"

"Maybe after Mrs. C explains them to me. She read one of them aloud today, and I thought I understood it, but as usual, she blew my mind."

"What was it about?" Ryan asked. "Oh, wait—don't tell Mrs. Crutchfield I said that. She'd disown me. I can hear her now: 'A poem is not *about* anything, Mr. Shelton.'"

"Right," I said. "Anyway, this poem called 'The Road Not Taken'—I thought Frost was trying to say that you should take an unusual path because you'd be glad you did. But really he's making a point about choices, like how you have to make a choice and hope for the best because you can't ever go back and change it. And years later, you have these mixed feelings because you'll never know how your life might have been if you'd made a different decision at some point."

"Man," Ryan said. "That's kind of cool, but it's also kind of depressing."

"Good poetry often is," I said. "You know what, though? I think it's so cool that I can talk to you about poetry without feeling like a freak. I wouldn't have expected it."

"Why not?" he asked.

Because I'm being the real me instead of Em, and you're still talking to me, I thought. "Well, your being on the baseball team and stuff—"

Ryan laughed. "So you expected me to be a dumb jock, huh? Believe it or not, Em, you can throw a baseball and still have a fully functioning cerebral cortex," he said.

"I didn't mean that the way it sounded."

"It's okay," Ryan said. "Some jocks are dumb. But not all of us. Listen, speaking of baseball, you know the state tournament is this Saturday."

"Of course," I said. Everybody knew that. Our high school varsity team had been state champs for the past few years in a row.

"Well, you know it's kind of a tradition for the girls to wear the team jerseys the Friday before the big game."

I knew that, too. It was a complete status thing—a way for the cool high school girls to showcase their ability to score a jersey from one of the players. Even at my school, the girls wore the gold jerseys of the middle school team that day.

"Anyway," Ryan continued, "I was wondering if you'd wear mine, number twenty. Kind of be my good luck charm?"

"Absolutely," I said, trying not to sound overly excited. I was stoked that Ryan liked me enough to offer me his jersey, but I didn't want to scare him off by seeming too clingy. Em was cool, not clingy. "I mean, anything to show school spirit, right?"

"You want to know something?" Ryan said. "I'd rather have you wear my jersey than any other girl."

How sweet was *that*? "Oh, Ryan!" I said. Clingy, schmingy—if he could go out on a limb, so could I. "There is no one else's jersey I'd rather wear."

"Cool," he said. Then there was an adorably awkward pause. "So, I'll drop it by your house tomorrow night, okay?"

"Sounds great."

Shelton, number twenty. Now officially my favorite number.

IX.
CAPTURING MARKET SHARE

Thirty-Three

Ryan's mom was waiting for him in the car when he came to the door and dropped off his jersey the next day. He seemed different; instead of making his usual quips, he was kind of shy. Maybe he felt vulnerable because he'd been so sweet on the phone. Or maybe he was embarrassed that his mom was with him. "You'll be at the game Saturday, right?"

"I wouldn't miss it," I said.

"Awesome," he said. "I'll be looking for you."

Shortly after he left, Dad came home. "It's only four thirty," I said. "You're home early."

"Don't you know what today is?" asked Dad.

"Thursday?"

"Thursday, April 16!"

"I'd completely forgotten!" I said. "Tax season is over!"

"I e-filed the last of the returns just before midnight," he said.

"You must be exhausted."

"I am," Dad said. "But I'm also excited. I booked us a chalet in the mountains of Tennessee for the weekend! We'll drive down as soon as school gets out tomorrow."

Uh-oh.

"Dad, I can't," I said. "I'm so sorry. I know it's tradition, but I totally didn't realize what weekend this was. I already have plans."

"Plans?"

"I'm going to the baseball tournament Saturday . . . with my friend . . . Kelsey."

"Oh," he said. "Okay, then. Another time. I'll cancel the reservation."

"You're not mad, are you?"

"Of course not. I'm glad you're making friends here, sweetie. You

167

and Kelsey have a good time."

Maybe I could retroactively untell my little lie if I got Kelsey to go to the game with me. I called her from my room.

"Hey, Em! What's up?" Kelsey said.

"Not much. I was wondering if I could bum a ride to the tournament on Saturday."

"Yeah, no prob. That would be fun."

"Cool. Thanks."

It was weird how unweird it felt. Three months ago, the very idea of calling the head cheerleader would have nauseated me with panic. But Em was so confident, so sure of herself. I loved that about her.

I had never planned on Ryan being part of Brynn's master plan, but his high school jersey created fantastic buzz for Em that Friday at school. Mine was the only green jersey on the middle school campus. For once, I purposely passed the spot where the Daisies hung out before school. Heatherly was wearing the jersey of the best-looking guy on the middle school team, but let's be honest: hot middle school guy, hot high school guy? No contest.

"How did you get that?" Heatherly snapped. "This is not possible. What'd you do, pay to rent it?"

"What's the matter, Heatherly?" I asked. "*Green* with envy? It's too bad that you have to wear a gold one. It's not your color."

"Is Ryan Shelton really your boyfriend, Em?" Meredith asked with humble sincerity.

"Shut up, Meredith," Heatherly said. "Of course he's not. Guys like him don't date losers like Plywood."

"You know, no one has called me that silly little name in quite some time," I said. "I find it mildly amusing that you insist on hanging on to something everyone else dropped three months ago. But if your wardrobe is any indication, you don't really keep up with current trends very well, do you?"

"Just because you've been sitting at the good lunch table for a little while doesn't mean anything. It won't last. I'll make sure of it," Heatherly said.

"You greatly overestimate your sphere of influence," I said.

"What does *that* mean?" Alexa asked.

"It means Heatherly keeps talking, but nobody's listening anymore," I said. "Except you two, apparently." I made sure to carry my backpack at my side so that the big, white twenty and the name Shelton would be clearly visible as I walked away.

As Brynn had predicted, Meredith and Alexa were the vulnerable part of Brand Daisy. The two of them were clearly considering Em as a viable brand alternative. To try to get her minions back, Heatherly had a B-list girl grab a seat next to me in the lunchroom and try to stir up some drama.

"Katelyn said your feet are too big," the girl said. "But don't tell her I told you." The other girls at the table waited for my response.

"Did she really?" I asked. Obviously, Heatherly had egged her on, but Katelyn saying something catty? That I could believe easily enough. She was petty and a social climber, always jockeying for position at other people's expense. And my first impulse was to say so.

But then I noticed how the Daisies were sitting perfectly still, pretending not to look at me, but making sure they could hear every word I said, and I remembered Brynn's coaching.

"Well, I've always thought Katelyn was so cute. I'm sorry to hear that she feels the need to say negative things about people. I hope she'll be able to deal with whatever personal problems she's having, because I truly wish her the best."

"You wish her the best?" one of the other girls said.

"Absolutely," I replied.

"Wow . . . I'd be mad if she'd said that about me." Then she added, "Em, you're so nice! And you know what? I think Katelyn maybe does have problems!"

The conversation continued without me, everyone talking about Katelyn's potential psychological problems, and how I was so generous to feel sorry for her.

After that, Heatherly did not attempt to play the gossip game with me again. And since the other girls had seen how diplomatically I'd dealt with the Katelyn situation, they were dubious about Heatherly's attempts to convince them I'd been talking about them. She was hard up for leverage.

Even the limo for Heatherly's big upcoming party paled in comparison to my supposed juggling of a movie star and a high school athlete. So with the exception of Heatherly, everyone at school was eating out of my hand from that point on, even the guys. While tabloid photos of me with a pretty-boy celebrity might have failed to get the attention of Wright Middle School's male population, a high school varsity player's jersey on my back was another matter.

It was funny how the same guys who'd never said a word to me before, except to call me Plywood, were suddenly all too eager to give me their seat at the lunch table or volunteer to get me a Coke or carry my tray when I'd finished eating. Even Chip Young, the quarterback who'd nicknamed me Plywood and thrown cranberry juice on my dress from *Flirt,* seemed vastly interested in every word that came out of my mouth and became obsessed with showing off in front of me. He'd attempt to regale me with boring football stories, and I'd pretend to be interested. I liked how Heatherly's eyes narrowed whenever Chip tried to impress me, so I gave him just enough encouragement to keep it up.

Dance, puppets.

Thirty-Four

Kelsey and I got to the game a little bit late, because, she explained, "You don't want to look like you couldn't wait to get there." She was starting to sound like Brynn. "Let's sit over here," Kelsey said. "That way, he'll be sure to see you when they go into the dugout for the next inning."

"Who?" I asked.

"Duh! Ryan Shelton!" said Kelsey. "The whole reason you came here?"

"Maybe I just wanted to enjoy an all-American pastime."

Kelsey laughed.

"What?"

"Em, I'm a cheerleader," she said. "I've been to nearly every game for nearly every sport Wright has. And I've never seen you at any of them."

I couldn't think of anything to say.

"Relax!" she said, elbowing me. "If there was ever a reason to come to a baseball game, Ryan Shelton is it. He's adorable!"

"I know!" I said. "Those freckles!"

"Tell me about it! He's so perfect for you!" Kelsey said. "He seems sweet, like you. Is he?"

"Totally!" I said. "When he called me about wearing his jersey, he said he'd rather have me wear it than any other girl! Can you believe?"

"Awww! What did you say?"

I'm gushing, I thought. *This is not cool. I have to stop gushing. Em does not gush.* "Oh, um . . . I can't really remember."

Kelsey looked serious and put her hand on my arm. "Em," she said. "I'm not going to tell anybody your personal business. I promise. I don't go around talking about people—especially not my friends."

I smiled. "So, I guess you're going to Heatherly's party next weekend?"

"No way!" she said.

"You aren't? But she invited you, right?" Heatherly would've had no choice but to invite the head cheerleader, just to give her party street cred.

"Yeah, but my mom called Heatherly's mom to check about the level of parental supervision. When she found out about the two-hour limo ride with no adults, she said hell would freeze over before she'd let me go."

"Get out!"

"Yeah, I know. I think she read some magazine article about what to do with teenagers, and now she's gone all Expert Mom on me. Quit laughing—authoritative parenting can be a major buzz kill!" Then her voice became quiet and serious. "But in this case, I'm kind of relieved."

Before I could ask why, we were interrupted.

"Who gave you permission to come to the game?" Heatherly, Meredith, and Alexa were standing in front of us, obscuring our view of the field. Then Heatherly turned to Kelsey. "Is it Take a Nerd to the Ballpark Day?"

"Heatherly, what's your damage?" Kelsey said.

"This is between she and I," said Heatherly. "Stay out of it."

"Her and me, moron," I said. "Objective case." Okay, so it wasn't very zen of Gomer, but I was starting to think maybe Gomer was overrated, a ploy not necessary for someone as cool as Em.

"Whatever," Heatherly replied. "Don't you think you need to quit stalking Ryan Shelton? I mean, just because he pitied you enough to let you wear his jersey doesn't mean you have to follow him around like a puppy. Do you have to embarrass him in front of everyone, too?"

"They're changing innings," Kelsey said.

I pushed past the Daisies and looked for Ryan. He was scanning the crowd as he jogged toward the dugout. When he looked my way, I held up my arm and waved. He smiled and waved back before disappearing under the concrete ceiling.

"He didn't look embarrassed," I heard Alexa say to Heatherly.

"Shut up, Alexa!" she answered. Then she said to me, "Maybe I should invite him to my party next weekend. He could sit beside me in the limo. Of course, it could be pretty cramped. Maybe I'd have to sit in his lap. I bet he wouldn't mind."

Just as I was about to lose it, I heard someone calling my name from the bleachers.

"Em!"

Kelsey and I, and the Daisies, turned around.

"Over here!" It was Caroline. She, MK, and Laura were coming toward us. "There you are, girlfriend!" Caroline said.

I looked at Heatherly right before I said, "Caroline!" and gave her a big, fake hug. "MK, you got your hair cut! And Laura, you look gorgeous as usual!" We exchanged compliments for a few seconds before I said, "Do you guys know Kelsey Brown?"

"Sure, you're Taylor Simmons's friend," Caroline said. "She has been the best Delts president *ever*!" MK and Laura agreed.

"Taylor was my cheerleading coach when I was little," said Kelsey. "She's been like a big sister to me ever since."

"And these are," I said, savoring the Daisies' pathetic shred of hope that I'd introduce them, "some other people who go to our school." The Daisies smiled nervously.

"Yeah, okay," Caroline said. "Em, where've you been hiding out? I tried you three times this past week, and you never even called me back!"

"I totally meant to," I said, "but this was the last week of tax season, and my dad was freaking out, so things were a little crazy at my house! Sorry!" Brynn had advised me to make Caroline work for my attention, which was easy since I really didn't enjoy her company.

"That's all right. I was calling you because you've got to come to my house next Saturday night! We're having Girls' Night In! We're going to watch the Teen Media Awards and do facials and stuff. Bring your sleeping bag, but don't plan on getting any sleep! Kelsey, you should come, too. Taylor's coming, so I'm sure she'd love to see you." The Daisies kept smiling.

"Will Allison and Brooke be there?" Heatherly asked.

Caroline looked at her strangely. "Who? Oh, Allison and Brooke. Um, no." Then she turned to me again. "So, you'll come, right? Kelsey?"

"I'm in! Thanks!" Kelsey said.

"Seems like there's some other party I'd heard about happening that night." I looked at Heatherly. "But I heard the girl who's throwing it is a loser. I wasn't planning on going, and I'd much rather come to your house anyway."

"You'd better come," said Caroline. "Or we'll hunt you down!" She laughed like that was *so* funny—and we all did, too, because dumb joke or not, she was Caroline Sanford. "Hey, there's plenty of room for two more if you want to sit with us."

"That would be great," I said. "I don't like the view here." I smiled at the Daisies as Kelsey and I walked away with Caroline and her friends.

Thirty-Five

Naturally, I had to get permission to go to Caroline's party.

"Of course you're going," Brynn said.

"I'm not playing hard to get with her anymore?"

"There's playing hard to get and then there's just exasperating the person beyond human limitations," she said. "You've got to give her a little encouragement if you want to keep her interest."

"Why do I get the feeling that you have more than a professional familiarity with this type of maneuver?" I asked. "You're not playing games with my uncle, are you?"

"Why? Do you think I need to work on keeping his interest?"

"Hardly," I said.

"Don't you worry about Uncle Sonny. Go to your party and have fun."

Since I had Brynn's go-ahead, all I had to do now was clear it with Dad. But once he heard it was an all-girl party, he didn't require a lot of convincing.

"Welcome to Girls' Night In!" Caroline said. "Go get changed! We're doing spa treatments!"

I changed into my pajamas, and MK began removing my makeup and smearing a clay mask all over my face. "This is so great for tightening your pores," she explained. Kelsey was applying an orangey pink polish to Taylor Simmons's toes, and the other girls were combing in deep conditioners, soaking their hands in paraffin, and plucking one another's eyebrows. The Teen Media Awards were on TV in the background.

"So, Em," Laura said, "is it true that you're going to have your own reality show on MTV?"

"Laura!" Caroline said. "We agreed we weren't going to ask about that!"

"What's the big deal? Everybody knows a film crew and a producer from MTV came to her school to get test shots or something. It's not like it's a secret!"

They all looked at me. "I'm really not supposed to talk about it," I said. "Sorry!"

"Well, if you did get a reality show, could we be on it, too?" MK asked.

"Um, I don't know," I replied.

"I think you guys need to change the subject," Taylor said.

"Okay. Hey, Em, Kelsey . . . did you hear that two other girls from your class are being rushed?" Caroline asked. "Heatherly Hamilton and Meredith Somebody?"

I wondered if she realized that Heatherly and Meredith were two of the girls from the ballpark, but I didn't say anything. Kelsey and I looked at each other.

"Heatherly's supposed to have a big party at her house—with a band and everything—when she gets in. Her parents are going to be out of town," added MK. "That could be fun."

"I hadn't heard that," I said. Heatherly really was working on it, just like she'd said she would. If she couldn't get their votes any other way, she'd bribe them with a party. Classic Heatherly.

"Allison and Brooke are sponsoring them," Caroline said. Then, checking to make sure Taylor couldn't hear, Caroline said to me, "Don't worry. Nobody listens to them."

"Allison's the one we saw at the mall, right?" I asked.

"Yeah. Total skank with money," MK said, a little too loudly.

"MK," Taylor scolded. "Let's be nice."

"Isn't Heatherly's dad a dentist or something?" Laura asked.

"Yeah, something like that," another girl replied. "I heard she's having a big party this weekend, and they're renting a limo and going to a club in Cleveland. Pretty cool. She definitely knows what to do with her dad's money. You gotta love that!"

Even though I didn't actually like the Delts, I didn't want Heatherly and Meredith getting in instead of me. "Kind of presumptuous, though, don't you think?" I asked.

"What?" MK said.

"Well, Heatherly's already planning a party, like it's a done deal that she'll get in. I mean, it's almost like you guys don't have any say in the matter, you know?"

"I hadn't thought of it that way," said Laura. "That really is presum . . . presum—"

"Presumptuous," I said.

"Yeah! 'Cause it's *our* decision!" Laura said.

"For real!" added MK. "Who does she think she is?"

"Well, like I said, I wouldn't worry about it," said Caroline.

"You're right," I agreed. "She's so not worth the time." I liked the way I'd been able to turn the conversation, but I wanted to really clinch it. "You know what?" I said. "You guys are so awesome! If I were going to have my own reality show . . . and I'm not saying I am, of course . . . but if I were, I'd totally make sure that you guys were on it!"

The girls beamed. "Ooh! We could have a big, fake feud!" Laura said. "And everybody would want to know the real scoop, but we'd just be all, 'I can't talk about it!' Oh . . . and I'd probably get some deal to design my own fashion line!"

"Yeah, and one of us would have to have a boyfriend everybody hated, and we'd get one of those run-together nicknames."

"One of you can have the boyfriend; I'm not tying myself down!" MK said, and everyone laughed.

"Speaking of which, MK," Caroline said. "Tell us about your hookup with that guy last weekend! How was it?"

"I've had better kissers," MK said. "But he was okay."

"I know!" said Caroline. "Let's go around the room, and everybody list every guy at our school that you've kissed, and rate him!"

After the initial feeling of being kicked in the stomach, I sat wishing the floor would open up and absorb me. How was I going to get out of this? Now all the Delts would know that I'd never kissed a guy and I'd look like a freak. Heatherly and Meredith would get in instead of me, and I'd never hear the end of it. I felt kind of sorry for

Kelsey, too, since she had the opposite problem. She was only in eighth grade, but she'd probably have a longer list than anybody, and that wouldn't look good, either. A really bad reputation could keep you out of Delts as easily as being a goody-two-shoes. It's funny: nobody ever specifically tells girls how many guys they're supposed to have kissed, but there seems to be an unnamed magic number. Below it, you're considered not desirable enough, and above it, you've got a bad rep.

Caroline started with Laura, who was sitting on the other side of me. Would they go right to left or left to right? If the former, the game might get old by the time they got around to me, and they'd get distracted by something else. Otherwise, I was up next. Laura had several guys on her list, which dragged out the suspense. When she finished, Caroline said the words I was dreading, "Em, how about you?"

"Well, I, uh—"

"Who cares about the guys she's hooked up with from school?" MK said. "I want to hear about Colby Summers!"

"Yeah, Em, we all saw the pictures. And we heard he sent you a present at school. So what's it like to kiss Colby?" Caroline asked.

"Colby. Well." I stalled. "All I can say about Colby is that he's definitely not what I expected." This sent them into a frenzy of high-pitched exclamations.

"What do you mean?" Taylor asked. "Elaborate!"

I didn't want to lie, but I couldn't tell them the truth about Colby. The whole truth, about his age and marital status, would ruin his career, not to mention that it would expose me as a fraud. And the partial truth, that he and I were nothing more than friends, was boring and wouldn't help me get into Delts.

"The thing about Colby," I said, "is that . . . "

"Yeah?" Caroline asked.

"He's not like he seems on TV," I said.

"In what way?" said MK.

"He's . . . uh . . . much more . . . mature."

The girls swooned a bit, with "ahhs" and "umms."

"Okay, bottom line," Laura said. "Is he the hottest kisser you've ever locked lips with?"

I didn't say anything.

"Yes or no?" said Caroline. Everyone was silent.

"The truth?" I said.

They nodded.

"No."

Because that was the truth. Since I'd never locked lips with Colby or anyone else, there was no way to quantify my best kissing experience, right? *Please don't let them ask me anything else,* I thought.

Taylor Simmons playfully pushed my shoulder. "So sophisticated, this one!" she said. "You must have kissed some pretty amazing guys if Colby Summers doesn't top your list!"

That wasn't officially a question, so I chose not to offer an answer. Instead, I smiled and kind of laughed.

"So what about Ryan?" Caroline said. "We know he's into you—he gave you his jersey to wear last week. Does he have a chance?"

"Or are you in love with Colby?" Laura asked. "You're wearing his necklace, aren't you?"

"Oh, this?" I'd been wearing it so long it had become a habit, and I'd all but forgotten I even had it on. "It's no big deal," I said, tucking it under my pajama top. "As for Ryan, I mean, he's great."

"Oh! That reminds me! He wants you to call him while you're here so he can stop by tonight!" said Caroline.

"Tonight? But look at me!" My face was covered in green goop, and my hair was pulled into a tight ponytail.

"Better go wash your face! I'm *so* calling him!" Caroline picked up the phone.

"No! Don't!" I yelled. I chased her around the room, trying to get the phone away from her.

"Hey, Ryan!" she said. "She's here. Come on over!" She and the other girls found this hysterically funny. "Oh, come on, Em! You know you want to see him! What are friends for?"

Thirty-Six

I ran to the bathroom and started washing the clay mask off my face. I was in such a hurry, I soaked my pajama top, so I went into Caroline's room and grabbed a T-shirt. It was the bright blue one with harlequins from last year's masquerade-ball theme party. Funny to think that I was actually wearing a Delts T-shirt—I had managed to slip into a world that had always seemed such a locked society. I wore the shirt with my pajama bottoms, not wanting to look like I was trying too hard. I had barely enough time to fluff my hair a bit and put on some mascara and lip gloss (I'd gotten to where I felt funny without at least a little makeup) before Ryan arrived.

"Emmm! Ryan's here!" Caroline called.

"What's up, Em?" Ryan said when I came into the den.

"Nothing. How 'bout you?" I replied. All the girls were staring at us, waiting to see what would happen next. It made me really uncomfortable, and Ryan didn't look too thrilled about it, either. He pulled a couple of paper clips out of his jacket pocket and began fiddling with them as he talked.

"So, uh, how'd you do on that science paper?" he asked.

"Good. I got a B plus."

"Oh, great. That's good."

MK became impatient. "You guys! This is so boring!" she whined.

"I know!" Caroline said. "They probably want to be *a-lone!*" She strung out the last word for emphasis. "Hey! Remember in middle school when we used to play Seven Minutes in Heaven?" All the girls shrieked with laughter, except for Kelsey, who seemed kind of nervous. "Come on, you two!" Caroline took Ryan and me by the hands and led us to a hall closet. She took out a vacuum cleaner and shoved Ryan inside. Then she whispered to me, "You can thank me later," before pushing me in next to him and calling out to everyone, "And we expect a full report when time's up!"

The closet was small and cramped and, of course, completely dark. We couldn't see each other at all, but we were crammed together against a bunch of coats, the wooden hangers jabbing me in the neck. I'd never been that close to a guy before, and it made me feel a little . . . it sounds ridiculous, but . . . scared. I liked Ryan, but I didn't like being shoved into a closet with him.

"Ryan, I'm sorry. They're stupid."

"You think so too? I mean, all the guys like them because they're pretty, but man, they're annoying," he said.

"Then why do you hang out with them?" I asked.

"I don't, really. I mean, I see them a lot at school and baseball games, and they're usually wherever my friends and I are on weekends, but it's not like I seek out their company or anything. Why do you?"

"It's kind of a long story," I said.

"Well, listen, I don't want you to think I don't like you, because I think you know I do. But I'm not really into, well . . . this. I'd like to kiss you—I mean, I really, really would. But not this way. I want it to be special."

"Me too!" I said. "I totally agree!"

"You do?" he asked, sounding relieved.

"Absolutely."

Ryan fumbled in the dark to take my hand. "You're really not like these other girls, you know that?"

Just then, Caroline threw open the closet door. She looked disappointed that we weren't doing anything. "Oh, come on! When you open the door early, you're supposed to get a show!" The girls laughed. Ryan pushed gently on the small of my back, letting me exit the closet before he did.

Ryan and I sat down on the couch, and Laura turned up the TV. "I can't believe she won favorite teen actress," she said about the girl walking off the stage. "I hate her." The other high school girls expressed their complete agreement that the actress was, indeed, a slut with flabby thighs.

Then the nominees were read for Favorite Actor in a Television Comedy. "And the winner is . . . ," the presenter said, "Colby Summers in *One Big, Happy Family!*"

"Em! Colby won!" Caroline said. I had completely forgotten that he'd flown out for the awards ceremony; Brynn had told me about it last week.

The crowd, both at the ceremony and in Caroline's den, went wild. Everyone in the audience stood up and applauded as Colby took the stage, and all the Delts yelled and then looked at me for my reaction.

"This is really overwhelming," Colby said. "Thanks so much to all my fans who voted for me. It means so much. I'd also like to thank everyone from the show. . . ." He recited a list of people I'd never heard of. "My wonderful family, and finally, I have to give a big shout out to Em, a new person in my life who's become very special to me. Em, thanks for everything. You're incredible. Love you, sweet girl."

As Colby left the stage with his little statue, everyone in Caroline's den turned to me with their mouths wide open.

"Ryan! Wait!" I called as he stormed off through Caroline's kitchen door. "Let me explain!"

But he was gone.

Thirty-Seven

Caroline and the others didn't seem to think that Ryan's reaction was a problem. "I love it when guys fight over me!" Caroline said. "I wish Colby could be here in person so Ryan could have kicked his butt!"

"I wish Colby could be here in person so I could steal him away from Em!" MK said.

"No way, MK," Laura said. "You heard him on TV—he's *in love* with her!"

"Oh, I know! That's so cool!" said MK.

Caroline asked, "How do you make it work?"

"We don't," I said.

"Right. When it's real love, you don't have to work at it," Laura said.

"Let's call him!" said Caroline. "I can't believe he hasn't called you yet! Can we talk to him, too? Where's your cell?" She started rifling around in my purse.

"Caroline," I said, "I'm not calling Colby. You have to help me convince Ryan there's nothing going on."

"Yeah, that's why you have this adorable picture of you two on your phone!" she yelled. It was the pic Brynn had snapped for me the day I'd interviewed Colby. I'd forgotten it was on there; it seemed like forever ago. All the girls crowded around to see. "Let's call him!"

"I told you, I'm not calling him!" The person I wanted to call was Brynn. Had she put him up to thanking me during his acceptance speech?

"You're probably right," Caroline said. "He probably couldn't talk over all the music at the parties after the awards show. But how come you didn't go with him?"

"Yeah, I totally would have been right by his side," MK said.

"When's your next date?" Laura asked.

"There's no date," I answered.

"Oh, my ███! She's dumping Colby for Ryan!" Caroline said.

"He'll be so heartbroken!" said Laura. "Em, he's in love with you!"

"I have a feeling he'll survive," I said.

"That's so cold!" Caroline said, laughing. "I wonder if he'll cry. Don't you love making guys cry? It's such a rush!"

I ignored Caroline and asked, "Look, can somebody drive me over to Ryan's?"

Caroline, MK, Laura, Kelsey, and I piled into Caroline's car. The other girls followed behind us in another car. They didn't want to miss anything. It was well after midnight, far too late for us to be going to Ryan's house. Dad would've freaked, but I couldn't wait. I had to try to smooth things over.

Caroline shut off her headlights and pulled up slowly and quietly into Ryan's driveway. Then she called Ryan's cell. "Come outside," she said. "Em needs to see you."

Ryan came out to the front porch a couple of minutes later. He was holding a white piece of paper. The girls sat in the car, probably straining to hear what we were saying. "Ryan, I'm really, really sorry," I said.

"Not your boyfriend, huh? Nothing to it? What, you think because I'm not some TV star or singer or because I live in Ohio instead of L.A. or New York that I'm stupid?"

"Ryan, you have to believe me. I'm not Colby's girlfriend!"

"Why would you string me along like this, Em? I've been honest and up front with you from the minute we met. If you didn't like me, you could have told me to go away."

"I do like you, Ryan. I really, do. Please believe me."

"I want to, Em. I want to believe you. But first the magazine picture with you and him, then he goes to your party, and now he's saying on TV that he loves you? What am I supposed to think?"

"I know it all looks bad. But it's not. He's a friend. That's all," I said.

"Then why would someone go to the trouble of emailing me this?" Ryan showed me the piece of paper. It had a picture of Colby wearing his trademark necklace, and under it, the sender had typed, "Ever seen this necklace b4 on NE1 u know?" The address was HHhottie. It wasn't hard to figure out who that was.

I put my hand up to my neck and felt the telephone token under my T-shirt. "Okay, here's the thing—"

Ryan put his hand on the cord and pulled it out so he could see. "You're wearing his necklace, Em."

"He let me borrow it." I unfastened it and put it in my jeans pocket. "I'll give it back to him. I'll never wear it again. I promise. It doesn't mean anything!"

"Come on, Em! The tabloid pictures didn't mean anything, the necklace doesn't mean anything . . . and I'm sure his declaration of love for you on national television doesn't mean anything either?"

"Ryan, I don't know much about the entertainment business, but I do know one thing: they 'love' everybody. I helped him out with something once, and he appreciates it, and we got to know each other a little, and we're friends. Nothing more."

"I have a lot of friends who are girls, but they don't wear my—well, I don't have a necklace, but if I did, they wouldn't wear it. And most of them don't wear my jersey. I thought that meant something."

"It did! It meant a lot to me!" I said. I wanted to tell Ryan all about the Em Campaign, tell him that all of it was fake and that the only real part was how crazy I was about him. But I was afraid—afraid that Ryan, like everyone else, was under Em's spell and could never like the real me.

Ryan looked at me for a long time. "I don't want to be some guy you hang out with when your movie star boyfriend isn't around."

"I'm not dating him. Please believe me."

He looked at me as though he wanted to. "Are you going to be seeing him again or not?"

The movie wasn't finished filming yet, and it was likely that I'd see Colby on the set when I went to see Brynn. "Do you mean, like, seeing him, or *seeing* him?"

Ryan let out a short, scornful laugh. "Forget it."

"Ryan—"

"Whatever. Look, it's late. I need to get some sleep. And do me a favor: don't tell all those girls in the cars what we talked about. I'm not interested in providing them with drama."

Before I could say anything, Ryan's dad opened the front door. "Ryan, what are you—oh, it's the tax girl!" he said. "Hello, Tax Girl. Isn't it a little late for you to be out?"

"Hi, Mr. Shelton. Sorry if I disturbed you. I was just leaving," I said. When I got back to Caroline's car, they asked what had happened. "Nothing. Everything's fine."

"You okay?" Kelsey whispered to me after everyone had finally started talking about something else.

"Yeah," I said. "Thanks, but I don't want to talk about it."

I tried calling Ryan's cell twice—once that night and once when I got home the next morning. No answer. Sunday evening, the text under his photo for the online community said, "Online," so I immediately sent him an IM:

Ryan? U there?

Two seconds later, the text below his picture said, "Ryan is no longer online."

I went to the set to see Brynn. We went to Colby's trailer to talk. Amy and Daniel were there, but Colby was filming a scene. "How'd the acceptance speech go over?" Brynn asked. "Colby completely improvised it! I can't believe I didn't think of it myself! Now everyone thinks you have the most amazing boyfriend ever!" Then she smiled and bit her bottom lip. "But really, *I* do! I'm so behind on all my work because I spent all my time this weekend with your gorgeous uncle!"

"Brynn, I need to talk to you," I said.

She snapped back to reality. "Something wrong?" she asked. "More problems with Heatherly? How could there be? After what Colby said about you at the awards show, the kids at your school—"

"Brynn, the guy I told you about—I *really* like him," I said. "But he won't talk to me after Colby's acceptance speech. I tried to tell him it was nothing, but he wouldn't listen. Tell me what to do."

"If he won't listen to you, then what can you do?" she asked.

"Colby didn't mean to cause trouble for you, Emily," Amy said. "He didn't know about that boy—I never mentioned it to him. He thought it might help you at school if he said something about you on TV. He meant what he said—he really does appreciate your keeping quiet about everything. You could have ruined him, but you didn't. Colby thinks a lot of you; we both do."

"Thanks, Amy. And I think you guys are the best. Really. I'm just so upset about this guy, Ryan." I turned to Brynn. "Isn't there some way you can fix it?"

"Emily, I'm good with smoke and mirrors, but I'm not all-powerful," Brynn said. "I can arrange a photo op with a cute guy, but I can't make someone have real feelings for you."

"I know. You're right," I said.

As far as Ryan, I was on my own, and it wasn't looking good.

X.
UNIQUE SELLING PROPOSITION, ANALYSIS OF BRAND CATEGORIES

Thirty-Eight

"*It wasn't me,*" Kelsey told me when I got to school on Monday.

"Em! Oh, my ██! We saw Colby's acceptance speech—it's all over YouTube!" said one of the cheerleaders. She was accompanied by a group of probably a dozen girls, including even Heatherly. No one seemed interested in talking about how her party had gone.

"My older sister said that MK and Laura told her that you chose Ryan over Colby!" one of the girls said. "Did you really? Even after what he said about you when he got his award?"

"Look, you guys!" another cheerleader said. "She's not wearing Colby's necklace anymore! It *is* true!"

"Come on! You don't really think she was ever dating Colby Summers, do you?" Heatherly said. "It's impossible! There's no way!"

"Um, hello?" Kelsey said. "There were pictures of the two of them on a date, he came to her party, she was wearing his trademark necklace for weeks, and last Saturday night he told several million people that he loves her! Where have you been?"

"It's some kind of trick," Heatherly said. "I don't know how she did it, but it's a trick!" Everyone looked at her in silence. "You guys! This is Plywood! Remember Plywood?"

"Oh, get over it already, Heatherly!" said Kelsey. "That was ages ago. Move on!"

The other girls giggled.

"Whatever, Kelsey," Heatherly said. "But I don't buy any of it for a second, and neither do Meredith and Alexa. Right?" She looked at the two of them for support, but they looked down. "Right?" she asked again. More silence. "I don't believe this!"

"Look, Heatherly, could you go have your freak-out someplace else? We're trying to talk to Em here," Kelsey said.

"So, Em, tell us why you broke up with Colby," another girl said.

"We want to know everything!"

Right before Heatherly was out of earshot, I managed to say, "I was never really serious about Colby. We're better off as friends."

At lunch, all the girls were still talking about Colby. All but one. I noticed that Jodi Franklin was kind of quiet. I didn't know much about Jodi, just that she'd moved to Wright about the same time I had, but unlike me, fitting in had never been an issue for her. Since she was so pretty and wore such cool clothes, she'd immediately been assimilated into the cool clique. "Is something wrong?" I asked.

"I'm failing algebra," she said.

"Oh, I'm sorry," I replied. "I guess your parents will flip, huh?"

"No, not really," she said with a sigh. "I'm going to get some water."

When Jodi walked away, the girl next to her said, "Jodi will wear a new outfit tomorrow."

"What?"

"Her parents never pay any attention to her. When she gets a bad grade, they tell her to cheer up and then send her shopping with the housekeeper."

I didn't know what to say. I remembered telling Brynn that people in the popular crowd didn't have real problems. I felt bad . . . not only because I'd been so stupid but because Jodi was hurting and people were gossiping about it. I wanted to say something to make her feel better, but how could I argue that Jodi's parents really did care about her? I didn't even know them, or her, really. I was actually glad for a minute when Chip Young sat down beside me and changed the conversation.

"What are you doing this weekend, Em?" Chip asked.

"Hanging out," I said. Let them continue to use their imaginations.

"Aren't you going out with Ryan Shelton?" he asked.

"Not this weekend," I said—or any other, apparently, since, besides the fact that I was still fourteen, Ryan wasn't speaking to me, a point better left unsaid. "But is there anything you want me to tell him?"

Chip swallowed kind of hard as he considered the prospect of my telling Ryan that he'd hit on me.

"Nah, that's okay," Chip said. I guess he didn't like being shot down, because he decided to turn his charm on someone else. "How about you, Kelsey?" Chip asked. "What are you doing this weekend?"

"I'm visiting my dad," she said.

"That's a real shame," Chip said, "because I was thinking you might want to do a little something for me to earn that jersey I lent you on spirit day."

Kelsey looked away and pretended not to hear him, but everyone got quiet to see what would happen next.

"Don't play shy with me," Chip continued. "You weren't shy at Sam's party a few weeks ago."

"Chip, that's such crap! I wasn't anywhere near you at Sam's party," Kelsey said.

"That's not what we heard," said one of Chip's friends, turning to give him a high five.

"Come on, Kelsey. Who are they going to believe? Me, or some girl who gets handled more than the team baseball?" The guys howled. The girls who were supposed to be Kelsey's friends grinned at one another. Kelsey looked like a wounded bird.

"Shut up, Chip," I said.

"What?" Chip replied. "What did you say to me?"

"I said, shut up, jackass."

"Listen, baby," Chip said, recovering. "You don't have to be jealous. There's plenty of the Chipper to go around. You'll get your chance."

"You'd better wake up before that happens, because clearly, you're dreaming," I said.

"Hey, you weren't at Sam's party," Chip said. "You don't know what happened. She was begging for it."

"When it comes to you, the only thing a girl would beg for is a restraining order," I said. "If you knew your way around the way you claim to, you wouldn't have to make up stories."

"Oh, baby, I know what I'm doing. I could teach you a lot of things." Chip flicked his tongue at me, a gesture that drew cheers from the other guys.

"Why don't you put that thing away?" I said. "I hear you're a lousy kisser anyway."

Chip grinned. "Oh, yeah? And where did you hear that?"

"From your sister," I said. As Chip paused in confusion, our entire back section of the lunchroom exploded with laughter and exclamations of "Woo! Burn!"

"Come on, Kelsey," I said.

Kelsey and I took the long way around to Mrs. Crutchfield's class to hang out for the rest of lunch. As we came down the long row of metal stairs, someone grabbed us from behind. In the space of about two minutes, they'd blindfolded us and dragged us to the empty lot behind the library.

XI.
BRAND DOMINANCE, BRAND CONFUSION

Thirty-Nine

"Em, what's going on?" Kelsey asked as we were pushed to the ground.

"I don't know; I can't see anything," I replied. I could hear our assailants breathing; there must have been four or five of them. I was scared: maybe Chip and his buddies had cut around the building to teach me a lesson about mouthing off to a jock. Where was psycho Warren when you actually needed him? As soon as I was able to collect my thoughts enough to start screaming for help, I heard a girl's voice.

"Silence, pledges!" she said. "You are commanded to submit to the will of your big sisters."

So that's what this was all about. I could hear the girls stifling giggles and the sort of sucking noise of an aerosol can. Then I felt something cold being rubbed into my scalp and greasy-soft pencils tracing paths down my arms.

When the blindfolds came off, Caroline, MK, Laura, and Taylor were laughing their heads off at Kelsey and me. We looked at each other. At first, I was angry. "You guys scared us to death!" I yelled. But Kelsey looked so ridiculous, her hair sticking straight out all over, eyeliner and lipstick all over her arms and face, spelling out stuff like DELTS 4-EVER and KELSEY ROCKS, that I couldn't help but laugh.

Kelsey hugged me and started jumping up and down. "We made it! We're pledges!" she said.

"Congratulations," Caroline said. "After you successfully complete your pledge period, you'll officially become part of the Delts' sisterhood." The four of them took turns hugging me and Kelsey.

"Here are your shirts and pledge pins," Taylor said. The white T-shirt had red Greek letters stitched across the front. Kelsey and I put them over our other shirts, and Taylor attached the small silver pins on the top left. "Wear them with pride."

"Em, this is so great! We'll be like real sisters!" Caroline said. For a moment, I felt a rush of acceptance wash over me. *I was a Delt! Who would have ever thought—Emily Wood, a Delt?* But then Caroline said, "As a Delt, we have a solemn responsibility to always help each other in any way we can. A Delt always seeks the good fortune of another Delt. Understand?"

I understood. For a moment, I had almost forgotten how I'd come to wear that shirt and pin. Caroline had helped me only because I could help her. I wondered if the other Delts knew or if they believed that Caroline really liked me. What if she'd told them the truth? But then I thought of Caroline's arrogance: she'd never have admitted to them, or probably even to herself, that she couldn't just snap her fingers and get a contract with a top modeling agency. No way would she want anyone to know that she'd had to scheme for it.

Besides, what did I have to feel unworthy about? If other girls got in because their families had money or because their gene pool happened to make them gorgeous, how was that any different than my getting in because I had good PR? Brynn had told me to stop overanalyzing everything, hadn't she?

"You're now officially a pledge," Taylor said. "During the next three months, you will be called upon by your big sisters to accept whatever challenges they set before you. Perform your duties well, as befits a Delt pledge, and you will be rewarded with full membership when the next school year begins." Taylor put her hand out, and the other girls placed theirs on top of hers. She motioned for Kelsey and me to do the same. We did. "So let us be worthy," Taylor said.

"So let us be worthy," Caroline, Laura, and MK repeated.

"So let us be worthy," Kelsey and I said.

I knew exactly what I would be considered worthy of doing: getting Caroline a contract with Ford.

Taylor broke the solemnity with one of those girly-girl yelps. "We totally ditched class to come kidnap you guys!" she said. "We've got to get back before we get caught!"

"I'll call you soon, Em," Caroline said. Of course she would.

When they left, Kelsey started jumping up and down again. I wondered if this was something they trained cheerleaders to do during summer clinics or something, to jump whenever they got excited as a means of staying in practice. "We're Delts! They take two pledges out of the whole eighth grade, and it's us! This is the coolest thing ever!"

"That means Heatherly and Meredith didn't get it," I said.

"Yeah," Kelsey said, grimacing. "I guess I should feel sorry for them, but I don't. Does that make me a bad person?"

"If it does, I'm right there with you."

"I've tried to find something to like about Heatherly, but she's so hateful," said Kelsey. "I'm glad I don't have to be a pledge with her." Kelsey looked guilty. "I'm sorry. I shouldn't talk about people."

It was strange. If Kelsey was so worried about what people thought of her, why did she get such a bad reputation?

"So what do we do now? Go to the bathroom and wash this stuff off?" I asked.

"Are you crazy? The whole point is for everybody else to know we made it! Why do you think they do this?"

Of course Kelsey was right. The purpose of graffitiing the new pledges was to make a point of who didn't get in. And this was going to absolutely kill Heatherly.

"I guess we'd better get to class," I said.

"Hey, Em," Kelsey said. "I didn't have a chance to tell you before, but thanks."

"For what?" I asked.

"For what you said to Chip. Why did you stand up for me like that?"

"Oh, please. It was so obvious he was lying. Besides, even if it had been true, he had no right to treat you that way. But he was lying, right?" Then I caught myself. "I'm sorry. That's none of my business. The point is, he's a jerk."

"No, it's okay. Actually, I appreciate you asking me to my face. Everyone else just spreads lies behind my back."

"What do you mean?" I asked.

"Last year, when I was named head of the squad, all these rumors about me got started. Stuff about how I wasn't smart enough to be in Vannies and how my mom had pulled strings to get me in. Then it got worse. First it was that I did something with a guy at the movies; next it was the baseball park. It was so weird, because none of it ever happened. I never even liked either of those guys, and I certainly didn't do what everyone was saying I had."

"But everybody said the guys confirmed it," I said.

"Well, duh!" Kelsey replied. "How many eighth-grade guys do you know who would deny getting some action?"

I felt so dumb. Of course the guys wouldn't deny a rumor like that—especially with the head cheerleader of all people. I'd believed it because everyone else had. And, if I was being honest, because I'd wanted to. When a girl is as pretty and smart and popular as Kelsey, if you can find something bad about her—if you can convince yourself that you're superior to her in some way—it makes you feel better about yourself. Like maybe she *didn't* get everything handed to her in that imaginary line where they distribute life's advantages—that there had actually been something left over for you. I guess girls think that if one girl is allowed to be really special, there's less special to go around for the rest of us, so we try to find some way to take away what she has.

"You're the only one who stood up to Chip," Kelsey said. "All my other friends just sat there."

"Maybe they're not real friends," I said.

When the bell rang and Kelsey and I walked to class, everyone stared at our graffiti with proper reverence. We split up past the main office since we didn't have the next class together. The teachers pretended they didn't notice us; they'd tried unsuccessfully for years to keep the Delts from "decorating" the new pledges. They felt the practice was divisive and likely damaging to the self-esteem of the girls who weren't selected—which was exactly what I was counting on when I saw Heatherly outside the computer lab, talking to Meredith and Alexa.

The blood drained from her face. "No," she said. "No way. This can't be happening."

"Oh, but it is!" I said with exaggerated bubbliness. "Guess you might as well cancel your big pledge party. How about a big glass of 'I got into Delts and you didn't'? Come on, Heatherly, drink it down."

"I hate you, Emily Wood! I hate you!" Heatherly said.

I winced. "Ooh, that's too bad," I said. "That's probably going to rule out any chance of my putting in a good word for you next year."

"I wouldn't be in Delts for a million bucks!" Heatherly screamed. She bolted through the sea of students.

When she was gone, Meredith said, "Em, do you think you could put in a good word for me and Alexa next year?"

"Yeah," Alexa said. "We're really sorry about all that stuff we did."

"Can't we be friends, Em?" asked Meredith.

"Didn't you guys pull this let's-be-friends trick on me a couple of months ago?"

"I'm sorry, Em. Heatherly made us do that," Meredith replied. "You know we've always liked you."

"Forget it," I said. "I have no reason to believe that this isn't another trick Heatherly has put you up to."

I started to walk away when Meredith said, "We can give you information."

"Not interested," I said.

"It's about Ryan," said Meredith.

I stopped and turned around. "What kind of information?" Part of me feared I might be walking into a trap, but I couldn't resist.

"Remember when Heatherly said she was going to get you?" Alexa said. "She's been spreading rumors about you. And she's been email-ing them to Ryan."

"What kind of rumors?"

"Like the kind she started about Kelsey last year," said Meredith.

"What do you mean, the kind she—" Of course! It made perfect sense. Kelsey had been too much of a threat to Heatherly: Kelsey was prettier, smarter, and nicer, and when she'd made head cheerleader, Heatherly couldn't stand the idea of someone edging her out as It Girl.

"Does Ryan believe what she's been saying about me?" I asked. "Does anyone?"

"I dunno," Meredith said. "But she's telling everybody that high school guys don't date eighth-graders for no good reason. And she's telling Ryan that a movie star wouldn't, either."

Great. I'd never even kissed a boy, and now I was the town slut. And what if Ryan actually believed her?

"But we'll tell everybody that Heatherly is lying," Alexa offered. "We'll even quit talking to her if you say so. Do you want us to start a rumor about her? We'll totally do it. She deserves it for the way she made us treat you."

"Spreading lies about someone doesn't seem right," I said. "Even if it *is* Heatherly."

"Oh, we wouldn't have to lie," Meredith said. "We could tell everybody what Heatherly's been saying about them behind their backs. You know, get everybody to freeze her out and stop talking to her."

"Look," I said, "I admit it's tempting. But no. It's not right. Can't you just tell Ryan the truth?"

"We don't know him," Alexa said. "Why would he believe us?"

"Then there's nothing you can do," I said.

"If Heatherly wins May Queen, she'll go after Ryan herself," said Meredith. "She's already emailing him and saying that she just had to tell him the truth about you because she felt so bad for him. She's laying the groundwork."

Alexa added, "You know Heatherly. She's good."

That does it, I thought. *I'm going to destroy Heatherly once and for all.*

"The May Queen voting is this Friday," Alexa said. "We can help you, but if you want to win, we have to work fast. You do want to win, don't you?"

Heatherly definitely needed to be punished, and all I had to do to strip her of everything she'd schemed and lied to get was simply give the word. If she was going to take Ryan from me, I was going to take everything else from her. Hadn't she always said that a guy like Ryan would never go out with a loser? So I'd make Heatherly the biggest loser ever. I envisioned her having to sit at the same lunch table where I used to sit, listening to the never-ending debate about superhero invincibility. "I'm intrigued," I told them.

"Say the word," said Meredith, "and we'll *ruin* Heatherly."

Mrs. Crutchfield interrupted our conversation. "Emily, there you are!" she said. "I need to talk to you about the literary magazine."

"I'll come by your room later," I said.

"It's fairly urgent," she said.

It's just a literary magazine, lady! I thought. *I'm sure it can wait!* "Let me just take care of this, and I'll come by your room later, I promise."

"Very well, then." Mrs. Crutchfield walked away.

I turned my attention back to Meredith and Alexa. "Let's see what you can do about Heatherly," I said. "For starters, I want you to undo all the rumors she's spreading about me—and while you're at it, the ones about Kelsey that have been going around since last year. After that, I don't want Heatherly sitting at the good tables in the lunchroom anymore. Understand?"

"Consider it done," Meredith replied.

"This assignment will serve as a test of your new loyalties. Show me what you can do. Impress me. And *then* maybe we'll talk about my putting in a good word for you with the Delts next year."

"You won't regret it, Em," said Alexa.

Could Meredith and Alexa really work fast enough to affect the May Queen votes? And were they even really on my side, or was this just another trick Heatherly had cooked up?

It was hard to tell. I saw the two of them whispering to girls who responded with looks of shock and disgust, but there was no way to know what Meredith and Alexa were saying; for all I knew, they could have been spreading more rumors about me. People would whisper when Heatherly walked by, but I didn't know whether they were saying they hated her or were going to vote for her for May Queen.

That Friday, during activity period, the ballots were collected and sealed. No one would know the results until Spring Fling, two weeks away.

I tried to call Ryan again that night. He wouldn't answer. I thought about leaving a voice mail, but I didn't want to say, "Hey, Ryan, contrary to what you may have heard, I never got busy with Colby Summers or with anybody else, and the girl who's emailing you about me is an complete demon, so don't trust her, okay? Call me!" BEEP.

All I could do was hope that Meredith and Alexa would deliver on their promise. It was bad enough to lose Ryan but to lose him to Heatherly would have been unbearable.

The next Monday, whenever Heatherly made a move to sit at one of the good tables at lunch, someone would move into the seat she tried to take or put a backpack in her way. Even the semipopular crowd had no use for her anymore. She had no choice but to sit with the geeks I used to sit with. *Please let them invite her to a sci-fi convention!* I wished. I really wanted to smile and wave, but Heatherly never looked up from her tray.

"Well?" Alexa asked. "How'd we do?"

"Not bad," I told her and Meredith. "Your work is quick and decisive. I respect that."

"Then we're cool with you?" asked Meredith.

"I wouldn't go quite that far yet," I replied. "I'm going to need a little more convincing."

"What do you want us to do next?" Alexa said.

"I don't know," I said. "Surprise me. Dazzle me."

The two of them grinned like children stealing a peek at their Christmas presents. "We'll think of something really good," Meredith said. "You can count on it, Em."

I was still trying to get my mind off the terrible notion of Ryan and Heatherly. It seemed like I was forgetting something. What was it? Ooh! The literary magazine. Other than the halfhearted edits I'd made during seventh period on days when Mrs. Crutchfield was in the room with me, I hadn't worked on it in ages. The days she was away team teaching, I'd kind of used the period to get homework done so I could have more time to focus on the campaign. There were still a lot of pieces that needed editing, I hadn't replied to people about which submissions of theirs we were using, and I hadn't even reformatted the files. When had Mrs. C said it was due to the printer? It had to be pretty soon if we wanted to distribute them before school was out. I figured I'd better find out.

Mrs. Crutchfield was in the room alone, grading papers. "Hey, Mrs. C," I said. "Sorry I've been so crazy busy lately. I'll stay after school today and get caught up. When did you say we had to have the magazine to the printer again?"

"Emily, I sent the literary magazine to the printer last Friday. I told you it was due the last week of April."

"But I hadn't finished it—not even close!"

"I've been reminding you about the deadline for weeks, and you kept promising me you'd take care of everything," she said.

"I know—I kept meaning to, but I guess I got distracted."

"In any case, it had to be done, and I couldn't wait for you forever."

"Oh, Mrs. C," I said. "I'm so sorry."

"No use worrying about it now," she said. "I was probably spending way too much time with my children anyway. And on the bright side, that band of gypsies who took them in has really taught them a lot of valuable life skills."

"Mrs. C . . ." I knew that even though she was making a joke about it, she was disappointed in me. "I let you down. How can I ever make it up to you?"

She removed her reading glasses. "Emily," she said. "I'm glad you've made some friends. Kelsey's a nice girl, and you have a lot in common. And I'm glad you're not target practice for those awful girls anymore. But . . ."

"What?"

"Remember that Frost poem, about choosing your path? I would hate to see you look back and regret the one you've chosen. Will you promise me you'll think about that?"

"I will," I said. *As soon as I've seen to Heatherly's ruin.*

I went to the set to see Brynn after school. I didn't mention the lit magazine.

"So how's life as a Delts pledge?" she asked. I was quiet. "Emily, is something wrong?"

"I don't know. It's weird," I said.

"Weird how?"

"I've always been opposed to socially exclusive clubs on principle, and I know good and well Caroline's using me, but still . . ."

"It felt good to get in, didn't it?" Brynn asked.

"Brynn, when I walked those hallways, with that Delts shirt on, with everybody looking at me like I was so cool, all of the other girls wishing they were me—I don't know—"

"It's called power," Brynn said. "It comes in many forms, all of which are seductive. It's okay to admit that it felt good, Emily. You are a human being, after all."

"It felt *great,* Brynn. Positively delicious. Heatherly was furious."

"Well, that was the best part, right?"

"Yeah, about Heatherly. She's spreading rumors about me."

"And you're surprised? That's how she operates. Nothing new there."

"Except this time, the rumor is that I was . . . *friendly* to Colby. Extremely friendly."

"Ewww!"

"Yeah. And she told Ryan, who still isn't speaking to me, by the way."

"Well, they say there's no such thing as bad publicity, as long as they spell your name correctly," said Brynn. "But in this case, that might not be true."

"What can we do?" I asked.

"I don't know, Emily. Colby's movie is almost finished—and your campaign along with it. I'll be out of here next week. Of course, I'll help you any way I can, but the Em Campaign is almost over. If you're going to stay on top of your school's social hierarchy, you're going to have to become your own spin doctor at some point."

"It's the Ryan situation that bothers me, not maintaining my status. That I've got covered: Meredith and Alexa offered to turn on Heatherly in exchange for being my friend. How hilarious is that? You totally called it with the whole divide-and-conquer strategy. I don't have to do a thing—they said they'd take her down for me."

"But you told them no," Brynn said. "Right?"

"Well, not exactly," I said. "I mean, they did say she'd been spreading rumors about me, after all . . . so I told them to make it stop and to make sure she didn't sit at the good tables in the lunchroom anymore. She deserves that, doesn't she?"

"Emily, the point was to *overcome* Heatherly, not *become* her."

"Oh, come on—she deserves it!" I said. "Besides, I didn't tell them what to do; I instructed them to surprise me, so whatever they do isn't really my fault." Then I couldn't help but laugh. "I'm telling you, they'll do absolutely anything to impress me."

"No, Emily. Don't go there. Remember the competitive benefit of the Em brand: cooler, and without the fascism. Your Unique Selling Proposition is your humanity . . . your kindness. You can give the kids at your school someone hip to look up to who doesn't oppress the masses. That's what your new brand can offer that the Daisies couldn't. If you lose that benefit, you lose your unique position in the marketplace, and you have nothing new to offer your audience. The result is brand confusion—your product becomes indistinguishable from the market leader it replaced. You become just another Daisy, a nasty, stuck-up jerk. You don't want to be that. Look, when you're elected May Queen, that will be the final nail in Heatherly's coffin anyway, all right? You don't need to stoop to her methods. By the way, when is the May Queen announced, again?"

"Next Friday," I said.

"The day after the film wraps. I'll stay in town through that weekend so I can be here for it," she said. "Listen, Emily, it's fine to enjoy yourself, but don't let selling the brand make you lose sight of who you really are—I kind of like her."

I couldn't help but think that Brynn had no idea what it was like to go from being Plywood to being Em, the biggest thing to ever happen to Wright Middle School. You could look at Brynn and know that she'd always been beautiful and confident and popular. How could she possibly understand what I was feeling?

"Anyway," Brynn continued, "Caroline has done her part, so I'll call my friend at Ford and tell him about her. She's earned it. Besides, it will be interesting to see what happens after she gets what she wants." I hadn't really thought about that. Caroline would get her contact and I'd still be a pledge? That definitely had the potential to suck.

At Brynn's instruction, I called Caroline and told her that a friend of my parents' who was working on the movie set thought she had potential and wanted to send her portfolio to Ford. Caroline pretended to be surprised by this, but she seemed truly grateful. I told her my friend had been really busy but that she'd promised to send the portfolio to Ford the next day.

Within seventy-two hours, Caroline had gotten a call from Ford and was scheduled to meet with them as soon as the school year ended. I'd have just over two weeks to be at her beck and call as a pledge. Now that Caroline was in the driver's seat, I wondered what she'd have in store for me before she left for New York.

XII.
PRODUCT
LIFE CYCLE
DECLINE

Forty

Meredith and Alexa didn't waste any time. They caught me as soon as I got to school the Monday of exam week. "Em! We did it!" Meredith said.

"Did what?" I asked.

"We came up with a way to surprise you!" Alexa said. "You said to dazzle you."

"Oh, yeah," I said. "I was studying for exams all weekend, and I kind of forgot about it." That was partially true—I had studied a lot, but I'd still wondered whether they'd really follow through, and if so, how.

"*We* didn't forget about it!" said Meredith. "Prepare to be dazzled!"

"What did you do?" I asked.

"Look!" Meredith pointed to the door of the guys' bathroom. It was covered with white stickers—address labels they'd run through a computer printer. They were plain except for a web address: www. heatherlydrools.com.

"What is that?" I said. "What does it mean?"

"We printed hundreds of them," Alexa said. "We stuck them everywhere!"

Whatever it was, Heatherly had earned it and more. There was no reason to feel nervous. So why did I have such a strange feeling in my stomach? "I need to get to a computer," I said.

I headed straight for the computer lab, with Meredith and Alexa following close behind. The technology teacher was in the server room and paid no attention to us. I typed in the web address, hoping I could get past the firewall. Immediately a huge picture of Heatherly came up. She was asleep, and white drool was oozing from her open mouth. There were other pictures of her, too—all apparently taken while she was asleep: one of a shot up her nose, another where they'd gotten a close-up of a huge, angry zit on her forehead. They'd written captions, too:

Heatherly Hamilton is soooo not cool. We can't believe we used to be friends with her!!!! We totally tricked her into spending the night with us this weekend even though we HATE her now!!!! Check out the nasty zit on her forehead! Now U know why she's wearing bangs this week! Heatherly, U suck!!!!! Meredith and Alexa

Though the pictures were unmistakably of Heatherly, I couldn't help but see myself three months ago. This was exactly like something they would have done to me. "Unbelievable," I said.

"I know! Isn't it the best?" Meredith said.

"No," I answered. "It's not the best. Not at all."

"Em, we thought you'd like it. We didn't mean to disappoint you," said Alexa.

"Don't worry. We can do better," Meredith said. "We'll think of something worse."

"No, that's not what I meant," I said. *Come on, Emily!* I told myself. *It's Heatherly! Heath-er-ly! She deserves it!* But I still felt humiliated for her. Humiliation—that nauseating feeling that made you wish you were dead—it was a feeling I knew only too well. A feeling so terrible you'd start a fight you knew you couldn't win or sell your own departed mother's heirloom jewelry for even a temporary reprieve. Though Heatherly was responsible for it, getting even still felt wrong. Just then, Heatherly came in. Enough of this: it was time to make things right.

"Heatherly," I said. "Listen, about all this—"

"Shut up! Just shut up! I HATE you! First you stole my seat at the lunch table, and now you steal my best friends!" Heatherly yelled.

The venom in her voice made me forget my pity for her. "You have the nerve to accuse me, after the emails you've been sending to Ryan?" I said. "I didn't steal anybody's friends. They came to me."

"You tricked them into turning on me!" she said.

"You lied to Ryan and everyone at school about me!" I yelled.

"She didn't trick us, Heatherly," Meredith said. "We're her friends now. You're a loser. Em is going to be May Queen, and you're going to be nothing."

"Yeah, everybody voted for Em for May Queen," Alexa said.

"You don't know that!" Heatherly said. "I'll make you all pay for this!"

When Heatherly ran out of the computer lab, Meredith acted as though we'd never been interrupted; she wasn't rattled at all. "So tell us what you want us to do to Heatherly next, Em. We'll do whatever you say."

But my pity, in spite of Heatherly herself, was starting to return. I'd never seen her like this—sure, I'd seen Heatherly cruel and vindictive, but not desperate and degraded. "I think you've done enough," I said.

The sarcasm was lost on them. "Oh, thank you, Em!" Alexa said.

"I've got to get to social studies," I said. When I left the room, Alexa and Meredith were popping high fives.

But I wasn't pleased with them. And I wasn't pleased with myself—whoever that was anymore.

Forty-One

I was studying for my algebra final Tuesday afternoon when the doorbell rang. I peeked through the blinds to see who it was. Caroline and crew. I opened the door.

"Come on," Caroline said. "We're going to Taco Casa."

"I'm prepping for my algebra exam," I answered. "I can't go anywhere now."

"But I'm craving a chicken chimalupa," Caroline said matter-of-factly.

"Em," said MK, "if your big sister is craving a chicken chimalupa, you have an obligation to get it for her."

So much for algebra. I wrote Dad a note saying I'd be back before seven, in case he got home before I did.

When we got to Taco Casa, MK and Laura spotted two freshman girls who were wearing silver pledge pins like mine. "Oh, good, you made it," MK said to them. She and Laura gave their orders to the pledges and went to sit down.

"I'll have bottled water with mine," Caroline told me before following them. "And extra sour cream."

I followed the other pledges to the counter, where they ordered for MK and Laura and paid for their meals. "You pay for them?" I asked.

"Of course," one of them said. "It's the least we can do for our big sisters, right?"

"Right," I said. "Sure." I ordered and paid for Caroline's food.

"Besides," the other pledge said, "it will all be worth it next year when we get to make *our* pledges do whatever *we* say. I'm going to be positively brutal to mine!"

"Me too!" said the first one.

"Don't forget the extra sour cream!" Caroline called.

When her order was ready, I took Caroline's tray to the booth where she and the other girls were sitting. "Didn't you get anything?" Caroline asked.

"I didn't bring enough money," I said.

"Oh, that's too bad," she said. Caroline had been eating for a couple of minutes when she suddenly put down her plastic fork. "Ugh! I've just lost my appetite." She nodded at something behind me. "That is the fattest pig I have ever seen."

"Who is that, anyway?" Laura asked.

"I don't know," MK said. "But somebody needs to tell her that she should get some liposuction or something. Gross."

"That's Susan Eaglin," I said. "She's in middle school. Seventh grade."

"You know her?" Caroline asked.

"Not really. I mean, I know her name."

"Well, I want to know how anybody gets to be that fat. Pledge, go ask her," Caroline commanded.

"What?" I said.

"Go ask her how she got to be that fat," Caroline repeated.

"You're kidding me. I can't go over there and ask her that. It's totally rude."

"Pledge," Laura said, "you will do your big sister's bidding or you will be relieved of your pledge pin."

I looked to Caroline for help, but she simply smirked. Now that she had her contact at Ford, I was of no use to her. She didn't have to play nice with me anymore. All those phone messages she'd left for me that I hadn't returned? The weeks of chasing after a mere eighth-grader who should have been kissing her butt instead of the other way around? I had no doubt she was fully enjoying this moment.

"Move it, pledge," said Laura.

I got up from my seat and walked over to the booth where Susan was sitting by herself. "Hey, Susan," I said. "I'm Em. We go to the same school."

"Well, of course I know who you are, Em! I went to your party, remember?" she said. "Awesome party, by the way!" All I could think was, *Thank goodness she's sitting far enough away that the Delts can't hear her.*

"Oh, yeah, thanks."

"So what's up?" When I didn't answer, Susan looked at me, confused. With some effort, she turned and looked behind her at the Delts, who weren't even trying to pretend they weren't staring at her.

"What's going on?" Susan asked.

"Nothing," I said. "Just thought I'd see what you were up to."

"Well, I'm not bowling," she said.

"Right! Bowling, that's a good one." I laughed nervously. I wanted to walk away, but Caroline was giving me a stern look. "Do you eat here a lot?"

"Sometimes. Em, why are those girls staring at us?" I looked down. "I knew it," Susan said. "Your Barbie doll friends dared you to come talk to the fat girl, didn't they?"

"Susan, I'm sorry," I said. "They made me come over to ask you . . ."

"Ask me what?" she demanded.

"You know . . . how you . . . how you came to . . . weigh so much."

Susan looked at me for a minute. Then, with no small amount of effort, she got out of her seat, picked up her plastic tray, threw her food wrappers away, and went straight to the booth where Caroline and the other girls were sitting. They pretended as though they hadn't been looking at her, hadn't noticed that she'd approached the table.

"You want to know how I got to be so fat?" she shouted.

"Excuse me?" Caroline said.

"Don't play dumb with me," Susan said. "I know you sent your little puppet over. You have a problem with the way I look?"

"I think *you* should have a problem with the way you look," MK said. "Besides, you don't talk to a Delt that way, you big, fat nobody."

"You think some letters on a T-shirt give you the right to treat other people like garbage?" Susan said. "I'd rather be fat than be in your stupid little club any day, because I'd never want to be like you."

"I can pretty much guarantee you'll never have to worry about being a Delt," Laura said, to which they all giggled.

"Whatever. I'm comfortable with who I am. I don't have to trash other people to feel good about myself," said Susan. "I feel sorry for you."

"*She* feels sorry for *us*!" Caroline said.

As the Delts continued their giggling, I stood there, stunned.

"Congratulations, Em," Susan said to me. "You obeyed your orders. Looks like you fit right in." As she turned to walk away, she added, "And to think I voted for you for May Queen."

I'd been paying so much attention to what was going on with Susan that I'd had my back turned to the order counter, but I had a sudden sense that someone was watching me. Standing there holding green plastic trays of beef burritos were Sonny and Brynn.

I opened my mouth, perhaps to say something, but nothing came out. The two of them looked at me with a mixture of shock and disgust.

"Oh, Emily," Sonny finally said. "What would your mother say?" I felt as though I'd been stabbed with a million tiny knives.

"So much for your USP," Brynn said wearily.

"Her what?" Sonny asked.

Brynn looked nervous. "Unique Selling Proposition?" she mumbled.

He looked at Brynn, confused, then at me. "What's going on here?"

Neither of us said anything.

"Come on, you guys!" MK said. "Fat Girl's too young to drive. She must be walking home. Let's drive past her and honk and wave!" As they scrambled to the exit, I stood staring at Sonny and Brynn.

"Now, pledge!" Caroline ordered.

I didn't know what to say to Sonny and Brynn, so I left with Caroline and the other girls. Susan was walking across the parking lot. When we drove by, Caroline and the others honked their horns, shouted, and laughed at her. She flipped us off, but her face was red and puffy. We'd made her cry.

My head was spinning when we drove away. All the other girls were laughing, but I was quiet, silently asking myself one question over and over: *Why had I gotten in the car with them?* I could have said no. I could have gone after Susan and immediately apologized.

To be downright honest about it, I could have chosen not to offer Susan up for ridicule in the first place. But I had . . . I had chosen that path. And once I was on it, I found I couldn't go back. What was done was done.

I thought about the Frost poem: *Yet knowing how way leads on to way / I doubted if I should ever come back.*

Caroline got me home before five thirty; Dad hadn't been home yet to see my note. I tried to go back to studying algebra, but the lines from the poem, along with the whole scene from Taco Casa, kept echoing in my head: *Your little puppet. Looks like you fit right in.* Caroline laughing. Susan's red face. And worst of all: *What would your mother say?*

I took a shower before bed, trying to wash it all away, to clear my head. But the words and images kept coming back to me.

I thought about what Mrs. Crutchfield had said about choosing a path. I could've refused to do what Caroline told me, but there was so much to lose, so much I'd worked for on the line. A few months ago, I'd never have done anything like what I did today—but a few months ago, the opportunity wouldn't have been before me, either. It's easy to do the right thing when you don't have the opportunity to do the wrong thing. Before, I'd never had the power to really hurt anyone because I'd never had any power at all. I'd wanted to get rid of weak, target-on-my-back Emily and become cool and untouchable Em.

But in trying to become Em, had I simply become the new Heatherly?

Forty-Two

I blew my algebra final. Since I begged to see my score early, Coach Baker let me wait in the doorway of the teacher's workroom while he ran the test papers through the scanner: D plus. He told me he was "very disappointed" in my performance. Luckily, my semester average was high enough that I'd still end up with a B- for the overall grade.

My other exams wouldn't be as hard as algebra, and maybe I'd get to study for them without Caroline having a Taco Casa attack. I told myself that I wouldn't think about all the other stuff. I even tried to rationalize that Sonny had been wrong, that he didn't know the whole situation, but I knew I was only fooling myself.

Dad hadn't said anything about it when he got home that afternoon, but I couldn't stand wondering anymore whether Sonny had called him and, if so, what he'd said.

"Did Sonny tell you about yesterday?" I finally asked.

Dad stopped reading the paper and looked at me with concern. "What happened yesterday? Is something wrong?"

"A lot's wrong," I said. I called Sonny and asked him to come by before his shift and to bring Brynn with him.

When they arrived, the way Sonny looked at me filled me with shame. "Hello, Emily," he said. "I hope we'll be seeing you under better circumstances today."

"What's going on?" Dad asked.

"Were you standing there the whole time?" I asked.

"Long enough to realize that the girl I saw in Taco Casa was not my sweet, kind niece," he said. "Emily, how could you?"

"What did you do?" said Dad.

"I know," I said. "I don't know why I did it. They told me to, and I was afraid to say no."

"Emily, what's happened to you?" Sonny asked.

"Will someone please tell me what's going on?" Dad was getting pretty worked up.

"I told Sonny the basic information about the campaign," Brynn said. "But I think it's time we told him, and your Dad, everything."

So we spilled it—all about how I'd found out Colby's secret, how I'd sold Mom's bracelet and sneaked into Brynn's firm to hire them, and all about the campaign.

"You sold your mother's bracelet?" Dad said. He looked at me as though I were someone he'd never met. "You sold your mother's bracelet—without even asking me—so you could be *popular*?"

"It wasn't about that—at first," I said. "I just wanted to be cool enough that they'd leave me alone. It kind of . . . snowballed."

Sonny and Dad looked at Brynn. "I'm very good at what I do," she said apologetically. "We may have gone a little overboard."

Once Dad had calmed down a little about the bracelet—and the idea of my running around New York City alone—I told them about Ryan and how he wasn't speaking to me anymore, and about heatherlydrools.com. Sonny and Dad were surprised, to say the least. Then, worst of all, I had to tell Dad what I'd done to Susan at Taco Casa and relive every minute of it. "I know—I'm a terrible person," I said. Dad sat there, stunned.

"No, Emily," Brynn said. "You're not the only one to blame here. Mr. Wood, I apologize for my part in this. I was trying to help, but I'm afraid I got caught up in the campaign and forgot that I was dealing with an impressionable young girl. I should have known this would be too much for her. That amount of power in such a short time would be overwhelming even for an adult. I've seen actors and musicians handle quick success quite poorly, so I should have known better. I'm as much to blame for this as Emily."

"No, you're not, Brynn," I said. "I didn't listen to you at all and I did these awful, mean things even though you warned me not to become like Heatherly." I finally looked Dad in the eye. "Please go ahead and lecture me. I can't stand the way you're not saying anything."

"If you've already figured out you were wrong, why do you need me to lecture you?" he asked gently.

"I didn't know you had it in you to be deliberately cruel, Emily," Sonny said. "That's what breaks my heart."

"But I didn't really tell Alexa and Meredith to do that stuff to Heatherly, and I had no choice about Susan Eaglin," I said. "They would've taken my pledge pin away."

"A few months ago you said the Delts were a bunch of snobs, and now you're worried about losing your pledge pin?" Brynn said. "I told you it was okay to enjoy yourself, and it is—but not at Susan's expense. Is being a Delt worth this?"

"No . . . I mean . . . I don't know. It's—it's so nice to be some-body."

"Is that really what you believe? That all of this makes you some-body?" asked Sonny.

"It sounds idiotic, I know. But you don't know what it was like before. Everybody thinks I'm so cool now."

"Apparently, not everyone—certainly not this poor girl Susan," said Dad.

Brynn said, "Remember, Emily, 'everybody' is a fickle entity. A few months ago, 'everybody' at school decided to treat you like dirt. Now you're making decisions based on what 'everybody' thinks?"

"I know you're right. But what am I supposed to do? I don't even really know how all this happened."

Sonny asked Brynn, "Do things like this ever happen when one of your campaigns goes awry? What do you experts call a mess like this?"

Brynn sighed. "I guess you could think of it as product life cycle decline. For various reasons, a product outlives its usefulness to the consumer. In this case, our product ended up not being such an improvement over the former market leader." Brynn put her hand on my shoulder. "I know you want me to tell you how to fix all this, but I can't.

"It's funny, you know. The clients at our agency ask all the time about projects they're offered—should they take this movie, record this song. There's a lot of expensive research that goes into trying to determine what will work and what won't, but there's no magic formula. The biggest budget film with the biggest stars can be a total flop, and some little sleeper with a bunch of unknowns can walk away with the year's top box office receipts. So I'll ask you the same question I ask my clients: What does your gut tell you your next move should be?"

"I don't know," I replied. "It seems like there should be some big way to fix things—something that would make up for the way I treated Susan. Something that would make Ryan understand who I really am and how I feel about him."

"Did you try telling him the truth?" Sonny asked.

"Yeah," I said. "Well, sort of. Not exactly. If I had, I would have had to tell him Colby's secret, and I couldn't do that."

"She has a point," said Brynn. "When we came up with our plan, we didn't exactly factor in a Ryan."

I buried my head in one of the couch pillows. "Everything is such a mess. I never meant to hurt anyone—except maybe the Daisies."

"Daisies?" Sonny asked.

"The tyrannical popular girls, led by Heatherly," Brynn said. "I'll explain later."

Sonny put his hand over mine. "Unfortunately, Emily, being sorry doesn't change what you've done. And as for some big gesture that would magically fix everything—you can't just bake someone a casserole in exchange for their dignity, or buy a greeting card that says, 'Sorry I humiliated you.'"

"On the other hand," Dad said, "I think saying you're sorry is a good place to start."

"I'm going to fix all this somehow," I said. "You'll see."

"What are you going to do about Ryan?" Brynn asked.

"I don't know. I was so afraid he wouldn't like the real me."

"That doesn't sound very fair to Ryan," Dad said. "You didn't give him a chance to get to know the real you. If he has any sense at all, he'd see how great my Emily is."

I loved the fact that, no matter what terrible thing I'd done, Dad would always think of me as his Emily and love me anyway. I hugged him and started to cry a little bit.

"Seems to me that for Emily to return, Em has to go," Sonny said. "Are you sure you're willing to do that?"

"I've changed so much in the past couple of months," I said, wiping my eyes. "Sometimes I'm not even sure where Em ends and Emily begins. There's a lot to like about Em—except for the whole drunk-with-power deceptive part, of course. Maybe there's a way to hang on to the good parts of Em and still get rid of the bad."

"I guess we'll see," Sonny said. Dad nodded.

I knew I wasn't off the hook yet. It would take a lot more to regain their faith in me.

XIII.
REPOSITIONING

Forty-Three

They blew up the old mental hospital the day before Spring Fling. The explosion was spectacular, thanks to the way the smokestacks crumbled slowly and dramatically, exactly as the director had envisioned. Colby shot his last take, where he danced triumphantly over the bodies of several terrorists while singing the jazzy number, "Better Not Mess with the U.S. (No, No)." I got to watch the whole, horrible scene, and after the director yelled his final "Cut!," Colby came over to say good-bye.

"Why are you looking at me like that?" he asked. Then he smiled. "I know—like I have to ask."

I was trying not to laugh because the whole thing was so ridiculous, but I felt sad for Colby at the same time, because even I could tell this was going to be terrible for his career. "Where did those women in red, white, and blue bikinis supposedly come from? Are we supposed to believe they climbed out of the rubble?" I asked.

"I'm trying not to think about it," he said. "Come on. Let's go find Amy and Daniel. We're flying out as soon as I get changed, and I've got something I need to give back to you." When we got to the makeup trailer, Colby handed me my Cool Stuff notebook. "Great stuff in here—just the kinds of things I was looking for," he said. "I'm going to run some lyrics by my producer, and if he likes them, you will have a cowriting credit, Miss Poetry Girl."

I should have been more excited, but I was still feeling like a jerk about Susan and everything else. "Thanks," I said. "Here's your necklace."

Amy fastened it back around his neck. "Emily," she said, "I'm really glad we got to know you. I hope you'll stay in touch."

"I will, Amy."

Brynn said, "Colby's booked solid all next week—a cover shoot, in-person interview, TV promos, but I'm staying in town for Spring Fling tomorrow, okay? I wouldn't miss it."

I hugged Amy and Colby and gave Daniel a good tickle. Brynn drove me home.

"Are you going to be all right?" she asked.

"Of course," I said.

Like I had a choice.

Forty-Four

Spring Fling was only slightly more than twenty-four hours away, and I still felt terrible about Susan, and even Heatherly, and I couldn't forget what Dad had said about Ryan. He was totally right: I'd never given him a chance. I'd been too afraid that he wouldn't like Emily Wood and that I'd blow it if I didn't sell him Brand Em. I knew I owed Em for attracting Ryan in the first place—I'd never even have met him if it hadn't been for her, and maybe I couldn't have kept his interest without her confidence and mystique—but for anything real to happen between us, I'd have to risk letting him see behind the facade.

I called Sonny after school. "I need a favor," I told him.

"What wouldn't I do for you?" Sonny asked.

"I need you to get Dad out of the house tonight so I can invite Ryan over."

"*That's* what I wouldn't do for you," he said.

"Why not?"

"You're asking me to arrange for you to be completely alone in your house with a boy?"

"So what's your point?" I asked.

"I don't think so," Sonny said. "As an officer of the law, I'm not allowed to discharge my firearm without just cause, but if I ever catch you in the house alone with some teenage lover boy, somebody's going to get a bullet in his butt."

"But Sonny, I have to talk to him. I can't do it on the phone."

"Then you'll have to arrange to meet him somewhere—a public place. But it can't just be the two of you, because that would constitute a date, and you're not old enough to go on a date."

"So what you're saying is, if I want to see Ryan in person, it has to be in a public place, with our peers in attendance."

"Yes."

I could hardly believe it when Ryan actually answered his phone. "Ryan," I said, "it's Emily."

"Something I can do for you, Em?" he asked.

"Are you going to my school's Spring Fling with Heatherly?"

"What? No!"

At least there was that.

"I need you to come to Spring Fling. Please."

"I thought you couldn't date until you were fifteen," he said. "Or was that something else you lied about?"

"Forget it," I said. "I shouldn't have called. I'm sorry."

"No, wait," Ryan said. "Tell me what's up."

"Look, I don't expect you to come as my date, but would you please come? You won't have to stay long. There's something I need you to see."

"I'll think about it," Ryan said.

"Please, Ryan," I said. "Please say you'll be there."

"All right, Emily. But whatever I'm supposed to be there for had better be worth it."

"It will be," I said. "I promise."

Forty-Five

The last day of school was a mere formality. The teachers had to be there, and we students were allowed to go by each teacher's classroom to get our final grade and to look over our exams to see which answers we'd gotten wrong. Hardly anyone took advantage of this courtesy since the last thing any normal student wants to do after exams is think about the material ever again. Most everyone skipped school that day altogether, but I'd gone mainly to see Mrs. Crutchfield.

"Hard to believe you'll be in high school next year," she said. "What will I do without my star pupil?"

"I'll really miss you, Mrs. C," I said. "And I want to apologize again about the literary magazine."

"Don't beat yourself up, Emily," she said. "It's in the past."

"I wanted to give you this, with my sincere thanks for everything you've done for me." I handed her a present.

Mrs. Crutchfield unwrapped it and said, "It's a collection of Auden! Oh, Emily, I was kidding about that! But thank you so much. It's very thoughtful. I'll treasure it." She opened to the front page. "But you didn't write in it."

"Oh, no—I couldn't. It's too beautiful. I didn't want to ruin it."

"Come on . . . dedicate it for me. That signature might be worth a fortune one of these days!"

I rolled my eyes and smiled. "Yeah, sure." I thought a minute, and then I wrote, *To Mrs. Crutchfield, who taught me about poetry and life. Thanks for always believing in me. Your friend, Emily Wood.*

"Thank you, Emily," she said. "Now I will truly treasure it."

As I left Mrs. Crutchfield's classroom, she called, "Emily!"

"Yes?"

"I just want you to remember to think carefully about which roads you take. Frost was onto something."

"I'll keep that in mind, Mrs. Crutchfield. I promise."

I had asked Dad to escort me to the dance that night, which wasn't weird because the parents of May Queen hopefuls always showed up to take pictures and such. "You're sure you want to do this?" he asked.

"I have to," I said.

Two hours before we had to leave for the dance, I took my shower. But instead of getting ready, I sat on my bed for a long time. I took out my Cool Stuff notebook. I hadn't even realized how long it had been since I'd written. I thought about what had happened over the last few months, of the things I'd said and done, and I wrote a poem. Mrs. Crutchfield had always stressed the necessity for revision. She'd said that she knew of only one poet who had ever been able to create a masterpiece in one draft, and that was John Keats. He was a young man who knew he was dying, and one night he sat outside and listened to a singing bird, and he contemplated his own mortality in a sublime poem called "Ode to a Nightingale."

Mrs. Crutchfield used to say, "Don't try to get by on a first draft unless your name is John Keats." Well, I was no John Keats, but I had something I needed to say and no time to revise. It was like everything that had been all jumbled up in my head for so long began to finally make some sense, and even when the words you need to say aren't perfect, if you really mean them, they're still pretty powerful. Writing that poem made me remember why I loved poetry so much, why it was such a huge part of who I was. It felt good to be writing again.

Someone knocked on my door.

"Come in," I said.

Dad peeked his head in. "Brynn's here to see you."

I asked Dad to send her in. "So what are you wearing tonight?" she asked.

"This." I pulled out a white shift dress with glittery horizontal stripes.

"Nice!" she said.

"It ought to be—two months' allowance, and Dad still had to kick in to cover the sales tax. I bought it weeks ago."

"It's a good choice. You're among the two percent of women who can pull off horizontal stripes, so you might as well work it. Accessories?" I pulled out some dangly earrings. "And to think, when I met you, you didn't know a diffusion line from couture. But this outfit needs one more finishing touch. I think I have just the thing." She pulled something out of her purse. It was Mom's bracelet!

I was completely stunned. "How? How did you ever get this?"

"You told me you'd sold it to an online dealer, so Sonny and I searched the Net for it."

"How in the world did you guys ever find it? You must've had to search every online jeweler. That would take forever!"

"Not when your boyfriend's a police officer. They're good at tracking things down. My business is supposed to be about knowing the right people, but cops have the real connections. Besides, you used the first place that comes up in a Google search."

"But it's too much—you can't afford to buy this back for me, and neither can Sonny."

"We didn't. It's a gift from Colby and Amy," Brynn said.

"What? Why?"

"Apparently, Colby's record label loved some new songs he'd written—songs with lyrics cowritten by Emily Wood."

"Wow! I can't believe it! He really did use some of the stuff from my notebook!"

"Yep, and the new songs are going to help a lot when he's the first client for my agency," she said. "With someone as big as Colby Summers, I can really make a go of it."

"You're going out on your own?" I asked. "But Noreen is so powerful. She'll ruin both of you."

"All this business with the Daisies kind of got me thinking," said Brynn. "Bullies aren't just in middle school. Colby's contract with Noreen's firm is expiring soon, and we're going to go to the media with his real age. We'll explain why he had to go along with the teen idol thing. Since you were so understanding, we're betting the rest of the American public will cut him a break, too."

"But won't this ridiculous movie kill his career?" I asked.

"Oh, that's the best part," Brynn replied. "We've decided to embrace the movie's stupidity, pretend it was meant to be a farce. *Monty Python* meets *Die Hard* meets *High School Musical*. We've leaked some early buzz to critics, and some of them are already predicting it will become an instant cult classic. There's a lot of anticipation already building, so by the release date, we might have a box office bonanza on our hands. Like I said before, you never know with movies."

I couldn't help but laugh. "You are nothing short of amazing," I said.

When I sighed, Brynn asked, "What's wrong?"

"I'm sorry. It's just that I don't deserve it—the bracelet, all the trouble you've gone to for me. And tonight, I could make an even bigger mess of everything. If I'm named May Queen, I'll have to give a speech. What will I say to all those people?"

Brynn said, "You'll know. No more trying to say what you think they want you to say. And no matter what happens, your dad and Sonny and I will be there to support you."

"I'm glad you guys are coming," I said.

"You're sure it's not dorky to bring adults?"

"No, but I wouldn't mind if you guys let me out at the door and then went to park the car. It's not that I'm ashamed of you or anything, but I'm still not comfortable in heels.

"Brynn," I added. "I do have one question. Why did you do all this for me? It was a lot more than Noreen had in mind, and you've kept with it even now that you're planning on leaving her agency. Is it only because you like Sonny?"

"Don't get me wrong, Sonny is . . . hmmm . . . 'irresistible' springs to mind. But you want to know why I really got so behind you on this?" Brynn pulled a photograph from her purse. "I brought this to show you." It was a girl about my age, with frizzy, uncontrollable curls, braces, and a huge brown birthmark that took up almost half her face.

"This is you?" I asked. "I don't believe it!"

"I know what it's like to be a middle school loser," she said. "Four years of braces—including headgear, mind you—and five separate laser surgeries to minimize the birthmark you now think is so cool."

"Sonny's wild about your birthmark," I said. "I guess you know he's nuts about you."

"Well, I am a pretty great catch," Brynn said. "And so are you, Emily. If Ryan doesn't see that, then it wasn't meant to be." She looked at her watch. "You'd better get ready. You can't go with that towel on your head."

Alone in my room, I looked in the mirror: no makeup, wet hair, and a bathrobe. It seemed as though it had been a long time since I'd really looked at myself without all the props. Could this girl have taken down someone as powerful as Heatherly Hamilton? Looking at myself now, it didn't seem possible. But I knew that tonight I had to be ready to face her, and Ryan, and the entire school at Spring Fling.

I had a plan, but if they put that crown on my head, could I follow through? Like I said before, it's easy to do the right thing when you don't have the opportunity to do the wrong thing. The May Queen crown came with a lot of opportunity, a lot of power. I could accept it, keep my Delts pin, and join the ruling class at Wright High. Maybe even come up with a way to get another chance with Ryan. Or I could abandon Brand Em for regular old Emily and lose everything I'd worked so hard for.

It was time to put on the Em costume—either for the last time or for good. I fixed my hair and makeup and put on my dress. Everything looked perfect.

Forty-Six

Ryan was waiting outside the door of the gym when I arrived.

"Ryan, you came," I said. "I'm so glad to see you. Thanks for showing."

"You look really nice," Ryan said, but he didn't smile. It was more like he was begrudgingly stating a fact.

"Thanks. Will you come in with me?"

"I guess. Are you going to tell me what you wanted me to come here for?"

"You'll find out soon, I promise."

When we walked in together, everyone turned to look. I hadn't even thought about the impression I would make walking in with Ryan, but I'd definitely made one.

"Em!" Meredith said as she and Alexa scurried to meet us. "You look so awesome!" They both hugged me. "Heatherly is over there with her parents. Nobody's talking to her at all! Don't you love it? And she'll completely freak when she sees that you got Ryan back!" The music was loud, and Ryan was looking away, so I couldn't tell whether or not he'd heard her.

"But where have you been?" Alexa asked. "We've been looking for you since the dance started."

"Alexa, look!" Meredith said. "It's the MTV producer—over there!" Brynn was standing with Dad and Sonny. "Are they filming this? Is this going to be the first episode of your reality show? Are we being filmed by hidden cameras? Where are they? Does my hair look okay? Do you need us to go into one of those confessionals afterwards and tell them what great friends we are?"

"No, thanks anyway. Look, I'm not staying long," I said. "Just came for the May Queen stuff."

"Right," Meredith said. "This must be so lame for someone like you! You're totally right—lame! We'll probably leave early, too. Yeah, we'll leave early, too. Hey—maybe we can all go somewhere and hang out!" She was like a Chihuahua whose owner has just returned home from a long vacation.

"I don't think so," I said.

"Duh, Meredith!" Alexa said. "She and Ryan want to be alone!"

"I'm going to get some punch," Ryan said. He hovered near the punch bowl, looking as though he wanted desperately to be somewhere else.

"Don't worry, Em," said Meredith. "We'll keep Heatherly away from him. We've got your back!"

"Yeah, with dagger in hand, no doubt," I muttered.

"What? I can't hear you," Meredith said.

"Nothing," I said.

Mr. Warren finally took the stage. "Attention please," he said. It took a few more requests for attention for everyone to stop talking. It was probably killing him not to scream "Shut up!" but since parents were present, Warren restrained himself. "It's my privilege to announce this year's May Queen. As you all know, the May Queen embodies Wright's core values of character, leadership, and service. You, the student body, had the solemn duty of electing the young lady who best exemplifies those traits. So without further ado . . ."

He made a big show of opening a sealed envelope. Heatherly was staring across the gym at me as she stood with her parents. The voting had, after all, come before her friends had turned on her and destroyed her for my amusement. It could easily be her name Warren would call out, and she'd be back with a vengeance, and this whole tug-of-war would start all over again. "This year's May Queen is . . . Em Wood!"

As I walked to the stage, everyone was cheering and clapping, chanting "Em! Em! Em!" over and over. Well, except for Ryan. And Susan Eaglin. And Heatherly, of course. She had buried her face in her dad's chest, and he was patting her back. I could see him repeating, "There, there." Kelsey caught me before I went up. "Congratulations," she said, hugging me. "You deserve it." She seemed genuinely happy for me.

I grabbed her hand and pulled her to the stage with me. "I need you up here."

Mr. Warren placed a rhinestone tiara on my head and gestured for the queen to address her subjects. As the crowd beamed at me with earnest faces, I couldn't help but picture them all in yellow T-shirts that screamed "Value me!" Brynn had been right: it was what every one of them wanted . . . and deserved. And it was the very thing no one ever really gave them.

When we'd started the campaign, with the Unique Selling Proposition that I'd value all the people at my school and find something I genuinely admired about them, I hadn't thought beyond the surface— nice haircut, cute outfit. But maybe it was supposed to be more. I looked at the people around me and realized that each of them had something I could respect. Even Mr. Warren. Yeah, he was kinda psycho, but you had to sort of hand it to him: nobody at our school ever got stabbed or anything. Maybe even Heatherly had something about her I could admire. She was sort of smart, in an evil genius kind of way. And could I really fault her for having become so ruthless? Yeah, a little . . . but I hadn't handled all that power so well myself. Maybe I could value her without having to actually like her. Maybe I could value other people in general, just for the sake of decency.

Maybe everyone was staring at me, wondering if I'd lost my mind while I stood there thinking about all this.

I took a deep breath and approached the microphone.

Forty-Seven

"**If you'd told me earlier this year** that I'd be standing in front of all of you, making this speech, I never would have believed it," I said. "I've thought and thought about what I would say if you offered me this honor, but I'm not really good at speaking off the cuff. I'm better at writing things down. I wrote this poem tonight before I came here, and if you'll let me, I'd like to read it."

The crowd applauded and cheered again, so I began reading.

"It's called, 'Apology.'"

Here is the part where I insist,
it is not only me.
We have all taken part—
sorting souls like a deck of cards,
creating categories of emblems and colors
with identical faces.

But this insistence changes nothing.
I cannot sweep my splintered glass
into a crystalline pattern,
making something lovely from the wreckage I caused.
I cannot pretend I never took into my eager hands
the treasure of the human spirit,
breaking it into pieces,
casting it among old wrappers and empty plastic.

And so I stand here,
muttering frustrated, failing syllables,
searching for a gesture that does not exist:
A quick fix to undo the damage.

I find instead
only low, wordless tones.
Finally,
my mouth forms one request:
Forgive me.

As I looked down and folded my paper, the audience was silent. Words.

Weren't words supposed to be my thing? The way I made sense of the world? But now I wondered if mere words could change anything . . . if there could ever be enough of them to undo a mistake.

There was nothing else written on my paper, but everyone kept looking at me, waiting for something more. For two and a half months, I'd been leaving things unsaid, letting people's imaginations fill in the blanks . . . or planting suggestions about what I might be up to . . . or spinning circumstances into a pseudo reality that put me in a better light or gave me the upper hand. It had been a long time since I'd said what I really felt.

"A few months ago, I was nobody at this school. But with the right clothes, the right hair, and a picture in a magazine of me with a famous friend—and just a friend, by the way—I suddenly became important. I became this whole product called Em, and everybody bought it. But I don't want to sell Brand Em anymore. I turned into a complete jerk, and I want to say I'm sorry for that. I wrote the poem I just read because I treated people like a means to an end, and that's wrong. I don't want to be a jerk anymore. You guys deserve better."

I took the crown off my head. "If you really want a May Queen, it shouldn't be me. I've gotten to know Kelsey Brown pretty well in the past couple of months, and I was surprised to find that she's one of the nicest people I've ever met. Seriously—I've never seen her do any of the unkind things that so many of us, including me, do to one another all the time. Maybe you think she deserves to have awful things said about her because she's pretty and a cheerleader, but she doesn't. None of the bad things you've heard about her are true; they were made up by someone who was as wrong about people as I've been. Maybe that someone didn't think she had a choice. But there's got to be a better way we can relate to each other. . . . I don't know, like maybe forming real friendships and being nice to people because it's the right thing to do not because of their position on the social ladder."

People in the audience were looking at one another and starting to whisper.

"I've talked too long. I don't know if what I've said will change anything. This whole idea of a queen . . . it's messed up, if you ask me. Why does one person have to rule over everybody else, anyway? Why do we constantly have to rank each other? But if you do want a May Queen—one who really represents the best our school has to offer—it should be Kelsey, not me."

I handed Kelsey the crown, and she stared at me, her mouth open. Then, as I began to walk offstage, she grabbed the microphone and said, "Not so fast, Emily Wood." The crowd began muttering. Kelsey said, "I don't know about you guys, but I'm with Emily. Who needs a May Queen?"

Someone in the audience yelled "Yeah!" and everyone started clapping.

Mr. Warren began waving his hands wildly. He pushed past Kelsey and me and took the microphone. "Hold on a minute! This is highly irregular," he said. "Wright Middle School has always had a May Queen! Someone has to wear the tiara for the newspaper picture! Now, who's it going to be?"

There was silence again for a moment, until Heatherly screamed, "FAKE!"

Everyone turned to look. Seizing their attention, Heatherly flashed a sinister smile my way and walked onstage. "May I?" she said to Warren. He shrugged his shoulders and handed her the microphone. "My fellow students," Heatherly said. "I think I speak for all of us when I say that I am outraged." There was a twitter in the audience as people looked around to see if Heatherly really was speaking for them. What was she up to now? "The May Queen is a treasured institution at

Wright Middle School," she continued. "And the fact that the student body has offered this honor to someone who obviously doesn't appreciate it . . . well, it makes me sad. How *dare* you, Emily?"

I looked at my dad and Sonny and Brynn, who stood there helplessly, with no more idea what to do than I did. I looked at Ryan, still over by the punch bowl, staring at me like he wanted to rescue me but didn't know how. Heatherly waited for her words to sink in, and I braced myself for what was sure to be her moment of triumph.

When someone finally broke the silence and yelled, "You suck!" I knew it was all over and that Heatherly had won, once and for all.

When the next person yelled, "Get off the stage!" I could barely force my legs to work as I made my way to the edge of the platform and began walking down the steps, my head down so I didn't have to look anyone in the eye.

That's when I saw a hand grab my arm. "Where do you think you're going?"

I looked up.

It was Susan Eaglin.

Could this get any worse? Not only had Heatherly turned the crowd against me, with everyone yelling at me to get out, but now I was going to be publicly pummeled by Susan. What could Warren really do about it? It was her big chance.

I guess I should have cared more than I did, but part of me knew that, despite my lame attempt at an apology, I deserved it. I remembered how I'd treated Susan that day at Taco Casa—how she'd cried in the parking lot. The fact of the matter was that she had every right to do what she was about to do.

"Where are you going?" Susan said, the crowd still booing. I looked up into their faces to embrace my defeat.

And that's when I realized . . . they weren't yelling at me.

They were yelling at Heatherly.

From the punch bowl area, someone began chanting "Em" again. It was Ryan.

And soon everyone was chanting right along with him.

When Heatherly finally slunk offstage and rushed out of the gym with her parents, they all cheered.

Susan looked at me and smiled and said, "Well, go on!"

I could barely believe it. I'd said what I really felt, and they got it. No tricks, no gimmicks.

When I went back up on stage with Kelsey, Warren asked again, "What are we going to do for the newspaper picture?"

Kelsey and I looked at each other and nodded. Then, together, we put the crown on Warren's head. The crowd went wild—laughing and whistling and catcalling. I knew he might give us summer detention, but it was worth it.

As usual, though, there was no predicting Warren's actions.

He stood right in front of the mike, the crown still perched on his head, and a stern expression on his face, until he suddenly said in a high-pitched voice, "I feel so pretty!" Then he blew kisses at the crowd and did all sorts of crazy poses for the newspaper photographer. The audience was in a laughing frenzy. The biggest shock of the night wasn't that I had turned down the May Queen title, but that Warren actually had a sense of humor.

As Warren continued mugging for the camera, Kelsey hugged me and said, "You were awesome! Thanks for being a real friend."

Spring Fling was alive with excitement. The music started again. Everyone was talking and laughing. Ryan met me as Kelsey and I walked offstage.

"May I have this dance?" he said.

"You don't hate me anymore?" I asked.

"I never hated you," he said. "And what you said up there took a lot of guts. Very cool."

"That's the thing, Ryan. I'm not cool. I'm just a poetry geek with a good makeover."

"I know," he said. "So are you going to dance with me, or what?"

I looked into his eyes and felt a genuine smile take over. "I don't know," I said. "Should I play hard to get?"

"Play?" He grinned. "You are hard to get!" He pulled me onto the dance floor.

"One hundred thirty-six days," he said.

"What?" I asked.

"Exactly one hundred thirty-six days until your fifteenth birthday, when I can take you on a real date. Of course, once school starts, you'll be in high school, so we can see each other every day."

"That seems like such a long time," I said.

"I know," said Ryan. "But maybe we'll see each other this summer, when you're out with the Delts?" I'd forgotten that Ryan didn't know about how I'd behaved as a Delt pledge.

"That reminds me," I said. "I have to do something."

I found Susan Eaglin in the crowd. "Susan," I said. "I want to say how sorry I am for the way I treated you. I wish I could do something to undo it, but I can't. I hope you can forgive me." The direct approach: nothing fancy about it, but definitely to the point.

"What you said in front of everybody tonight—and to me just now," said Susan. "It means a lot."

"Thanks," I said. "I've wanted to apologize ever since it happened."

"Let's put it behind us," she said.

"Susan, why are you being so nice about all this?"

"I don't know," she said. "I guess I'm a nice person." She smiled.

"Yeah," I said. "You really are." Then I added, "And I want you to know I'm totally quitting Delts. I don't want to be part of something like that."

Susan said, "I'm kind of sorry to hear that."

"You are? Why?"

"You worked so hard to get in, why don't you do something with it? You know, change the system from within?"

"I'll have to give that some thought," I said.

After Susan forgave me, I smiled so much at everyone that my cheeks were actually a little sore. It felt awesome—an incredible lightness. I didn't have to worry about whether the people I was talking to were A-list or D-list and how that would affect my reputation segmentation, and I also didn't have to worry that someone talking to me was part of a master plan to humiliate me, either. It was all just . . . normal. Like we were all just people and nobody was any more important than anyone else.

Dad, Sonny, and Brynn found their way through the crowd and told me how proud they were of me.

"Thanks," I said. "There's someone I want you all to meet."

I waved Ryan over and introduced him.

"With your permission, sir," Ryan said to Dad, "I'd like to take your daughter out on her first date when she turns fifteen. That's one hundred thirty-six days from now. I've calculated it."

"A math whiz!" Dad replied. "My kind of guy. You know, one hundred thirty-six days seems like an awfully long time, doesn't it?"

"You mean, you're going to relent?" I asked.

"How about . . . I don't know . . . one hundred thirty-five days?" he said.

I groaned.

"You showed an awful lot of maturity tonight, Emily," he said. "I think we can probably work out a little compromise—a compromise involving a group setting, perhaps? Or maybe I could come along?"

"Dad!"

"Thank you, sir," Ryan said.

"Maybe we can talk more about it when we're in Tennessee?" I asked Dad.

"You still want to go?"

"I wouldn't miss it," I said.

"Okay if Em and I step out a moment for some fresh air?" Ryan asked. We walked just outside the doors, and when he saw that Dad and Sonny and Brynn had stopped looking, he grabbed my hand and quickly pulled me to the side of the building away from the entrance. We could hear the music pulsing through the walls, but otherwise, it was quiet and we were alone.

"You know how tonight feels?" Ryan asked.

"How?"

"Special," he said. Then he gently took my face in his hands and kissed my lips. "Very special."

I'd always wondered what my first kiss would feel like. It was soft and warm and left me so weak-kneed, I couldn't even speak. Then Ryan looked at me with a puzzled expression.

"I still want to know how all this crazy stuff happened, though."

"I'm relieved to say that I now have clearance to bring you up to speed on the entire campaign, from SWOT analysis to brand dominance to the severing of client loyalties," I said. "But not tonight, please."

"What did any of that mean?" he asked. But he didn't seem to really want an answer at that moment, because he leaned in to kiss me again. "You're definitely the most interesting girl I've ever met, Em."

"Do me a favor," I said. "From now on, call me Emily."